PANDORA'S SUCCESSION

RUSSELL BROOKS

PANDORA'S SUCCESSION

By Russell Brooks

13-Digit ISBN (print version): 978-0-9867513-1-8

Acknowledgements

I would like to acknowledge these individuals without whose help this novel would not have been possible:

Editors: Victory Crayne, Lisa Martinez, and Alethea Spiridon.

Publishing and marketing associates: Jeff Rivera and Jerry D. Simmons.

Book formatters and cover designer: Signe Nichols and Carol Webb of FirebirdMediaManagement.com.

Parents Stanley and Cynthia Brooks and other immediate family members (too many to list here).

Friends in The Artist Lounge, without whom *The Russell Show* would not exist.

Also the following: Randall Brooks, Ron Muka, the Centers for Disease Control (CDC), Eric Black, Ben Kockerman, Gumbowriters.com, Joseph Finder, Barry Eisler, JA Konrath, Wim Demeer, Jim Gessner, The Rainiacs, Jill Delbridge, Gary Smailes, Nelson Christensen, Cheryl Tardif, Steve Bick, André Chevalier, Hélène Mayotte and Fabien Dépres.

And especially the bloggers who helped spread the word.

Chapter 1

Somewhere near Groznyy, Chechnya,

The blow to the side of his head dropped Ridley Fox to the floor. The cold surface against the side of his face, the jarring pain and the spinning were the last things he remembered before he blacked out. When he awoke, the throbbing pain remained, as he was dragged by his legs across the floor, the concrete scraping the back of his scalp. He opened his eyes, to stare into the barrel of a Russian AK-108 assault rifle less than a foot above him.

His fiancée, Jessica, had died at the hands of his captors, two years before, just hours after he had proposed. Unlike her, he knew they'd torture him first. He had promised to give up his career in the Joint Task Force Two (JTF2)—Canada's equivalent to America's SEALs—to settle down with her. The heavy drinking and bar fights began, and then ended shortly after, with Fox in a prison holding cell. That's where he met his current CIA superior, General Paul Downing, and learned everything about the weapons consortium known as the Arms of Ares—his captors.

Fox mentally shook away that memory, as he watched a tangled web of exposed pipes and cheap wire mesh-covered light bulbs that ran along the ceiling while he was dragged along. One of the guards yelled at him in Russian. Although Fox was fluent in the language, as well as a few others from each continent, he was too disoriented to listen. All he did was concentrate on getting his strength back. But even if he got most of it back, he still would've been mentally unable to focus on overpowering his captors.

Moments went by, and Fox felt his legs being dropped just as he succumbed to the blow of a boot tip to his side. The kick forced a loud grunt out of him as the guard yelled profanities at him. Fox blinked rapidly as the pain subsided, taking slow deep breaths and waiting for the guard to kick him again. It didn't come. Above him he couldn't see much but a yellowish flickering reflection of light. Then he heard footsteps walking away from him. The thundering boom of the slamming metal door was accentuated by its echo in the cold, dry room.

"Is that it? Why don't you come back and finish me off?" At least that's what Fox wanted them to understand, even though it came out sounding different. Except for the occasional knocking within the pipes that snaked throughout the structure, there was silence.

The ceiling spun above him. Fox closed his eyes, but the throbbing in his temple and his side continued. He thought back to three days before, when he was contacted by a man named Gregor Sokolov—a scientist working for Ares—who offered him the opportunity to put Ares out of business. In return Fox would help him and his wife defect. It was an offer Fox couldn't refuse. Presently, he was in the underground facility where Ares was developing something so deadly that Sokolov didn't even want to discuss it in their correspondence.

He heard a metallic creaking sound as the door was reopened. Fox noticed that the person who entered the room was a bit more discreet, right down to the sound of the latch to lock it. When he opened his eyes he saw the silhouette of someone kneeling beside him, seconds before he tasted a dry cloth being tied around his head, covering his mouth. Although he was trained not to panic in such a high-stress situation, his breathing intensified when the individual pulled Fox's shirt up high enough to expose his chest and held a needle inches above it.

He struggled to move his arms and legs, as the person lowered the needle, the sharp edge touching his skin—but his damn limbs weighed a ton. He made one last attempt to move, and the needle thrust into him, puncturing deep into his heart. The simultaneous mixture of pain and rush of energy he felt brought instant flashes. It was though the goddamn room was in flames around him. He felt the burning inside of him, coursing through his veins to his arms and legs, at such speed that he was literally thrown up off the ground.

"Fuck!" The gag muffled his curse along with the screams. Seconds went by before he stopped.

"Mr. Fox, thank God." It was a woman's voice. Her thick Russian accent added to her broken English. "I just shot you with adrenaline. Oh my God, I thought they would kill you."

Fox clutched the syringe that protruded from the left side of his chest and pulled it out gently, waiting a bit longer until the sharp pain subsided. His hands quivered as he undid the cloth that was tied around his mouth and looked around him—it was all concrete from floor to ceiling. It all came back to him—even his strength. He touched the bruise on his temple, his hand jolting away as he felt the sting. Fortunately the guard did not strike him too hard with the butt of his gun, or else he could've been left with a concussion. A well-informed guard would've known to have done so, considering how much of a threat Fox posed to these people.

"Listen to me. Do you remember where you are?"

Of course he remembered. He didn't even look at her as he breathed hard. He couldn't fathom how he could've been so sloppy. There was no room for mistakes in his line of work. He didn't have a wife and kids to go home to. There were definitely no colleagues an outsider could call and expect to get an honest answer as to his current whereabouts.

"Fox," the woman said again as she grabbed his shoulders tightly.

Fox looked into her pale, white face. The coffee stench in her breath caught him head on.

"Yes, I know where we are," Fox said, referring to the underground facility they were in.

"Yes, but we don't have much time. Somehow they knew you were coming, but I couldn't warn you. So I come back. Oh my

God. I had to be sure you were okay."

Fox's left hand lashed out and clutched her throat.

"Fox...please...I cannot breathe."

"That's the whole idea. Now tell me who you really are."

"I'm Sveta," she struggled, "Doctor Gregor Sokolov's wife. The late Dr. Sokolov. I've been using his name to contact you. I didn't know what else to do. It's the truth."

Fox unclenched her neck slowly, just enough so that she could breathe easier. "The code."

"The...code?"

"I won't repeat myself."

"One tulip in May for every hundred raindrops of April past."

That's good enough. He released her. She gasped for air and cupped both hands over her mouth. Her eyes watered as she coughed.

Fox looked at his watch. It was 12:52 AM. "Wipe your face. It'll draw attention to you."

She sniffed as she took a tissue out of her lab coat pocket and dabbed her eyes. "Do you have backup?"

There was no sense patting himself down. He knew his weapons were gone. "I'm here alone."

"You can fight six armed guards by yourself?"

"You have a better idea?" She didn't answer. "Yeah, I didn't think so. I'm going to need my weapons. Where are they?"

"They're in storage. Make a left outside and they're in the third door on the right-hand side."

Fox heard the clacking sound of the lock on the door. *Shit, someone's coming in.* Without a moment's hesitation he dropped to the floor, tucking the syringe under him and he assumed the same position he was in before Sveta revived him. He closed his eyes while he listened to the sounds of footsteps. There was the clapping of heels as they hit the floor. The sound was familiar— it was the boots the guards wore. One set was heavier than the next—there were two of them.

"What's going on? What are you doing here?" said one of them in Russian. The proximity of his voice alerted Fox that the guard stopped within two feet in front of him. His cue would come at any moment now.

Sokolova placed a hand on her hip while she pointed at herself with the other. "I should be the one to ask you what this man's doing in here." She then pointed to Fox. "How could you allow him to get in here undetected?"

The guard seemed to be at a loss for words for a moment. "We're not sure as of yet."

"Not sure? You mean you don't know. Do you happen to know who he is or who sent him? No, I guess you wouldn't know that either. Not after you nearly killed him."

"He...uh...we were given last-minute warning. We took necessary action."

A raging fire burned within Fox as he kicked out his left leg in a semi-clockwise rotation, hooked the guard's ankles and swept him off the ground. Using the momentum from the kick, Fox sprang up just as the guard hit the ground. He quickly lunged towards the other guard, whose first instinct was to reach for his AK-108 Assault Rifle. Fox struck him in the forearm, making him lose his grip on the rifle. He followed with a palm-heel strike to his nose—breaking the cartilage. The blow snapped the guard's head backwards and left his neck exposed. Fox followed through with an edge hand blow and shattered his trachea. As though his skeleton had lost its density, the guard folded over like a wet towel and dropped to the floor.

Fox didn't have to hear the other guard's movements to know that he should re-engage him. The guard didn't have a moment to get up before Fox slammed the heel of his boot onto his solar plexus. He then turned to Sokolova who stared at him wide eyed while she took two steps back. A few weeks ago he would've killed her too, and the bitch would've deserved it. He saw the fear in her eyes and the paleness of her face. *Woman, you better not slow me down.*

Fox brushed a lock of his auburn-colored hair that has fallen over his left eyebrow. "That's two down. Four more to go."

Sveta was still at a loss for words as she looked down at what Fox had done. *Goddamn you, woman.* He snapped his fingers in front of her face to redirect her attention. "Listen, we're going to get through this together. But I'm going to need you to stay focused, or else you're going to get us both killed. You understand me?"

She gave a set of short, quick nods.

"Good. I'm going to change into his clothes. I just hope they fit."

Fox looked at both guards and visually measured each of their heights. The one with the shattered nose appeared to be close to his height of six foot two. His clothes should fit. Fox knelt down in front of him and pulled off his boots. "I need to know something."

"What?"

"Why are you doing this? Why now?"

Sveta cupped her hands over her mouth and her nose before she let out a huge breath. It was as though she was trying to hold back more tears. "My husband, Gregor, was killed two days ago in an accident with the bio-weapon that we're working on. I never wanted any part of this, but he was greedy and easy to corrupt. The organization we belong to—the Arms of Ares—paid us a lot of money for our skills as microbiologists. I never imagined so many deaths would result from the weapons we've built and sold to terrorist groups and rogue nations. But I want no part of it anymore."

"Let me get this straight. You're helping a criminal organization develop weapons strictly to market them illicitly, and it never occurred to you that innocent people would be killed? You're something else, lady, and you took a huge risk contacting me. Why me, anyway? Why not MI-5 or the FSB?"

"The Arms of Ares has infiltrated many top-level organizations and agencies, including the British and Russian intelligence agencies you just named."

Fox was unbuttoning the guard's shirt when she suddenly grabbed onto his hands. *What the hell are you doing?*

"I lost my husband to Ares, and you lost your fiancée. I wanted to have ordinary life too, with children and even grandchildren. Ares stole that life from you—that's why you joined CIA. Am I right?"

Fox stared at her, incapable of ignoring the comment. *Jessica,*

not again. She knew one hell of a way of tapping into my soft side.
No. Remember what I'm here for. Just focus.

"That's why I trust you," Sveta continued. "I know you cannot be led astray by these people like me and my husband were."

She let go of his hands and allowed him to finish unbuttoning the guard's shirt, remove it and put it on. It was a tight fit, but it would pass. Fox soon had on the guard's pants. "When you first contacted me, you said there were other labs. Why didn't you want the CIA to focus on those?"

"Those are sleeper laboratories. If there's a problem in one, they can easily drop everything here and set up shop in another lab where the facilities are already established."

Fox tucked his hair under the guard's cap. "Then it ends here. This is where we'll bury everything."

"It won't stop them. They'll go elsewhere. Continue their research and development without problem."

"Yeah, but it'll take a while for them to recruit more scientists. Taking out everyone in this lab could cripple their production."

"True, but not for long. Ares has many resources."

"Yeah, no doubt," said Fox. "So what kind of R and D are we talking about? Weaponized Ebola? Anthrax?"

"Something far worse. It's a microbe called Pandora. All I can say is that small amounts of it introduced into a populated area can produce a death toll similar to that of a nuclear bomb. Ares has set new standard in biological warfare."

"If there's more of it out there then we'll have to find it, starting with you telling me where to locate those sleeper labs, the biology behind Pandora, and any means of immunizing ourselves against this thing."

"I've forwarded some of that information to the secure email you gave me. If you get me out of here alive, I'll forward you the list of all the active members of Ares and their clients. As for a defense against Pandora—there is none."

"None? Or none that Ares wants to find?"

Sveta shook her head. "There's no known protection against Pandora unless you want to outfit six billion of the world's inhabitants with anti-contamination suits."

"You're funny."

"I'm not trying to be." Sveta paused as though she was in thought. "One more thing, Ares is ready to sell Pandora on the black market. A demonstration is supposed to take place in Darfur sometime tomorrow afternoon. That's about twelve hours from now."

"One done against innocent villagers, no doubt. They're going to try to sell it to those who are against the peace process."

"With this weapon, they could strengthen terrorist organizations such as Al-Qaeda in their attacks against the US. They'll be unstoppable."

Fox removed the ammunition clip from one of the rifles and picked up the other. "Everyone's stoppable. We strike them fast and we'll strike them hard."

"What you need to know is included in the email I sent you, as well as the location of the demonstration."

"Good. I'm going for my ammo. Now get the hell out of here."

"Oh yes, before I forget. You should also know that this laboratory doubles as a containment unit to prevent any contagions from getting out. In other words, if there's any type of disruption in the confines in which Pandora is stored, the place will go on lockdown. There are sensors throughout the facility that are sensitive to the slightest change in the atmosphere. Setting off an explosive close to Pandora can cause the lockdown very quickly."

"Then that's where I'll place the explosives. Are you sure there isn't anything else you need to tell me before we leave this room?"

She stood silent for a moment, as if deep in thought, and then nodded. "I'm sure."

"Go wait for me outside." Fox opened the door and let her pass first. The hallway was clear when she walked out. He closed the door behind him and walked in the opposite direction.

Fox found the storage room easily and collected the two C-4 flat explosives, the cigarette-box-shaped detonator, and his Heckler and Koch USP Compact Tactical handgun. He unscrewed the noise suppressor and dropped it on the shelf, knowing that using it now was pointless. He tucked the handgun behind him, in the waist of his pants, where he could easily reach it. He then immediately stuck an explosive to the back of the storage rack and activated it. He would later detonate this with the remote. Maximum damage could only be achieved if the explosives were placed in the same room as Pandora. He walked back to the hallway, not making eye contact with those who passed him.

Fox came to a window where he could see into the main research room. There was a huge contrast between the cleanliness and brightness of the laboratory versus the hallway where he was. There were several men and women in white coats who seemed to be assembling several objects he couldn't describe, but he knew they had something to do with the large set of metal canisters along the back wall with the N2(l) label affixed to each of them. He counted four of them and they were all about two feet wide and over eight feet tall. From his limited scientific knowledge, he was sure the liquid nitrogen in those canisters had something to do with the storage of Pandora. Within that room was another room, also separated by a large glass partition where a green glow emanated.

Pandora.

Fox realized the glass partition most likely acted as a seal to protect the white- coats from exposure. That theory was soon confirmed when he saw an airlock chamber that led into the inner room with the green glow. That's where he had to plant the other explosive, which was close enough to breach the inner chamber. The C-4 in the storage room would take care of the rest of the facility.

Fox opened the metallic door and walked in. Everyone inside seemed too preoccupied to notice him. He stayed out of the way, making no eye contact, staying close to the walls until he came to the first set of liquid nitrogen canisters. He planted one of his bombs behind it.

"Are you mad?" Behind him someone cried out in Russian. "Get out! You can't bring weapons in here."

Fox turned to the man and replied to him in Russian. "We caught an intruder earlier. So we're making a precautionary sweep to make sure everything's the way it should be."

"No one else has come in here. Leave now," the man ordered.

He must be the head scientist.

"My apologies. I'll leave," said Fox as he nodded and exited the room, closing the door behind him.

There was a commotion ahead, a lot of yelling followed by shuffling feet. Fox recognized it as his cue to hurry. They obviously found the two guards he had taken out earlier—and that he was missing. He picked up the pace as he saw two guards running towards him down the hall, searching the rooms. Five white-coats kept clear by sticking to the walls as the guards swept by. Fox imitated the other guards by running and checking one room after the next, but he couldn't afford to do it for long—someone was bound to see through his disguise.

That came soon enough when he heard someone yell, "There he is. Stop him!"

He turned around and ducked to the opposite wall, grabbed his AK-108 and fired off a few rounds at the two guards behind him. They ducked around the corner as bullet pockmarks spread across the walls in a straight line, sending a mixture of dust and cement chunks ricocheting off the walls. The others would soon be drawn to his location like bees regrouping to form an assault.

He spotted the entrance close by and he palmed the detonator. Once the structure started to cave in on itself, he'd still have time to make his escape. The euphoria of the thought overwhelmed him, until he heard screams.

"Zacrute," Fox heard someone yell in Russian—this meant shut up.

"We have your partner. Come back now and throw down your weapon!" yelled the same man, again in Russian. Fox assumed him to be their leader.

Shit, why'd she have to get caught? What the hell didn't she understand about waiting for me outside?

She had already risked her life to rescue him—it would be inhumane to leave her. Along with knowing everyone in Ares, she might also know who set him up. Fox sighed and tossed the rifle across the floor so that it slid to a stop in the middle of the two intersecting hallways. He slowly walked to where he'd thrown the gun, keeping the detonator closely hidden inside his shirtsleeve and his hands held high enough, but not too straight, to avoid letting the detonator to slip too far inside his shirt. He walked out in full view of the enemy, who were all strategically positioned. Two guards were down on one knee while the other two stood behind them, one beside Sveta, with the tip of his AK-108 inches from her. Further behind them, a few white-coats peeked from around the corners.

"We've been given orders not to execute you. But it doesn't mean that we won't shoot off your kneecaps if you give us reason to," yelled Sveta's captor. "Put your hands behind your head and get down on your knees!"

Fox did as he was told. He went down on his knees and slowly put his hands behind his head and discretely let the detonator slide out from the inner sleeve into his hand. The moment that he would push the button, he knew he wouldn't have long before the blast caused a lockdown. But he couldn't do it as long as Sveta's captor pointed his rifle at her. An explosion would startle him and might cause him to unintentionally pull the trigger. Fox only needed for him to point the rifle away from her for a few seconds.

Although he was a quick draw with a sidearm, his HK versus their AK-108s wouldn't give him much of a chance surviving. However, their weapons were bigger and heavier than his, making it more difficult for them to aim both quickly and efficiently. The sound of an explosion could distract them even more—buying him more time to react.

Fox played a scenario in his head. The three guards would most likely approach him while the other stayed with Sveta. He'd detonate the explosives when one of them was close enough—using the extra one to two seconds of bought time to grab him in a chokehold with one arm while simultaneously using him as a human shield—then draw his HK with his free hand to dispose of the other guards. Sveta's captor would most likely use her as a shield, so he would have to be taken out first. Speaking to him in Russian would be a start. "I'm unarmed, and so is the woman. What threat is she to you right now?"

The guard appeared to think about it for a few moments, and then lowered his gun. Fox knew, at least right now, that any misfire would go into the floor a few inches from Sveta's feet. She'd be fine as long as she didn't move.

But rather than three, Sveta's captor only sent the two front guards after Fox, while the other remained behind with him. It wasn't the scenario Fox had expected, but he'd still have to detonate the explosive to distract them. He only hoped that they would momentarily point their guns away from him, making it harder for them to aim at him properly if he were to rush them.

The two guards were over thirty meters away from him. Fox only needed twelve meters from a dead start—a distance that he could clear in two seconds—in order to gain the necessary momentum to attack the first guard. Sure, using his sidearm might appear to be more efficient, but the chance of hitting his mark was lessened while they were moving. If Fox were off by a fraction of a second, one of the guards might be able to take a decent enough aim to at least put a few rounds in him.

The guards closed the distance to about fifteen meters from him and Fox's thumb slid over the button of the detonator. The guard to the left was a half step in front of the other. Fox would base his timing on that one. Right before the guard on the left reached twelve meters away, Fox pressed the button on the detonator and an explosion occurred further back in the lab. Fox dropped the detonator and simultaneously launched from his position. He kept low as he drove forward, swinging his arms rapidly as his knees pumped into his stomach. He straightened up prematurely— slightly reducing his forward momentum—as he swung his arms outward a split second before he was between both guards. In a double clothesline move Fox struck them both in their heads— flipping them onto the floor.

Fox used the impact from the second guard to pivot around while he drew his gun from his waistband. As he rotated, he fully extended his arm while the third guard was still in the process of aiming his rifle. Fox squeezed the trigger and watched as the guard's head snapped back before he lifted off the ground. The guard had not yet hit the ground before he had Sveta's captor in his sights. Fox pulled the trigger just as he saw a flash of light come from the guard's rifle, quickly followed by a staccato noise and objects whistling by him. However, Fox's shot was on target. He saw the guard go down, holding onto the trigger as he did, and shots pockmarked the ceiling and burst one of the pipes.

Sveta was crouched over with both hands covering her ears, as steam from the damaged pipe blew clouds of vapor around her. Fox saw that she was in shock and felt it pointless to yell for her to join him. He yanked her away—nearly dislocating her shoulder in the process. The floor shook as they ran—the chain reaction would catch up to them very soon. Fox heard staccato shots and Sveta cried out. It wasn't long after that Fox realized he was pulling dead weight. *Damn it, she's been hit.*

When he looked down at her, blood stained the back of her lab coat. Fox saw the perpetrator, lying sideways on the floor in the middle of the intersecting hallways. It was one of the two guards he had clotheslined. *Why didn't I kill that son-of-a-bitch?* A rumbling caused Fox to nearly lose his footing. Then bits of the ceiling collapsed around him, and a huge futon-sized block crashed down and crushed the guard before he was able to fire another shot.

"Sveta...Sveta." Fox knelt down beside her. Still no answer. *Shit, don't die on me now.* "Who set me up?"

She was gone.

When he looked over his shoulder, he saw a metal door sliding down from the ceiling. He broke out in a sprint and threw himself under it, seconds before it touched the ground. He was now outside, but still underground. A metal ladder was a few feet away. He ran for it and climbed to the top. He struck the wooden trapdoor hard, and it bounced once before settling open.

The scent of hay and fresh manure struck his nostrils as a small number of horses stomped and whinnied in their stalls. The ground shook, rattling the wooden walls of the stable they were in. *A stable and a farmhouse fronting for an underground bio-weapons facility. Who would've guessed?*

He climbed out onto the hay in the middle of the stall and ran for the door. The five horses in their stalls stomped and whinnied wildly at the tremors.

Fox ran out of the stable into the crisp, cool air, and stopped at the splintered wooden fence that bordered the driveway. He hopped over, turned left, walked six steps, turned right and walked another three. He knelt down on both knees and dug up a wallet-sized tracking device. Then he bolted across the moonlit field, to the woods where he'd hidden his motorcycle. He pressed a button on the tracker and followed the sounds of a huge flock of grasshoppers that died down a few seconds later. He then came to the camouflage net that covered his motorcycle. He yanked it off and lifted the seat. Underneath it was a lit dial pad. He punched in the numbers 062176, which was followed by a beeping sound and a click. He lifted the cover to remove a satellite phone and dialed a number. The phone on the other end rang once and then he heard the recorded greeting.

"Welcome to Spade Insurance. Please listen carefully for our menu options have changed." Fox dialed in his code, 062176. The voice recording ended and there was a short pause. A pleasant voice with a slight Jamaican accent replied.

"How can I help you, Mr. Fox?" It was Marie Vasell, General Downing's secretary.

"The lab's destroyed. I need to speak to General Downing immediately. We're going to have to scramble a team to Darfur ASAP. This so-called simple assignment I was given—it just got a whole lot more complicated."

Chapter 2

Odessa, Ukraine, 8:57AM, the day after.

The gentleman stubbed out his second cigarette in the ashtray. The outdoor terrace to the café he was at was one of many in this tourist area of the city, within walking distance of the Black Sea.

He wasn't in town to enjoy the eighteenth and nineteenth century architecture, or the popular beaches. Even back in the days as a KGB operative he rarely took the time to enjoy himself in many of the places his work took him. But those days were long gone. Although he had several aliases, he was best known as Valerik. This was the ideal place for him to meet his Ares colleagues, the first time since getting back from the bombed out facility near Groznyy, Chechnya.

Valerik recognized his ride, as the black, fleet-sedan stopped several feet away. As he got up, his protruding gut bumped the table, a constant reminder of how much weight he had gained since his deactivated status as KGB. It was then that he noticed a black espresso stain on his white shirt. Had the spill been on his brown jacket it would be better concealed. But he left it unbuttoned since it fit him more comfortably. He grabbed his handkerchief and dipped it into a glass of water belonging to another patron as he walked by. He worked on the stain, ignoring the angry protest behind him.

A man dressed in an overcoat stepped out of the front passenger seat to open the back door for him. An overcoat in this weather? He might as well have placed a sign on his forehead that read *I'm hiding a gun.* Valerik got in and sat down beside his white-haired superior, who was also a former KGB operative. The doors shut and the car drove off.

"What's your assessment of the Groznyy lab?" asked the white-haired man in Russian.

"The laboratory was on lockdown, indicating Pandora was unleashed inside. I didn't dare use the override codes to open the blast door to inspect the damage," Valerik replied in the same language.

"You should've gotten there quicker. We'd be rid of Fox once and for all. Now he's gotten away, along with how much intelligence on us? Only God knows."

"The guards reported they had captured him. Apparently Sokolova helped him escape."

"Of course she did, just as she led Fox to our lab."

"We still have our satellite laboratories—"

"Which we'll have to abandon immediately," the white-haired man took out a larger than normal pen-like object and twirled it.

Valerik looked away from him, out the window to hide his frown. *That damn toy of his.* He couldn't stand seeing him play with that pen.

"With Fox's escape, those locations may be compromised. See to it that Pandora's taken to another location until we can set up some new satellite laboratories."

Valerik looked back to his superior. "I can do that. In the meantime, we should delay the demonstration."

"If we do that, we risk losing the confidence of our clients— and the billions that Pandora could bring in for Ares."

"What if Fox knows the location of the demo? If he disrupts it, we'll lose our clients for sure. We should send a few of our men to accompany our clients while they set up Pandora to be tested."

"The only Ares members involved will be those that deliver Pandora. Beyond that, if we start chaperoning our clients they'll ask too many questions about the security of our organization. So far, I haven't heard from our source that Fox knows anything about the demo or its location. Just concentrate on getting Pandora moved."

The white-haired man signaled the driver to pull over beside a small marketplace comprised mostly of small tourist shops. When the car stopped, Valerik got out and held the door open as he peered inside. "I'll contact you once everything's done."

"See to it that you do. With positive results, of course."

Valerik shut the door and walked in the opposite direction. The sedan drove off. When the car was out of sight, he walked into the marketplace and went to a mobile phone vendor. He walked up to the counter that doubled as a display case, pointed inside to the mobile phone, then slapped the cash down on the surface. Once the clerk handed him the phone with prepaid minutes, Valerik left the store. He removed the uncharged battery from the phone and replaced it with a charged one—same brand—that he kept in his jacket pocket. Once outside, he activated it and dialed a number. After the first two rings, the call was answered.

"What do you have to report?" asked an electronically disguised voice.

"It's me. Are your men on standby?"

"They are. Did anything else go wrong?"

"Not at all. It's only a minor setback, that's all. We'll just have to begin the operation earlier than expected."

"Do not disappoint me. The success of our operation depends on you getting the package."

"Yes, sir." Valerik's phone went silent as his real superior switched off.

***

Heathrow Airport, London, England.
Dr. Tabitha Marx sat alone in the VIP lounge as she waited to board her flight to Entebbe Airport in southern Uganda. She downed the last of her Black Russian, rested the glass on the table beside her, got up, and walked to the floor to ceiling window that overlooked the runway and the dozens of stationary planes.

She had cut down significantly on her drinking since she had arrived from Ayles Ice Island in the Canadian arctic two years ago. Before she had arrived, two cryospheric researchers had accidentally exhumed a prehistoric man that was infected with a dormant microbe. Their exposure to the microbe and their eventual death—as well as the deaths of some that came to their rescue—would have made international headlines had she, her colleagues at the Centers for Disease Control and Prevention (CDC), and both Canadian and American governments not intervened. Fortunately, the outbreak was contained without any repercussions of a mass panic.

Marx's six-foot stature mostly attracted wealthy and powerful men to her, the rest were intimidated. As she watched the planes take off, her flowing, dirty-blonde hair draped down the shoulders of her pantsuit.

So much had changed over the years. Born to American parents forty-four years before, she was used to travelling, since her father worked at the American Embassy in Islamabad, Pakistan. He was later killed by the Soviets in an air-raid in neighboring Afghanistan, near the end of the Soviet-Afghan war.

Her hatred towards the USSR and Communism increased tenfold that day—so did her bonding with her mother, but it wasn't meant to last. Her mother was hospitalized, a few years later, with severe heart complications.

It was then that her mother disclosed the horrifying truth. Marx's father was a CIA agent that had aided the mujahedeen to run their training camps in Afghanistan in their fight against the Soviets. What was more devastating was when her mother also told her that she had been recruited by the KGB to spy on her father, and that furthermore, the intelligence that she had provided the Soviets ultimately got her father killed.

It was the most emotional day of Marx's life. She had screamed at her sobbing mother, telling her that her sickness was well deserved. It was last time that she saw her mother alive. She was bawling as she ran from the hospital room, pushing hospital staff out of her way. She made it outside of the hospital where she collapsed, only to be aided by a few motorists and pedestrians. It was the last time she remembered crying.

The lounge doors opened and a group of men in business suits walked in and headed straight for the bar. Marx glanced briefly at them and sighed, assuming them to either be businessmen or diplomats—the latter she detested—as it was a constant reminder that all the world's problems could be linked to politics and religion. It was what eventually destroyed her family.

It wasn't long before one of them approached her. "Good morning. Would you care—"

"No, I wouldn't." The man withdrew from her immediately, muttering something under his breath. Just then she heard her boarding call over the PA system. Marx walked back to her seat and grabbed her single travel bag. In a few days, she would make history, and the face of the world would be forever changed.

Chapter 3

West Darfur, 10 AM, local time

T he townspeople crowded the town square on market day. Most of the residents of this small dusty town—one of the few on the United Nation's endangered list that has avoided attacks from both government and militia forces—had left and were making their way in droves to the refugee camps that bordered Chad to the west. For many, this was the last opportunity to stock up on rations before they migrated.

Over where the adults bargained for everyday items, three young boys kicked around a soccer ball between the stalls. The shortest of the three was the last to kick the ball. He sent it flying out of the market and into a clearing. They ran after the ball which had rolled under the feet of a man dressed in a traditional pastel-colored robe, and a skullcap, with most of his head and face covered by a length of cloth.

They stopped a few feet away, gawked at the giant, but did not run. He was leaning against a stack of empty boxes in the shade, and his eyes were visible as he peered down at them. He was not dark-skinned like them, but had more of an olive-colored complexion. They had never seen anyone of that complexion before, but knew he must be from a land beyond the desert, possibly even further than where the devils on horseback came from.

The giant kicked the ball back towards them and looked away.

The shortest of the three picked it up and walked closer to the man. "Where are you from?" he asked in Arabic—the most common language that was spoken in the region.

Fox looked at the kid and saw in his eyes that he ached to know who he was. The boys must have known right away that he wasn't from here.

"Did you come to save us from the devils on horseback?"

Fox glanced at the other two boys and then back at the one that spoke to him. They were all familiar with *the devils* or The Janjaweed—their official name. The Sudanese government had continuously denied being linked to the militia group, for carrying out the most atrocious attacks that had left scores of innocent people dead.

"What do you know about the devils on horseback?" Fox replied in Arabic.

"They're very bad men," the child replied as the other two approached.

"Really?" asked Fox. "What's your name?"

"I'm Musa."

"I'm Adam," the boy to Musa's left quickly said.

"I'm Ibrahim," said the other.

"Where are you from?" asked Musa.

"Did you come from the other side of the desert?" asked Adam.

"Where's your horse? How did you get here?" said Ibrahim, as the others joined in, flooding Fox with questions.

Fox held out his palm. It appeared that the size of it, in the children's eyes, was enough to silence them. "Are they the same ones that come every time?"

They nodded.

"How many usually come?"

"Ten," Ibrahim said first.

"I saw eight last time," said Adam.

"That's good enough," said Fox.

"We haven't seen them in a long time," said Musa.

"Did you come to save us from the Janjaweed?" asked Ibrahim.

"My mother told me that help would come. And that they would be men from far away, just like you," said Musa.

And their bombardment continued. These kids and their families had next to nothing and they depended on outside help. His fight wasn't with the Janjaweed. He wouldn't even be here if it weren't for Ares.

"Are you here to help us?" asked Adam.

Fox couldn't avoid looking into their pleading eyes. "You shouldn't need any help. After all, you just said that they haven't been seen in a long time. You should all be safe. Now run along and play with your ball."

The boys didn't appear to be convinced.

"The last time they were here they scared everyone with their guns," said Ibrahim.

Musa's ball slipped from his hands, but he was quick to pick it up. "They took clothes that my mother was selling at the market and didn't even pay for them."

Adam nodded. "I heard they set fire to villages."

Fox looked past them, in the distance, where he thought that he heard something. He waved the boys away with his arm. "Run along." Fox walked off and left them. *This is their civil war, not mine, who am I to get involved? I'm just here to fuck Ares over. I would've done the same had they gone to Somalia or Zimbabwe.* He didn't dare look back at the boys. They would only make him go soft, and he couldn't afford another blunder such as the one in Groznyy.

He rubbed his forehead with his sleeve, wiping off some sweat. He then took a swig of cold water from his canteen that he had well hidden under his robe.

Fox turned to the sounds of a diesel engine gunning, and saw thick, black smoke belch into the air. A truck with a small open-end payload drove around the stalls, into the town square. Following it, on horseback, were five more men in army fatigues. The Janjaweed—the devils on horseback themselves—were here.

The bustling market came to a complete standstill as the men passed through. But Fox's focus was on the truck and its cargo. His facial scarf began to drop and he fixed it to cover above his nose, as he dashed through the crowd, keeping his eyes on the truck.

During his pursuit, he saw a stall with women's clothing. He reached inside his robe and took out a few bills without counting them. He tossed them on the table in front of the merchant saying the standard Arabic greeting, "Izeyik." Simultaneously he grabbed three garments off the rack. He didn't hear any protest from the merchant.

The Janjaweed drove about a hundred meters past the marketplace and stopped in front of an old, school building that had seen its share of assaults—from the dilapidated rooftop to the pockmarked outer walls.

Two men hopped out from the back of the truck. They waited as two more inside handed them an object on a tripod, and then a metallic briefcase. The driver came around back to help them and they all carried everything into the single-storey structure. Three of the horsemen doubled back towards the marketplace. The other two dismounted their horses, walked them to the side of entrance, and stood guard with their assault rifles.

Fox hid from sight as the horsemen rode by. He kept his face covered as the sand and dust that the horses kicked up blew about him. Before the dust settled, he was meters away from the men that guarded the school entrance. He had the green, red, and blue garments in each hand, holding them high for them to see.

"Izeyik, Izeyik. Quay-Seen?" *Hello, hello. Are you well?*

The two men didn't answer, but approached Fox, their rifles pointing downward.

"I'll offer you an excellent bargain on these beautiful robes for your wives or mistresses. Name your price," Fox said in Arabic.

"Get lost. We're not buying anything from you," grunted one of the men in the same language.

"All right, all right. I won't sell. I'll offer these free and then half price on the rest of my merchandise. Anything you want." Fox held the robes high enough to block their view.

With the clothes dangling in front of them, they didn't see Fox's attack coming. Fox leaned forward slightly, forcing his legs into the ground, and then he burst forward into the devil on the left, driving one arm downward onto his arm, forcing him to point the rifle away from him. With his forward momentum, he used his opposite hand to strike his opponent causing him to stumble backwards with a collapsed windpipe.

As expected, the second opponent thought of using his assault rifle against Fox at close range. But Fox was able to move his hands faster than the devil could lift his weapon. Fox struck him in his upper torso while wrapping his opposite leg around his opponent's—hooking him and creating a loss of stability. Gravity then took over and the devil was thrown onto his back, causing him to lose grip on his rifle, which slid a few feet away. The devil had no time to react, as he was left vulnerable to Fox's downward heel strike to his nose. His head rolled to the side as blood poured out from what was left of it. Fox shook the stinging pain from his hand—that happened less now than it did when he had first joined the military.

He used the robes he'd purchased from the merchant to tie their arms and legs together, and then he dragged them by their collars inside the school, where they would be out of sight should the other devils return.

He ran outside and grabbed their assault rifles, removed the ammunition clips, and brought them into the school with him. He tossed them into a classroom. Weaponry made these men fierce, and they used this against defenseless women, children, and elderly villagers. But these guys were no match for Fox. He was not only skilled with a gun, but also with knives and hand-to-hand combat. Their mistake was doing business with Ares, because now, it put them on Fox's hit list.

Fox walked down the darkened hallway. There were no lights in any of the classrooms he walked by, and none in the hallway either. He heard voices, and it sounded as though the men were quarrelling. *So much the better.* Fox took out the HK from inside his robe. He removed the suppressor and screwed it on as he approached the classroom where he heard the voices.

Fox reached the doorway of the classroom and stood to the side of it. He took out a dentist's mirror and used it to see into the classroom. He didn't see any wooden tables, chairs, or teacher's desk, as he was used to in elementary school. But he spotted his targets—five of them that had assembled the tripod. A few feet away from them, on the ground, lay an open briefcase which had a fluorescent-green glow emanating from it. It was the same as he'd seen in the underground lab outside of Groznyy.

Now that he knew exactly where each of them stood and that Pandora was safely in the briefcase, he put the mirror away and casually walked into the classroom with the HK raised. Two of the men were quicker to spot him than the other three. That didn't matter to Fox. He popped a single bullet into each of them first, before nailing the other three, who were slower to react.

There were only three devils left and they were in the market. As long as the merchants distracted them, he could easily slip out of town and make it peacefully to his rendezvous point. If they got in his way he would deal with them.

He examined the bright-green light that shone from inside the briefcase. Fox couldn't believe that a vial as small as the test tube he saw could wreak so much damage. It was well incubated in thick foam to prevent the slightest scratch. Whatever horror was about to be unleashed on these people, Fox didn't want to know about it.

One of the devils had a key attached to the waist with a chain. It must be the one used to unlock the metal case. Fox placed his foot onto the devil's waist at the end of the chain, grabbed the end with the key, and broke it off. He then closed the metal case, locked it, and took it with him.

Fox went back to the marketplace where he suspected the three remaining devils were. There was still minimal activity at the marketplace, just as when he had left it. Then he saw them, each of them taking things off the tables of the stalls and looking at them. They kept what they wanted and threw to the ground what they didn't, just as Musa had described.

Speaking of Musa—he unexpectedly heard loud bawling...It was Musa. He was running after one of the men who had taken his soccer ball and was holding it high above his head, making Musa jump for it.

"Please, he's only a child. It's the only toy he has. Aren't the clothes you took from me enough?" pleaded a woman that ran up to the bully and grabbed onto his other arm.

"You dare touch me, filthy peasant woman." With a single blow to her head, he sent her to the ground. Musa rushed to her, as the man spat on her.

"Is that your mother, you silly little boy? Tell her you'll get your ball back once you've earned it," said the man, as he tossed the ball in the air repeatedly, laughing.

That was none of Fox's concern. These villagers went through these problems on a daily basis. Fox had what he came for—there was no time for pit stops.

Less than a dozen paces later, Musa's crying still went on. A few more seconds went by and Fox closed his eyes hard, hoping somehow it would block Musa out. It didn't.

Christ, this wasn't some kid that was crying over a video game he didn't get for his birthday. Some asshole just slapped his mother right in front of him. The same guy would probably kill Musa's mother in front of him, too. He sighed as he turned to look at them. *Fuck. How did I become so selfish?*

"Leave my mother alone." This was all Fox heard from Musa as he looked back and saw him on the ground beside his mother. The devil took out his assault rifle and waved it in the air. Musa screamed and quickly jumped on his mother as though to shield her.

The sight of the gun even startled Fox. *You got to be shitting me.* He headed towards them and clenched a fist that grew tighter as he got closer to the devil from behind.

Fox put down the briefcase. "Hey!"

The devil hardly had time to turn and look in Fox's direction before the rifle was pulled out of his hand. By the time he had fully turned, Fox's left fist was already in full flight. The blunt of the impact got both the upper level of teeth and the lower bridge of his nose and lifted him into the air briefly before he hit the ground. Heads turned and people rushed from way inside the marketplace to catch what was going on.

Fox looked down at him as he shook out the stinging of his hand. He pulled the magazine out, pocketed it, and looked at the gun. It was a QBZ-95 Chinese Assault Rifle. He then looked at Musa who looked back at him with a tear-stained face.

His mother sat up and pulled her son into her tightly. Musa glanced at the unconscious devil and then back at Fox. "You came back. You *did* come to save us." Fox felt a rush of heat to his face as Musa's face lit up with a smile.

Fox breathed heavily and looked to the growing crowd. The two other devils would be showing up soon. And he knew they were coming, when people in the crowd dispersed, as two men in fatigues emerged.

Fox turned to Musa and his mother and motioned them to the side. "Move away, quickly." Musa backed up as he helped his mother slide backwards in a seated position as Fox stepped away.

The bullies glanced down at their fallen colleague and then at Fox. He could've easily disposed of them with his HK, but doing so in front of the children would have been inappropriate. That's a line he would never cross.

He tossed the empty rifle aside, picked up the briefcase and held it out in front of him while he faced them. "You know what's in here, don't you? You know you can't risk damaging the contents of this briefcase?"

There was a pause from the two men as they appeared to think about what he just told them. They both looked at each other briefly before lowering their rifles. The one on the left handed his gun to the other, and from inside his robe, he withdrew a machete and rushed Fox with a war-like cry.

What an amateur.

The man was quick with the blade as he swung downwards to the left. Fox leaned back on his right leg and pivoted to the right to dodge it. He did the same thing but to the opposite side as the man swung the machete downwards to the right, missing him again. The man swung across, but Fox raised the briefcase and caught the blade with it, then kicked his assailant in the groin. The man doubled over, dropping the machete. With his free hand, Fox grabbed the devil's head and pulled it downwards into his upward swinging knee, dropping him.

Fox looked up at the remaining devil. He seemed to have trouble managing both assault rifles. Fox was about to rush him as he fumbled with them, but a frying pan suddenly crashed down on the devil's head from behind. When he dropped to the ground, a few others jumped at the opportunity to have a go at him by kicking him while he was down—including the woman who had sacked him with the frying pan.

The confrontation was brief, but ended with the three devils being lifted and carried overhead by small groups of men. Fox observed this and decided that the townspeople would take care of them as they saw fit, now that they were unarmed and posed less of a threat.

Fox felt something at his feet and saw Musa's soccer ball. He picked it up and walked over to Musa, who stood next to his mother. She was back on her feet, surrounded by a few more of the villagers. Fox knelt down and handed Musa his ball.

Musa took it with both hands and smiled. "Thank you."

"You're welcome. That was very brave what you did, standing up to that Janjaweed bully. You're a good kid, Musa. Take care of your mother. She'll always need your help." Fox rubbed Musa's bald head, making him laugh. "I'll see to it that some help comes soon to keep those bad men away."

Just then, Ibrahim and Adam ran up to him, laughing as they all threw their arms around Fox. For a second, Fox felt an emotional attachment to the three boys that made him not want to let them go, but he had to. For the moment he couldn't do anything more for them.

The boys let go of him and Fox stood up, walked up to one of the horses that belonged to one of the devils and climbed onto its back. He then waved to the crowd before he rode off.

The entire village waved back to him and cried out their thanks and praises. Musa, Ibrahim, Adam, and dozens of other children ran after him, up until the edge of the village, cheering and waving their goodbyes to Fox as he rode away into the desert.

Fox didn't quite reach a mile before he pulled the reigns of the horse to make it stop. He dismounted and took out his satellite phone from under his robe.

"There's no need for that, Warrant Officer," came a voice from the sand.

At that point, five figures sprouted up from the sand, dropping their sand-colored robes to reveal their army fatigues.

Warrant Officer Pat Hiller, Fox's friend in the SEALs, walked up to him. "I take it things went smoothly."

Fox handed Hiller the metal briefcase without answering. Something stirred at the bottom of his gut and it got worse. A familiar acidic taste followed and he ran off to the side, fell down to his hands and knees and threw up.

Hiller ran to him. "Whoa, buddy. You okay?"

Fox waved him off without answering. *A mother and son were nearly slaughtered, maybe more, and I was about to walk away. How the hell could I be okay? Shit, Jessica would still be alive had I followed up on my instincts on her employers instead of ignoring them.*

Fox spewed his stomach contents into the sand a second time. Tears soon followed. He'd become a killer with a single-minded purpose—not the man Jessica was going to marry.

"Listen, buddy. You don't look so great," said Hiller. "Extraction's supposed to be in precisely four minutes. The Chad border ain't too far away. Are you sure you can handle the helicopter ride?"

Fox took out a handkerchief, dabbed his eyes, and then wiped his mouth. "I'll be okay. It's probably just traveler's sickness."

"Traveler's sickness my ass. We're getting you to a medic." Hiller helped Fox get up. Fox walked back to join the other SEALs and looked at each of them. He didn't know their personal stories, only their individual skills. Looking at them, he saw himself as he was five years ago. Those were the days when testosterone drove him, rushing into battle—whether he was rescuing hostages from Somalian pirates, or from other terrorist cells. Those were the days, when he killed an enemy, it was out of self-defense. Since Jessica's death, self-defense for him was nothing more than a euphemism. It was only now that he began to realize this. It must be why he threw up.

A helicopter would be arriving soon to pick them up. He'd know by the time it landed whether or not he could continue with this life.

Chapter 4

Novinsky Boulevard, 121099, Moscow, Russia, 12:03PM local time

The white-haired man twirled his pen as he gradually squeezed the phone harder by the second.

"Yes, I heard you the first time. Just remind them that we're not responsible for the safety of their men or any breach in their security."

"They're arguing that the security breach came from our end," said the man on the phone.

"Pandora was in their possession when it went missing. You tell the Sudanese officials that we have an endless supply, which we'll sell to other clients that we regularly do business with. Let them know that if they want to continue doing business with us, they'll have to guarantee that there won't be any more security breaches, especially since it puts us at risk also. And tell them that whether we choose to accept them as clients again will be at our discretion." He slammed the phone into its cradle. *Bloody salespeople, don't know when and how to control the clients.*

He got up from his desk and walked over to the window. He was on the ninth floor of the modern office building at the corner of Novy Arbat and Novinsky Boulevard. Thirty years ago he never would have imagined working in a clandestine organization, much less being the leader of one of its cells—the October Cell— named after the month it was established.

There were other cells throughout Europe, mostly consisting of ex-intelligence and military officers. He told himself that nations rise and fall, but wars are common, and have been since the beginning of time. He mused that war would always yield great business. He might consider the fall of the Soviet Union, and his inactivity in the former KGB, as a mixed blessing. The knowledge and experience he had acquired had allowed him to help jumpstart the Arms of Ares, which had seen worldwide revenues of over four billion in the last eight years in arms sales. He expected those revenues would triple with Pandora in their possession.

There was a knock at the door. He stopped twirling the pen and inserted it into the breast pocket of his charcoal-gray suit.

"Enter," he said, without taking his eyes off of the traffic below. Through the window, he saw the reflection of one of his staff members, closing the door behind him.

"Excuse me, sir. There's been some troubling news."

"If it's about our loss in Darfur, I'm fully aware of it."

"It's not about Darfur, sir. It's about our satellite laboratory."

The white-haired man turned away from the window to face him. "What do you mean?"

"There's been an attack. We're not sure when, but it must have been recently."

The white-haired man approached him slowly. "Pandora, is it safe?"

The man didn't answer immediately. Either he didn't know or he was afraid to tell him.

"Is it safe?" he yelled.

"We don't know, sir," the staff member said. "We got a distress signal that was cut off within seconds of it going off. When we tried to contact them, there was no reply."

"Valerik, where is he?"

"He cannot be reached, sir."

"Find out what happened there. I want some answers within the next half hour. I want you to also contact the unit and have them assembled and waiting for me at our usual rendezvous point. Have my car waiting for me downstairs."

"Yes, sir." The man then walked out the door, closing it behind him.

The white-haired man took out his pen and twirled it, trying to calm his agitation. This couldn't have been Fox—again. If it was, he would've known in advance from his mole in the CIA, unless Fox caught onto him. But then, a more dreadful scenario occurred to him, and the more he thought of it, the faster he twirled his pen. *Valerik stole Pandora to sell it himself, and it was the last remaining stock.* If he was out there hiding, his cell would track him down and he would personally end the traitor's life.

Chapter 5

US Air Force Base at Entebbe Airport, Uganda, 5:40 PM local time

The two F-16 Fighter Jet escorts broke away as the C-130 Hercules turboprop aircraft made its final approach to the runway, touching down nearly ten minutes later.

"Welcome to Entebbe Airport, the latest in new American bases," said Hiller.

"Any place where I could avoid being shot at for the next forty-eight hours will do," said Fox, eager to get off the plane.

"Is this your first time here?"

Fox nodded. "I haven't been to many bases here on this continent. Most of my time has been hopping around Europe and the Middle East."

"Well, we ain't going to be needing those bases much longer—the European ones, that is. The Soviet threat's not the big issue—the terrorist threat is. Over the next few years the Pentagon's going to be relocating those bases right here in Africa and the Middle East."

Fox nodded. *Makes sense. It's a better way to keep a close eye on terrorists and oil resources.*

Once the Hercules aircraft had taxied to a stop, Fox and the SEALs didn't waste time unbuckling their seatbelts, getting up, and lining up at the back cargo door.

Hiller motioned Fox forward with his right arm. "Ladies first."

"Dumb blondes in back," Fox quipped, which was followed by laughter from the other SEALs.

Hiller patted Fox on the back. "It's good to have you back. You had me worried back there in Darfur."

"I'm fine. I told you not to worry."

The back cargo door lowered and touched the runway. The heat hit him as though an oven door had just been opened. It wouldn't be long before he'd need another cold shower once he got indoors. It'd been a while since Fox wore army fatigues. He remembered that he wore a similar pair while with Hiller after they had rescued Canadian and American hostages from pirates in the Indian Ocean in a joint SEAL-JTF2 mission a few years back. But it was the only clothing they provided him with back at the Chad-Sudan border base.

He looked at the red-colored sky that surrounded the setting sun over the forest. A commercial plane roared overhead as it took off. Soon afterwards he heard a Jeep approach. "Here's our ride, right on time."

"Correction, Warrant Officer. That's *our* ride. We've got to get this here weaponized virus, or whatever you want to call, it out to the CDC compound northwest of here." Hiller pointed to another Jeep that raced along the tarmac and screeched to a stop beside the other. "I believe that's your ride coming right now."

When Fox saw the Jeep's driver, he looked the other way. "Oh Christ, it's Walsh."

"So you know him, one of your pals I take it."

"Not exactly. I think I'd rather be back in Darfur, than ride with him."

"Hey there, Foxy!" yelled Tom Walsh.

"Damn, I feel sorry for you, buddy," said Hiller as they reached the tarmac. "When we get back home, I'll set you up with my sister-in-law. She's as stubborn as they come, but I'm sure you'll take anything at this point, right?"

"As long as she doesn't wear your shoe size, I might take her."

Hiller laughed. "I'll remember that. My wife and I are having a barbeque next weekend. You plan on joining us?"

"You know I'm always there."

"Cool, we'll see each other then." They shook hands.

Fox walked to Walsh's Jeep as Hiller and the other SEALs got into theirs and drove away to a UH-60 Black Hawk Helicopter.

"What's going on there, Foxy?"

Fox climbed inside as Walsh jetted off. "First of all, stop calling me *Foxy*."

"Oh come on, what's going on with you? You should be proud of yourself. You managed to stop a case of genocide and piss off our enemies again. This time, all at once."

"All in a day's work."

"All in a day's work? Are you kidding me? Wait a minute, let me guess. You dated and dumped another woman again, didn't you? Come on, you can tell me."

Fox rolled his eyes. "It's over and that's all I have to say about it."

"Damn it. You know what your problem is? You let yourself get too close to women and when you have to let them go, it's too painful for you. I mean, you change women more often than most men change their underwear."

"Except for you, of course."

Walsh shot a glance at him. "What's that?"

"Just drop it. I don't need this right now."

"Jesus, I was just trying to make conversation." Walsh parked the Jeep crookedly and took up two parking spaces. Fox stepped out of the Jeep, and he looked at the newly-built military intelligence facility, which was still undergoing construction in certain parts.

Walsh joined Fox and led him to the entrance. "Here we are, probably the most technically advanced and secure facility in the entire country."

Fox didn't comment. He got out and followed Walsh inside. They both came to the security checkpoint where Fox emptied his pockets and placed his wallet and an envelope in a basket that was put on the conveyer belt. He walked through the x-ray booth behind Walsh. When the two marines at the checkpoint were satisfied, Fox took back his wallet and walked off.

"Sir, you forgot this." When Fox turned, one of the marines

held onto the envelope. Fox thanked the marine and took it.

Walsh nodded as Fox pocketed the envelope. "What you got there, a love letter?"

"Yeah. That's what it is," lied Fox. It was a letter of resignation he planned to give Downing. He wrote it while he was in Chad. *I delivered Pandora and Ares would lose billions from that loss. Let the CIA take care of the rest, I'm through.*

Walsh buckled his belt as he led Fox down the hall. "Tell you what. I'll make it up to you. It won't be long before we head back home. Why don't we check out a Redskins game?"

"Thanks, but no thanks."

"Jesus, aren't you hard to please. Don't tell me you're still upset that I brought up your last fling."

"No, I'm just not into football," Fox lied again. He was the team's MVP the last two years in high school. He even dabbled with rugby while on a training mission in Scotland, back in the days while he was in the Canadian Army.

"Fine, then we'll check out the opera. How about that?"

Fox rolled his eyes to the ceiling and sighed. *He's relentless.*

Walsh pushed open one of the conference room's double doors, and Fox followed him into the room. He saw his superior, General Paul Downing at the head of the conference table. To his right, he saw the more stoutly built, Post Commander Bell. To Downing's left sat a blonde woman who looked up at Fox and Walsh as they entered. Fox didn't know her personally, but could only guess her to be Dr. Tabitha Marx, from the CDC. Her name was mentioned a few times in his initial briefing before he left for Chechnya. Her violet pantsuit accentuated a certain sense of authority as it mixed with the dirty-blonde hair that hung past her shoulders. He guessed her to be in her mid-forties, at most.

Fox always pictured women with high levels of education to be a bit on the plump side when they hit their forties, due to the stresses of balancing both work and family. But not Dr. Marx, who was widowed a year after she married a wealthy industrialist. She still kept her shape and youthful appearance. Maybe it was camouflaged by her height—being over six feet tall—or maybe it was the grace in her movements when she swiveled around in her chair, exposing the length of her crossed legs. But when she looked back at him and smiled, Fox noticed her icy-blue eyes.

"You can both have a seat," said General Downing. "You both know Colonel Fred Bell." The Post Commander poured himself a glass of ice water from the pitcher on the table as he nodded. "Sitting in on this meeting is Dr. Tabitha Marx from the CDC."

"Good evening, gentlemen," Marx said. Fox and Walsh nodded.

Downing turned to Fox. "As you probably know, Dr. Marx is a specialist on the bio-weapon you've successfully retrieved. She has come here to see to its proper disposal."

"I have a question, Doc. What Fox brought back was small enough to fit in a briefcase. How bad a weapon is it?" asked Walsh.

"It's one of the deadliest weapons ever known to man," she replied. "The small amount of the Pandora microbe Fox retrieved is enough to wipe out an entire city the size of New York. Imagine if you were attacked by a single microbe that's virtually invisible to the naked eye. It finds its way inside you, either through your mouth, ears, or the nose, and eats its way inside, ingesting tissue and organs in order to self-replicate. All you feel is the inside of your body collapsing while the microbes increase exponentially in numbers. Huge boils appear all over your body, seconds before they erupt and spray the billions of offspring your body helped to produce. The casual observer would see fluorescent-green smoke blowing out of an infected victim. Then again, if you were close enough to see this, then you're good as dead within minutes."

Walsh recoiled in his chair. "Jesus, Doc. Is this your idea of a bedtime story?"

Marx looked at Walsh with a half smile. "Does the scenario frighten you?" She dropped the grin. "It should. Because this is exactly what Mr. Fox retrieved."

Fox noticed her as she ended the sentence looking at him. *What was it about those eyes of hers? It was as though she were trying to read my thoughts.*

Bell took a gulp from his glass. "Jesus Christ! You mean to say, what fit into that briefcase is enough to start World War Three?"

Marx leaned forward and placed an elbow on the table.

"It's anyone's guess as to how far terrorists would go to attack America. Imagine Al-Qaeda agents going on suicide missions not just in New York, but also in Los Angeles, Washington, and Chicago. Add to the fact that it would be followed by a massive panic across the country. Nine-eleven would be reduced to just another paragraph in a high school history book."

General Downing cleared his throat loudly. "Uh, thank you for the explanation, Dr. Marx."

Fox had a sense of relief. It wasn't just him who felt uncomfortable around Marx after all. His own boss was even freaked out over her explicitness in detail. God forbid she became one of the President's advisors. America would be on a year-long state of emergency.

Fox noticed her stare again. She was really starting to freak him out.

General Downing turned to Fox. "Despite the loss of our informant, and some very crucial intelligence about Ares, we've been able to proceed with what you were able to get about other possible Pandora laboratories. I've put Tom in charge of handling the task force units to conduct simultaneous raids on them."

Fox turned to him, a bit tense out of excitement. "So that's it. We're done."

"Not quite," began Walsh. "Less than three hours ago, teams were dispatched to two other laboratories, one in the northern part of the Republic of Komi, in Russia, and also in Belarus, north of the city of Polatsk. Both teams reported that nothing was left of them when they arrived. However, the lab north of Polatsk was on lockdown. The blast door wouldn't open once we entered the codes."

"Something happened inside," said Dr. Marx.

Downing looked at her. "What makes you think so?"

"It's obvious why Ares would use bunker-like blast doors at the entrance of their underground labs," Marx replied. "It's not to keep certain people from getting in, but in order to keep Pandora from getting out in the event of an accident."

"An accident? I doubt that. That's rather unlikely," said Fox.

Marx turned to him. "And why's that?"

"Their lab in Groznyy is destroyed. They've lost Pandora over there. I'd think they'd be more cautious, especially since it might be their last sample of Pandora. It just seems too good to be true that they'd be that careless as to lose such a valuable commodity by accident."

Walsh turned to Marx. "Fox may have a point. With the timing of those raids, whether Ares was setting up shop in either of those labs, we should've nailed them."

Marx leaned back, away from the table. "Another explanation is that Ares could've set off the accident deliberately in order to send us off course. Meaning that there's possibly more sleeper labs."

Fox put an elbow on the table, and he let his head drop into his hand, massaging his forehead. "I doubt it. My contact was very accurate in the intel she shared with me. She never mentioned the possibility of her intel being faulty."

"Then how else do you explain the lab being on internal lockdown?" asked Marx.

Fox paused for a moment. He looked up at her. "I can't be sure. Maybe...I don't know...another disgruntled agent in Ares, like Sokolova. The person or persons could've deliberately caused the accident."

"That may be true, Ridley," said General Downing. "But the intel your contact would've given us, had she survived the escape, would've helped us identify the person, or persons, who could be potential defectors." He pushed his chair back from the table and grabbed his cane. "Are there any more questions?" No one answered. "Then this meeting's adjourned. I believe you must go report to the CDC's compound, Dr. Marx?"

"I told them to start without me," Marx replied. "They should know what to do without my help." She got up and addressed everyone before she left. Walsh, Fox, Colonel Bell, and General Downing returned the address as they also got up.

As Fox and Walsh walked to the door, Walsh whispered to Fox, "So what do you think about her? I'll bet you haven't had a catch like her yet, have you?"

"She's not my type, Walsh, so lay off," Fox angrily whispered back to him.

"Tom," said Downing. "Could you excuse Fox and me for a minute?"

Fox looked back at his superior. *Intel your contact would've given us, had she survived the escape, would've helped us identify the person, or persons, who could be potential defectors. That was what Downing just said.* Fox knew that comment was directed towards him. And now he was going to get it.

Walsh agreed and closed the door behind him, as Fox walked back towards his boss.

Downing rested both elbows on the table and cupped his hands. "I've known you for about five years, ever since I first recruited you from the Canadian Special Ops. I've watched you make mistakes until you learned how fatal they could be. But I still can't get around how you could've been so careless, to allow yourself to get caught, when you were in Chechnya."

"I can—"

"You know I hate it when you interrupt me."

Fox cleared his throat. "I'm sorry."

"You were able to accomplish the mission because you got lucky. A civilian rescued you—a civilian. Your blunder could've caused a serious threat to national security, and possibly an international crisis, if Ares had succeeded in selling Pandora to our enemies." Downing leaned back and took a breath. "I turned fifty-six ten days ago, I'm walking with a prosthetic leg, and I put three children through college. Over the years, I've dealt with all types of threats to our country while you were doing the Moonwalk in elementary school. I've also dealt with all kinds of people, and you're unique, Ridley. You're tough and you can be sadistic. But you also have a soft side that allows your emotions to get the best of you. That's what happened in Groznyy, didn't it?"

Fox shook his head slowly. "Not so much, sir."

"Oh really? Then how do you explain what happened?"

"They were expecting me. Sokolova confirmed it, just as I had mentioned in my report. It all points to someone setting me up."

"I'm not talking about that. I'm talking about the fact that Ms.

Sokolova is not here with us. My God, the intel she could've provided us with is invaluable. It may be months, if not years, before an opportunity like that happens again."

Fuck. Didn't you just hear me? We may have a mole in the agency and all you want to do is blame me for what we lost. "Then we find out who's the mole and get the info out of him."

"What mole?"

"As I said earlier, I was set up. The details of my mission were tightly sealed. No one was supposed to know about it—which means that there was a leak somewhere in the ranks."

"You *assume* there was a leak," Downing shot back.

"I know there was a goddamned leak because Sokolova confirmed it," said Fox, losing control of his tone of voice.

"Really? What were her exact words?"

Fox thought back to what she said. *Somehow they knew that you were coming.*

"Well?" asked Downing. "What were her exact words?"

Fox looked away and sighed. "She mentioned that Ares has already infiltrated other foreign intelligence agencies." *He's not going to buy that.*

"*Foreign* intelligence agencies? Yet she'd contacted you specifically. If she knew for sure that there's a double agent within the CIA, why didn't she warn you then?"

Fox shook his head. *I knew he wouldn't buy it.* "I don't know."

Downing slammed the table with his hand. "This is pathetic. You've gotten yourself so wrapped up in your personal vendetta against Ares, after what they did to your fiancée, you can't even concentrate. I don't know why I thought that you'd be fit enough for this assignment. I'm going to recommend a full psychiatric evaluation be done on you."

Maybe Sokolova got it wrong and there is no mole. Maybe I'm just fishing for any damn excuse after all. "That won't be necessary."

"And why's that?"

Fox reached into his pocket. Just as his fingers touched the envelope there was a knock at the door, followed by Walsh bursting through, breathing heavily and covered in sweat.

"I'm sorry to barge in like this, sir. But we've just gotten word that something's happened at the CDC facility. And I'm afraid it's not good."

Chapter 6

CDC Facility, northwest of Entebbe International Airport, 30 minutes earlier

Hiller's stomach growled as the UH-60 Black Hawk bobbed through some turbulence. He hadn't eaten a full meal since he left the Congo-Sudan border. Now all he thought of was some fall-off-the-bone ribs, some potato salad, maybe some Cajun-style chicken, and a cold beer straight from the keg. While this imaginary meal kept his mind wandering, the pilot spoke to him. Hiller didn't even pay attention and he straitened his headset.

"You mind running that question by me again?" said Hiller.

"I asked you if this is the first time you've been to the CDC compound?" asked the pilot.

"Yeah," Hiller answered.

"Then I'll update you on a few things. When I set us down, you just walk up to the gate where the guard will let you in. Dr. Cole will meet you outside the domed tent so you won't have to go inside. You just hand him the package and come back. Any questions?"

Hiller smiled. "Will I be chased by rhinos?" The other SEALs with him laughed.

"You're funny, but no. All wildlife has been temporarily displaced in accordance to agreements between the Ugandan and American governments. They even had to spray the ground with a very powerful insecticide to kill any insects on the surface and the ones in the ground. They couldn't do much about the flies though."

Hiller looked at the metal briefcase. "Damn, this weapon must be some real contagious shit."

"I don't know any more about it than you do, sir," the pilot answered. "Once whatever in the package is neutralized, and hopefully soon, the CDC will have to haul ass out of here before the animal rights and the other environmentalist groups start poking around."

The Black Hawk swooped down from the night sky outside the fenced area. Hiller got out carrying the briefcase and saw the domed tent. The area wasn't as big as he expected, maybe slightly smaller than a soccer field. It was was bordered by a twelve-foot high, barbwire fence. A twenty-foot wooden tower to his left, inside the fenced area, had two guards posted, accompanied by ten others on the ground. The six flood lights—swarmed by hundreds of insects—kept the grounds bright.

One of the guards opened the entrance just as a white coat emerged from the dome's double-doorway access. Hiller met the white coat halfway.

"Dr. Cole?" he asked loudly, above the noise from the propellers.

Cole nodded. "Warrant Officer Hiller?"

Hiller handed Cole the metal briefcase and the key. "She's all yours."

"Excellent. We'll take it from here."

The SEAL ran back to the helicopter, and it lifted off seconds later.

***

When Cole reached the doorway and pulled it open, the cool air greeted him. He walked towards the isolation chamber that was at the center of the dome where two of his colleagues were. It was twenty feet in length and width but only nine feet high.

"All right guys, we got the package. Let's get started," Cole said. It was only then that it dawned on him that they were not dressed in their HAZMAT gear. "Why aren't you two dressed?"

"It won't be necessary," the one nearest to him answered, as he rushed toward Cole while he opened his lab coat to grab the hidden D-W73 Cold War era Russian Air Force Officer's Dagger, and plunged it into Cole's stomach. With his free hand, he covered Cole's mouth to muzzle him. He turned the blade and pulled upwards, maximizing damage to his internal organs, before he released him and let him drop to the ground.

***

The assailant picked up the briefcase and handed it to his partner who carried it over to a table in front of the isolation chamber, unlocked it with the key, and opened it. The assailant went to another table with a communications port and a telephone which linked him directly to Entebbe Base. He picked up the phone and there was a ringing on the other end.

"Entebbe Base," came the reply.

"We're under attack...send help...quick. They're Russian—" He screamed loudly and hung up. The assailant then turned to his partner. "Was I convincing enough?"

His partner stood beside the open briefcase. "You couldn't have been more perfect." He took the fluorescent-green vial and let it drop gently on the ground without breaking. He then hit the alarm button. The siren was heard for miles.

It was not too long after, that ten of the guards burst through the doorway with their assault rifles in position. They fanned out to cover the inside of the dome.

"What's the emergency?" yelled the leader to the two scientists, and then he saw Cole's body with the dagger protruding from his stomach. His assault rifle shot up immediately. "Both of you, hands in the air. Do it, now!"

This brought the other guards running. Within seconds, they had encircled the two scientists.

"I repeat," yelled the leader. "Put your hands up, or we will be forced to shoot you."

The two white-coats didn't obey him, but instead looked at each other and smiled. "For The Promise?"

"For The Promise." The partner already had the vial under the heel of his shoe. As he slowly raised his hands along with the assailant, he breathed his last breath and crushed the vial. It wasn't long before what felt was millions of microscopic teeth tearing away at the flesh, starting with his foot and then moving to the rest of his body. His body convulsed erratically as he dropped to the ground, as his vision was clouded by a fluorescent green dust. He faintly heard the screams from the guards before his eyes burst and oozed out of their sockets along as the metallic taste of blood filled his throat. The pain caused him to scream a voiceless scream as he felt the inside of his body being torn apart.

***

The SEALs were no more than three miles away when they were notified of an attack at the CDC compound. A few minutes later, the base was below them, as they made their descent to give air support, only to see the soldiers hightailing out of the dome.

The pilot opened the side door from up front, while Hiller and two other SEALs covered the doorway, taking aim with their assault rifles. The multiple screams preceded the green-colored smoke that exploded from the dome's entrance, making its way to the Black Hawk.

Hiller jumped back and the other two followed his example. "Shit! Pull up, pull up!"

They were not able to rise fast enough before the plume enveloped the helicopter. Even with the propellers at maximum, it couldn't slow down Pandora's momentum as the SEALs all suffered the same fate as the men below. Nothing was left of their bodies by the time the Black Hawk crashed and burst into flames.

Chapter 7

CDC compound, Northwest of Entebbe, 9:50 PM

Fox stared at the charred remains of the helicopter as he stood a dozen feet away. Warrant Officer Jack Hiller and he went back a few years, to the time when he was recruited into the CIA. *Shit.* Only God knew how many more he would lose in his quest to stop Ares. He squeezed Hiller's dog tag in his left hand and felt the edges dig into his palm. Hiller was the closest friend he had—pals both on and off the job. In his other hand he had the envelope he nearly gave to Downing. *Fuck it.* And with that thought he tore up the envelope and threw the pieces into the wreckage.

"Hey, buddy," said Walsh as he approached. "I'm sorry about your friend."

"I'm fine. You don't have to apologize." Fox turned away from the wreckage. But he was far from being all right. They walked towards the dome. "Any leads yet?"

"The General's all over it. All of the airports are on high alert and there are checkpoints on every highway leading from here, but I doubt that at this point we'll ever catch who did this."

"Yeah, whatever. Hopefully they died along with the rest of them." Fox couldn't help thinking about what his superior had told him earlier about his emotions interfering with his work. *Why didn't I kill the guard that killed Sveta while I had the chance? The names and faces of every Ares operative would be known.*

When they were both inside the dome, they saw Dr. Marx, in an overcoat, talking with two of the men from Entebbe Base. Their colleagues were all over the compound searching for more casualties and evidence.

As they got closer to her she turned to face them. She extended a glove-covered hand to both of them and greeted them. "I appreciate you coming so quickly."

Walsh was the first to extend his hand to hers. "We couldn't come any earlier, for obvious reasons."

Marx then shook Fox's hand. "I know. I and a few others came here first to inspect the area in HAZMAT gear. I was airborne when the SOS was sent, and I was forced to turn back. We used lab mice as a way of ensuring safety for you to come. It took close to three hours before all visible signs of Pandora dissipated. Come with me, you'll want to see this." She led them to the isolation chamber. After they passed through the decontamination airlock the crisp frost air hit them. "Don't worry. We'll be out of here long before we all freeze."

Along one side of the floor sat four trays holding black anti-contamination bags with the yellow bio-hazard symbol on each of them. Each of the bags was about the size of a regular duffle bag. "The temperature's being regulated at minus three degrees Celsius to help keep what's left of these bodies in one piece."

Walsh squinted as he looked at Marx. "In one piece?"

Marx nodded. "Precisely."

Fox listened to her as he looked down at one of the trays. Walsh did the same with another tray. As Fox looked at the bags, he questioned their small size, seeing that they looked too small to contain an average-sized man that would have fit on the trays that they were on.

"Aside from the inorganic components of their skeletons and Pandora's slimy by-products, all that was left of them were their clothes, and a few other personal items."

"Jesus!" Walsh jumped back from one of the bags he had unzipped. The sight of the mess in front of him was enough to throw anyone back. Walsh hopped between the trays and around both Marx and Fox as he ran for the door, his right hand over his mouth.

If this was going to be one of many embarrassing moments with Walsh, Fox was ready to ditch him the first chance he got. He looked back at Marx who was looking down at the body bag. The woman wasn't showing any kind of emotion.

"I should've warned him about that. I guess I was wrong to assume that anything with a visibly large bio-hazard symbol would be enough to keep anyone away," said Marx with deliberate sarcasm.

"As I said, nothing much that would identify the victims was left." Marx knelt down in front of the same tray from which Walsh had run, put on a pair of latex gloves from her coat pocket, and stretched them over her fingers. She then pinched and lifted a section of the cover before she continued to unzip it halfway.

It wasn't what he saw that almost made him react like Walsh— he'd already witnessed unspeakable acts against human beings— but the more Marx unzipped the bag, the more he pursed his lips and squinted. *Dear God* was all that came to Fox's mind. The dark and thick, slimy mass had sparse amounts of hair and bone. It clung to the inside of the bag and bubbled as more air was exposed to it. *No wonder the bags were that size. It was most likely pumped through a hose.*

"Zip it up!" Fox turned away.

Marx raised an eyebrow, shrugged her shoulders, and zipped it back up. She stood up, took off the latex gloves, and dropped them on the cover.

He stormed away a few paces and then doubled back. Fox knew he was not being fair to her, but it made him feel better to act as though it was her fault. *How could she be so close to such a stomach-turning sight and be unaffected? She didn't even flinch. Maybe it was an act.*

"I must admit that I haven't seen anything like this since 1987," said Marx. "I was just starting out with the CDC when I accompanied my colleagues to Northern Canada where the first outbreak occurred in a small Inuit community. There weren't too many deaths, since Pandora is less effective in the cold. We were able to contain the outbreak and also keep the incident out of the papers to prevent a widespread panic. But when our research revealed exactly how dangerous Pandora was, our government at the time thought they had found an alternative to the nuclear bomb. The Department of Defense had contracts with the CDC for R and D funding."

Fox glanced at all of the body bags. "Looks to me that it didn't need either more research or development. After what's happened here, I'd say it accomplished what it was supposed to."

"Only too well. You see, there was fear that if we were to release it on the enemy that it might find its way back to us because we had limited control over it when it was airborne."

"What do you mean?"

"Once released, wind currents, for example, can blow Pandora almost anywhere. We could potentially harm a friendly nation. You've seen how easily it spreads."

"Therefore, Pandora can't be controlled once it's released."

"That's exactly what all the critics said about the project. The best my colleagues and I were able to do, was to freeze its replication by immersing Pandora in liquid nitrogen. That's how it's stored. Before it was released, it would be fed with small doses of a protein supplement which would give it longevity before it came in contact with a potential host."

"So it *does* have a weakness—starvation. That's why none of it was found by the time we arrived, because it starved to death."

"Correct. That's why it was so important for us to choose this location to set up this compound, far away from any populated areas. Other than starvation, Pandora's virtually indestructible. Unlike a regular missile, shooting down a missile containing Pandora won't do anything but release it into the atmosphere where it will inevitably drop to earth."

"If you were to feed it a large amount of its supplement, how would that affect its reproduction rate versus feeding it a smaller amount of the same supplement?"

"An increase in supplement is directly proportional to its reproductive rate. The more food it ingests, the more offspring it produces." Marx then motioned in the direction of the door. "Judging from the distance between here and where the helicopter was, whomever used this weapon must have fed Pandora with a fair amount of the protein supplement in order for it to increase in such numbers that it would've reached it so quickly."

"But wouldn't the force of the helicopter's propellers be strong enough to fan away the microbes?"

"Not necessarily. As I mentioned earlier, the reproductive rate of a single Pandora microbe is directly correlated with the amount of food it ingests. If a large enough quantity of the complex protein supplement were fed to it, it would not only reproduce so extremely rapidly as to appear as a green-colored explosion."

"Which is probably what happened here," said Fox.

"No doubt," Marx nodded. "And the wonderful thing about Pandora is that energy from the parent is transferred to its clones, only gradually decreasing in each generation."

"I don't know which school of thought you come from, but I don't find anything *wonderful* about Pandora."

Marx gasped at the comment. "I'm sorry. I didn't mean to say it that way. I was only speaking from a scientific point of view."

Fox followed her out of the isolation chamber as she continued with the conversation. She put her hands into her pockets. "A few years ago there was a second outbreak, again up in Northern Canada, near the north pole, when two university scientists accidentally exhumed a Pandora-infected prehistoric man, buried under the ice for what could've been a few millennia. Their SOS was intercepted by the National Security Agency's Echelon system. You could imagine the horror I felt when my phone rang soon after."

Echelon was the National Security Agency's computer program that automatically intercepted keywords in regular conversation, either on a regular phone or through cyberspace, used to track potential terrorist threats. The system had been updated to include references to Pandora.

"I flew up there with a team and fortunately arrived on time to contain the outbreak. I thought that was the last we'd see of Pandora, until now," said Marx.

Fox ran a finger over his left eyebrow. "Pandora wasn't created, after all."

"Most definitely not. The ice man's discovery suggests that Pandora is a microbe that existed in prehistoric times. It managed to survive over time by lying dormant in the ice man. My guess is that at the time that he and members of his community were infected, he either fell through a frozen lake or was buried under an avalanche while the rest were wiped out."

They reached the doorway to the dome and exited where Walsh was.

Fox walked up to Walsh. "You all right? You've lost some color in your face."

"I'll live, and I tan easily," Walsh replied. "What I still can't figure out is how Ares managed to get their hands on Pandora."

"Ares has spies everywhere, unless they discovered it on their own." But Fox felt that the latter explanation was the least likely.

"No matter how they discovered it, whoever's responsible for this disaster went far enough to kill everyone to cover their tracks," said Walsh.

Dr. Marx turned when she heard a cleanup-crew member shout out to her. "Dr. Marx, we found another victim."

"I'll be right there," she replied. She turned to Fox and Walsh. "I have to go. I'll send you my results when I'm done."

"Sure thing, Doc," replied Walsh.

Fox nodded to her. He was about to walk away when Marx called back to him. "Oh, Fox, watch your back. You never know what or who may turn up."

"I'll make sure of that." Fox checked the ground to make sure he didn't step in anything gelatinous as both he and Walsh walked back to their transport helicopter that was outside the compound.

With no survivors or any retrievable data so far, the trail was about to run cold. And those responsible wanted it that way. Fox knew he would go sleepless for several nights knowing that a surprise attack was imminent.

Chapter 8

West Tokyo

Hideaki Hashimoto usually read the morning news from his laptop computer at 6:00 AM while he sipped on a cup of hot tea. He preferred sitting outside at the gazebo in the garden when it was sunny and warm. But this morning was different. It was 5:35 AM, and he was inside his office tearing through webpage after webpage on his laptop as his tea sat untouched on his desk. Three hours ago, a telephone call woke him up, alerting him of the incident in Uganda.

He must have checked the same news pages several times over, convinced he had missed something. CNN.com, BBC. co.uk—they had nothing. Maybe news on the Pandora outbreak in southern Uganda would only break later that morning, unless the officials wanted to keep the incident under tight wrap to avoid a worldwide panic.

There was a knock at the door.

"Enter," Hashimoto said in Japanese. His personal secretary walked in holding an envelope and an agenda. She then closed the door behind her. "Come in, Ms. Miyake." His eyes never left the monitor.

Ms. Miyake removed her heels at the door as she crossed the Kars rug on her way to her boss's desk and handed him a manila envelope. "Good morning, sir."

Hashimoto placed the envelope on the edge of his desk. "Any

news worth telling me about?"

"Yes, sir. The approval of Hexagon's recent purchase of Warner-Parke Pharmaceuticals in the US has yielded great results. Shares have shot up from $820 US to $1027 US per share."

"Anything else?"

"There's another testing of Project Clarity this morning."

"At nine o'clock?"

"Yes, sir."

"Make sure my driver knows I want to be there at least half an hour early. I personally want to meet the two test subjects."

"I'll see that he gets the message," said Ms Miyake as she scribbled notes into her agenda. "There's also your scheduled teleconference with a Nick Archer from *Financial Planet Magazine* at—"

"Cancel that meeting. I'll conveniently be busy during that hour."

"I'll email him the message right away, sir." More notes were scribbled into the agenda.

The desk phone rang and Hashimoto snatched it. "Moshi moshi?"

"I've arrived a few moments ago with the package. I couldn't contact you sooner for security reasons," said a Russian-accented voice in English. Hashimoto covered the ear piece and gave a head signal to his secretary to leave. She quickly obliged, understanding his need for privacy.

"That's understandable," Hashimoto replied in the same language, recognizing Valerik's voice.

"Not too much trouble, I expect."

"Of course not. I know these people. It was a piece of cake, as the Americans say. Nothing complicated. I only wish the two men you assigned to accompany me would relax a bit. A shot of Vodka to celebrate wouldn't hurt."

"My men were not trained to drink, but to obey. The Undertaker would be very disappointed to hear you talk like that, after everything she's done for us. I trust they've done everything you've asked?"

"Yes, and all too well. They were both a bit more passionate than I was. Anyhow, I'll see you later this morning after I get sleep. It was a long flight."

"Excellent work. Your brothers and sisters have much to be grateful for. By the way, I was notified not too long ago of a certain incident. Our friends are searching for two men." *Men that don't exist, of course.* Hashimoto was careful to avoid using words such as *Americans, manhunt* or *Uganda* in the same sentence. "Do you have any concerns?"

"My former comrades will also be kept so busy running from our friends that they won't have time to come look for me."

"Don't be too sure of that."

"I know."

Hashimoto hung up the phone, more assuaged than when he had answered it. Pandora was finally in his possession, the online news could wait. He knew his tea would be cold by now. That was nothing to stress over, he would send for another cup later.

Hashimoto was a handsome man, standing five-foot-seven inches and he was relatively fit for sixty-four. He had a doctorate certificate in Pharmaceutical Sciences from the University of Tokyo. That and his numerous awards took up an entire wall. The other side was covered with awards and framed newspaper articles related to Hexagon Pharmaceuticals, of which he had been the CEO for the past twenty-three years. He was one of the youngest CEOs to have ever been given that title in the history of the company dating back to 1860.

Hashimoto's association with Valerik went back as far as the early 1980's, when the Soviets had recruited him based on his unique knowledge of brainwashing techniques. Hashimoto's human experiments during the Soviet-Afghan war would've had him arrested for war crimes several years before had the secret gotten out. In addition to the handsome salary the Soviets gave him, they facilitated his climb up the corporate ladder to become CEO of Hexagon Pharmaceuticals.

This was all threatened the day Dr. Tabitha Marx—otherwise known as the Undertaker—had him kidnapped and brought to a warehouse. She told him that she knew everything about him and Valerik after she rummaged through her late mother's belongings.

But her goal was to use an earlier variant of the Clarity drug—turning him into one of her followers. Hashimoto would later lure Valerik into an ambush where the same would be done to him.

Since his encounter with Marx, Hashimoto was able to see that religion and politics were the root of all of the world's problems. The world only needed one belief system, and that's why she told him that he should establish his own cult, The Promise, and use Clarity to help recruit members. Hexagon was the perfect front.

Hashimoto wasn't surprised that Dr. Marx hadn't called him yet. She was on an American Military base and wouldn't risk calling over an unsecure phone line. Valerik would've text-messaged a code to her that should've passed under the Intelligence community's radar, illustrating his success in acquiring Pandora. This would in turn let her know that it was all right to disperse of what she had obtained. Framing Ares for it was a bonus.

Stealing Pandora from the weapons consortium, known as the Arms of Ares, would be a serious blow to that organization. Valerik was a professional. He'd proven himself several times before and wouldn't be so careless as to lead a trail to either him or Hexagon Pharmaceuticals.

Even if he did, Hashimoto was more than equipped to handle them should they ever come looking for him.

Chapter 9

Hexagon Pharmaceuticals Head Office, West Tokyo, Japan, three hours later

D octor . Nita Parris parked her car in her reserved parking spot. It was the first time in days that she had chosen to drive to work. Most of Hexagon's employees took advantage of Hexagon's shuttle bus service from the nearby train station that dropped them off at each of the building's four main entrances. She remembered the orientation session she had to get—mandatory for new employees and overseas transfers, like herself. Her guide even spoke English to her when he gave her a personal tour. All that was important to know about Hexagon Pharmaceuticals was that there were four Plexiglas-covered buildings that took up an area of ten football fields, named each according to orientation.

The south building was the tallest and had a two-storey lobby area with five office floors above it. The north building had residences on its two floors and a basement for compensated human trials. The east building had a ground floor and four sub-basements where chemicals and other products were manufactured and stored. Then there was the two-storey west building which consisted of conference rooms, auditoriums, and a cafeteria. All four buildings were easily accessible by horizontal escalators inside. Someone that could memorize that would never get lost inside. If they couldn't, then they could refer to the maps.

With her black golf umbrella in one hand and her Madison Avenue Tote hanging from her opposite shoulder, she walked up the divided, flower-adorned walkway to the south entrance and joined a group that poured out of a shuttle bus. The crowd that surrounded her was a portion of the 105,000 that were employed worldwide in the United States, Great Britain, Canada, and Brazil, making Hexagon one of the largest pharmaceutical companies in the world.

Being the only black woman among mostly Asians wasn't the only thing that made her stand out—it was how fast she walked. Even in her four-inch-high stacked heels, she moved quickly. Seven years after she had hung up her track spikes, she still couldn't slow down. But to her, it was everyone else who was slow.

As a young girl growing up in Barbados, she easily out-sprinted the boys, even the older ones. And although it'd been more than eight years since her last track meet, she couldn't resist finding an outdoor, galvanized-rubber surfaced track to do some wind sprints on—just for the rush she used to have. She joined a gym that was a fifteen minute jog from where she lived and managed to go twice a week. She was flattered every time someone had trouble guessing her age, but she knew that most of the men did so just as a cheap pick-up line.

When she had competed for the Princeton University Track Team she was always hunted by the boys on the football and basketball teams. They'd always been present at home competitions, in packs of eight to ten, and always tried to get the phone numbers of the girls on the team.

Even today, things hadn't changed in terms of how men looked at her. Such as the four men she had caught in her peripheral vision since she'd left her apartment earlier. It wasn't a natural habit, it was a CIA-based trained habit to be able to spot people that either observed her or followed her inconspicuously.

She liked the flowers in the center median. They reminded her of the ones that she and her aunt Pauline had planted around the house, back home in St Phillip parish in Barbados. Those were such innocent times for her, when she would share everything with her aunt, whom she owed everything to.

She never knew her parents. Her mother had passed away a few days after she was born, and her father was a ghost. Aunt Pauline, with the exception of a few other aunts, uncles, and cousins who lived in Barbados and England, was the only family that she knew.

After she passed through the revolving door to the South building, she glanced at the large digital clock that hung above the security guard's round counter in the center of the atrium. It was 8:35 AM. She was well ahead of schedule. These past several weeks she had played to perfection the role of a senior researcher for Hexagon Pharmaceuticals. On the books, the company had several legitimate research contracts worth millions of dollars. But General Downing sent her there to spy on her boss, Dr. Hideaki Hashimoto.

The National Security Agency always suspected that illicit human trials were conducted by the Soviets during the Soviet-Afghan war and that they had recruited Hashimoto to run the experiments. Every investigation turned up a dead end. Nevertheless, the NSA's paranoia led them to believe that if he had perfected his brainwashing techniques, it would likely fall in the hands of an enemy nation or terrorist group.

Downing felt that her background in biology and chemistry would make her a perfect fit. While she pursued her Biochemistry doctorate at Princeton, she had singlehandedly discovered a bio-weapon threat against the US. Downing wasted no time recruiting her. The CIA and the FBI's top guns still could not figure out how they overlooked what she saw. To him she was a perfect candidate—no parents and an aunt for a legal guardian.

But what took her out of the labs at Langley, Virginia, and into the field, was the night she was nearly fatally wounded after a carjacking. It was all because some jerk stood her up on a date. She drove home after waiting for him for over an hour, finally arriving at the traffic light at the DC-Maryland border on Pennsylvania Avenue. It didn't take too long until she heard someone tapping at her window, only to turn and stare into the barrel of Lorcin 9mm semi-automatic pistol. The next thing she knew, she lost her car and wound up having to be taken to the hospital with a mild concussion.

The CIA managed to get her into Hexagon, in their San Francisco branch first, until she got herself transferred to West Tokyo's International Headquarters. Fortunately, she didn't have to speak Japanese since she worked with bilingual colleagues.

She got on the horizontal escalator that carried her to the north building where she hopped on the elevator. There was a ping before the doors opened one floor below, to a white hallway with several doors on each side. The strong scent of lemon stung her nostrils as her heels clapped across the recently washed floor. She stopped once she got to the third door on her left, entered, and closed the door behind her.

She reached to her right and grabbed a lab coat from one of the brass hooks. She removed her jacket and put on the lab coat, leaving her brooch exposed. The events would also be inconspicuously filmed with the miniature camera that was in the brooch pinned to the lapel of her pantsuit. She was there for one reason—to brainwash the two new test subjects with the latest variant of the Clarity drug. After submitting a report, she would meet with her colleague, Tomas Levickis, who was no doubt in his van somewhere doing surveillance as well as recording everything from the brooch.

To her right was a door to the monitoring station, and the one ahead led to the testing room. Both rooms were separated by a one-way see-through window. She walked ahead, pushed the door open, and saw her two test subjects, Dewan and Eva, and her boss, Dr. Hideaki Hashimoto, as he spoke to them.

"Hexagon has patented more than twenty over-the-counter medications and is one of the leading researchers in drugs that could reverse the effects of Alzheimer's disease."

She heard the door click shut as it closed automatically behind her. She smiled. Dewan and Eva were in two dentist-like chairs and beside them was a table with a metal box.

Hashimoto turned to the sound of the clicking door. "Dr. Parris."

"Good morning, sir. I didn't expect to see you here." Parris walked over to the table, laid down her tote, and dropped her jacket on the back of the chair.

"I wanted to chat a bit with Dewan and Eva. Yesterday's meeting was so brief that I wanted to get to know them better." He looked at the two subjects, one a twenty-one year old African-American man and the other a nineteen year old Caucasian woman.

Parris walked up to the one-way mirror to fix the collar of her lab coat. On the other side of the mirror, there would've been at least two other scientists, both male, in front of computers recording everything from blood pressure to brainwave activity in the two subjects.

Levickis had already run their background checks the day before when Parris first met them, and both of them had criminal records. Dewan had a previous charge for marijuana possession in Brooklyn, New York—one that he denied by claiming the drugs belonged to his college roommate. Eva had been arrested in London, England, for hacking into an Italian bank's computers and transferring over one hundred thousand Euros to different accounts she had set up worldwide.

"Did I mention before that Dr. Parris moved here from San Francisco where she conducted research for our sister company?" asked Hashimoto.

Eva rolled her eyes. "You have."

Parris, now back at the table, glanced at Eva briefly and pulled the metal box closer to her. Although she tried to hide it, she actually stared at Eva's circular nose ring. She had three other studs in both ears and even one through her tongue. *Uggh. What was so exciting about puncturing holes all over your body?* She flinched at the thought of having a piece of metal protruding through her tongue. Then there was Dewan—a handsome young man. He wore the typical baggy jeans and a Los Angeles Lakers basketball jersey. No tattoos.

"Now that Dr. Parris is here, I'll leave you three alone." Hashimoto got up and smiled at Parris before he exited, leaving a trace of his aftershave behind.

She'd successfully brainwashed two others like Dewan and Eva, a little over a week ago. But this time she would use a more recent variant of the drug, and the guinea pigs in front of her would be her first experimentation with it. "So tell me, how do you like your new surroundings?"

Neither one answered her. *All right, time for a different approach.* "Do you miss home?"

Dewan and Eva looked at each other as though they were silently trying to determine who should answer.

Parris looked at Dewan. "How about you, Dewan?"

"Me?"

"Yes." Parris immediately dropped the sarcasm in her voice. "Yes, you, dear." Parris clenched her teeth behind closed lips as though to catch her last word from leaving her mouth.

Too late.

Dewan shrugged his shoulders. "It ain't Brooklyn, but hey, it's a free trip. Anything to get away from there. It's starting to become too *bougie* for me."

"Why do you say that?" Parris asked.

Dewan sighed. "I mean, New York's becoming a place for rich people only. Living in Brooklyn today, you might as well live in Manhattan. Damn rent is so expensive that it's harder for people like me to get ahead, 'cause I'm always broke."

Parris looked him in the eye. "No offence, Dewan, but is that why you were selling dope on the side?"

"Aw shit, man. I'm going to tell you like I've told everyone else," said Dewan. "It wasn't my weed, I don't smoke it, and I told my roommate to stop keeping that shit in our apartment. The police messed up their investigation and I go down for it. So much for justice."

Parris did not notice any change in his eyes that made her believe that he lied to her. "I'm sorry to hear that, Dewan. I wasn't trying to offend you. You're right, life's unfair. And injustice always tends to happen to the better ones. Trust me, I've met others. As a result, you've found yourselves on the other side of the law."

"So what does that have to do with us?" Dewan asked.

So now he wants to talk. "I was just coming to that, Dewan—and this concerns you too, Eva. After three days around your new brothers and sisters, what is your own personal take on the group?"

Dewan sighed. "First of all, they aren't my brothers and sisters. Second of all, they're weird."

Parris raised an eyebrow. "Weird?"

"Yeah, weird," answered Dewan. "You know. Strange, odd."

Parris put her hands in her lab coat pockets. "How are they weird?"

Dewan looked over at the table before he looked back at Parris. "They all act so happy, like they've all been visited by Mary Poppins or something. And also this 'end of the world' thing they keep talking about. That it's coming and that they'll be all saved."

"And you find that hard to believe."

Parris then turned to Eva. "How about you, Eva?"

"Well, yeah. I just wonder how everyone, or why everyone, in that group seems to think that the world's coming to an end," she answered.

"I had enough listening to that 2012 crap already," interjected Dewan. "And now this. Then there's the leader they all follow who says, 'The wicked, they're all going to be punished.' Whatever that means."

Eva moaned. "And they never stop."

"No offence, Doctor," said Dewan. "I just want to get paid, see a bit of Tokyo, and then go home. I've seen enough. That's what you all promised in your agreement, right? I can quit this so-called experiment whenever I choose and you'll fly me back home for free. That's the agreement."

Parris raised her index finger as she looked at both of them. "It is. But you haven't come to the fun part yet."

"Oh, so now there's a fun part?" Dewan said sarcastically.

"Yes," she replied. "The part where you get to try our new drug. This is the main reason why you're both here."

Dewan looked away to the door. "Yeah, yeah. The sooner we get this over with the better."

"Talking about your experiment, what's supposed to happen in these chairs?" asked Eva.

Parris walked up beside Eva and touched the headrest of her

chair. "The visor attached here will fit over your eyes where you'll see a variety of images. The electrodes that I'm going to attach to your head and chest will record everything from heart rate to brain activity."

Parris strapped them both into their seats and then attached the adhesive electrodes to them, one on their temples and one on the left side of their chest.

Parris walked to the table and opened the metal box. She took out a bottle of rubbing alcohol, a small bag of cotton balls, a pair of latex gloves, and two bandages, and she placed them each on the table one by one. There were also two twelve-milliliter graduated disposable syringes with hypodermic needles and caps attached to them that were alongside two small sealed glass vials filled with a clear solution.

She snapped on the latex gloves, removed the cap from the hypodermic needle, and picked up one of the vials with the other hand. She looked over at Dewan. He'd been staring at her for a few seconds and frequently rolled his eyes. She would treat him first. She stood to his side and rubbed the cotton ball in a circle on the back of his upper arm. She then took the syringe, filled it with the drug, and injected him. Not to her surprise, Dewan didn't flinch. He was in no way like the stereotypical African-American males you'd see on some primetime television networks back home, where they're portrayed as being obscenely foul-mouthed, low educated, trouble-making individuals. On the other hand, whether he was innocent or not, he was prone to violent outbursts. If only he knew who she really was and what she could do to him, he probably wouldn't be in the same room with her.

"Ouch, be careful," said Dewan as she pushed the plunger in a bit too hard.

"Oh, I'm sorry," Parris lied, as she held back a smile. *I could do a lot worse.* She pulled out the syringe, immediately placed the cotton ball on the injection spot and applied pressure for thirty seconds. She reached over to the bio-hazard pail that was beside the table and pushed the syringe through the flap. She then stuck a Band-Aid to Dewan's arm.

"What's that supposed to be for?" Eva asked.

"This is a drug we call Clarity. It'll help you to listen and comprehend things much better," Parris answered.

Eva smiled. "You mean, make us smarter?"

"Not quite." Eva looked convinced. Dewan frowned. Parris took another cotton ball and alcohol and did the same thing to Eva.

***

While Dr. Parris continued with the experiment, Hashimoto and two scientists observed from the adjoining room through the one-way see-through window. The sound of a turning door handle caught his attention and Hashimoto turned to see Valerik holding open the door, munching on a sandwich. He left the room with Valerik and walked down the hall to a vacant laboratory where they had more privacy.

"Is there something wrong?"

"Not at all," Valerik answered. "But I felt more comfortable seeing you in person instead of speaking over the phone."

"I thought our phone lines were secure. No one's supposed to be able to crack through."

Valerik shoved the rest of the sandwich into his mouth. "Nothing's ever completely secure nowadays."

"Then why did you call me this morning if you knew of the risks?"

"The conversation was kept brief." Some crumbs fell from his mouth before Valerik wiped it with the back of his hand. "There was no mention of Pandora, and you did not call me by name either, as I had told you. The Americans have their supercomputers set up to zero in on key words and trace the location of conversations. But they won't find us as long as you continue to follow my instructions."

Hashimoto sighed with relief. "You're right. Now, what's so important that you had to come here?"

Valerik licked his fingers. "As you know, the Americans are investigating."

Hashimoto reached over to the counter and handed him the tissue box. "I would think so."

Valerik snatched a tissue and wiped his hands. "I received

word about one of them."

"Who is he?"

"His name's Ridley Fox. He's the one responsible for disrupting our plans in the Chechnyan laboratory. He's one of their top agents, if not the best."

"And you're supposed to be *our* best agent. I assume that you'd know how to handle him if ever he gets too close?"

"I can handle him." Valerik balled up the tissue, tossed it to the waste paper basket and missed. "Besides, I doubt that neither he nor the Russians know where to start looking for me."

"If Fox is as good as you say he is, then, I hope not. And with your countrymen on the case—"

"I am a man without a country. The Russians are not my countrymen. My loyalties are and will always be to The Promise."

"I'm sure that's what Dr. Marx would want to hear from you. So would I." Just then, Hashimoto's cell phone rang. He flipped it open. "Moshi moshi."

"Sir, you need to come back to the lab," said one of the scientists from the monitoring room.

"What's wrong?"

"Maybe you should come and see for yourself. Dr. Parris has gone on with the experiment a bit differently and Dewan's readings are somewhat awkward."

"Awkward? In what way?"

"She's gone off on a tangent. She's doing things that were not planned and Dewan's readings are unusual. That's why I think you should come back and take a look for yourself."

"I'll be right there." He flipped his phone shut and looked back at Valerik. "Wait here. I'll send for you when I'm done."

Chapter 10

"I'm curious, Dewan. When you go back home, what are your plans?" Parris lowered the visors over their eyes and pressed the small button over the nose piece to activate them.

Dewan glanced up at the ceiling and then down at the floor as though in deep thought. "I haven't figured that out yet. Get another job, whoever'll hire me, and then try to get back into school, unless I find something better. With what I'm supposed to receive from doing this experiment, my rent should be covered for the first few months anyway."

"I see." Parris nodded. "And if that doesn't work out, what then?"

Dewan sighed and shook his head. "I don't know. I haven't thought that far ahead yet."

"I'm concerned about what you said before," said Parris. "That New York is getting too bourgeoisie for you that you can't handle it. And with a criminal record, it's going to be hard for you to find a job and possibly pay for your schooling."

Dewan rubbed his right eye. "So what are you saying—that I should just give up?"

Parris placed the alcohol and the plastic bag of cotton balls back into the metal box and closed the lid. "Not at all, I was just curious. You're so anxious to leave this place and go home. I just wanted to know what you have left to go home to."

Dewan didn't say anything as she placed her hands in her lab coat pockets and paced in front of the table. She then turned to

Dewan. "Tell me more about your parents, Dewan. Your mother's a nurse and your father's a truck driver. When's the last time you spoke to them?"

"About a couple of weeks ago," he answered. "They don't even know I'm here."

Parris tilted her head to the side. "Why's that?"

He sighed. "'Cause they'd get mad at me."

Parris nodded. "So you feel comfortable lying to them."

"I don't want to," Dewan answered. "But I had no choice this time."

"Did they believe you when you told them you were innocent of the drug charge?" she asked

"I don't know. Things have been different between us since that time. But they'll be fine. It'll blow over. I know I'm innocent."

Parris walked back to the table, opened her tote, took out a file folder and placed it on the table. From inside the folder she took out a copy of a newspaper clipping from the *New York Times*, held it up and looked at it. "Edwin Douglas. Does that name mean something to you?"

"Yeah, that's my dad. What about him?"

Parris didn't answer him right away as she watched Dewan's frustrated expression fade to worry.

"What's wrong? Why's he in the paper?"

Parris took a deep breath and let it out slowly. It was the only way she knew how to prepare herself to give him the bad news.

"I was doing some research on you. I took a look at some of the newspapers back home on the Internet and ran a search on your name. Your father's name came up in the obituaries section from a newspaper that was published two days ago. This is just a printout of the newspaper's online website. I believe you should look at it." Parris walked over to him and lifted his visor and held the folded newspaper article out in front for him to read. Parris watched him carefully as she prepared herself for the inevitable.

"No!" He screamed as he tried to force himself up out of the chair. "How do I get out of this chair? Let me out!"

"I'm sorry, Dewan. You're here among friends."

"I told you to get me out of this stupid chair," he yelled.

"Okay, give me a second." She removed the electrodes from his chest and face, then the straps.

He got out of the chair, walked beside the table where he slammed his fists. "Not my dad. Hell no!"

"I'm sorry, Dewan." She had to calm him down and restrain him. It was the only way to continue. At least let Hashimoto and the others think that the experiment was still her primary objective. The pain that this young man felt, it was inhuman for her to still treat this as an experiment. She was not even supposed to have shown him that article and she knew she'd be in Hashimoto's office afterwards trying to explain herself.

Parris glanced briefly at Eva—who could not hide her concern.

"Don't worry," she mouthed without speaking. It was only then that Eva appeared to relax.

***

Hashimoto walked back into the observation room just in time to see Dewan get out of the chair and slam his fists on the table. Dewan then walked over to the wall where he put his back to it and let himself slide down to the floor, landing on his rear end.

Parris walked over, knelt down beside him and put her arm around him, pulling him closer to her. As tall as he was, he still went to her willingly as he cried. She sat with him in her arms, cradling his head close to her as though he was her little brother. Instinctively, she stroked his shaved head as the tears poured onto her lab coat.

"The experiment's ruined. We need to stop," said one of the scientists.

Hashimoto turned to him. "What do you mean ruined? What's going on?"

"Dewan's out of the chair. Dr. Parris has gone on a tangent, and I doubt he wants to take part in the experiment any longer. We should terminate this and replace him with someone else."

Hashimoto watched as Parris continued to talk to Dewan. *Why didn't she follow the procedure? She knew that keeping him in the chair was essential. She was up to something. He'd know soon enough exactly what it was.* "No, not yet. I believe Dr. Parris knows exactly what she's doing. She's just using a different approach."

"But, sir, didn't you see his readings—"

"Wait. I want to see where she's going with this."

***

It was all a part of the act on her behalf, anything to get him to calm down. At first anyone would've thought that Dewan was hot-tempered, but the way Dewan gripped Nita's upper forearm said otherwise. *This didn't feel right.*

"I'm...I'm here for you, Dewan. We're all here for you. I can only imagine the thoughts that must be going on in your head right now, but you've got to listen to me. Is it all right if we still talk? We can stay right here or we can sit back down at the table, whichever you prefer."

Dewan kept clinging to Parris, but he stopped bawling.

"I'm assuming you want to stay here. That's all right. We can talk right here," said Parris as she stroked the top of his head. It was so smooth that she couldn't resist continuing. "Your father had a weak heart. He'd already suffered a heart attack five years ago. It could've happened to anyone."

Parris glanced over at Eva. She stared blankly back at her, as though she was beginning to get bored.

Dewan started to sniff as he tried to utter a few words. "It happened because of me. My arrest, that was too much for him to handle. And I was innocent and still am."

Dewan sat up and wiped the tears with the sleeve of his shirt. Parris kept one hand on his shoulder.

"There are few people for you to go back home to, Dewan. It's going to even be more difficult for you when you go back." Parris turned to Dewan and crouched beside him. "Back home, all you've experienced is a half-rate justice system that lets the guilty walk, and hard-working individuals like yourself fall to the bottom of the barrel. The people you met yesterday, maybe they don't mean much to you, but they are good people. They've all suffered at the hands of injustice like you have. And one way or another, they've all come from similar backgrounds like you, and even Eva." Parris held his hand as she continued to speak to him.

"Hazel," he said.

Parris's eyes widened as she heard him say the name. "I beg your pardon?"

Dewan sniffed. "Hazel. That was my sister's name. Her perfume smelled just like yours. She's the only one at home whom I was close to before—"

"Shh! You don't have to talk about that." Parris already knew about Hazel. She had been killed in a hit and run. The police never found the culprit. She felt that Dewan blamed himself for not being able to save her.

"The important thing, Dewan, is that your new friends can and will be your family, because they are just like you. Just from different parts of the world. I think one of them is from New Orleans and lost everything to Hurricane Katrina. They were nice to you yesterday because when they look at you, they see themselves. And trust me, they want to help you get over the pain. You might be labeled a criminal, but you're far from being one." Parris noticed Dewan had stopped crying and had started listening. *Is this Clarity taking effect on him?* "Look at what the outside world has done. It's destroyed your family and kept you down. And the ones responsible for all your family's problems got away with it."

Dewan wiped his forehead with his sleeve.

"Your sister died a senseless death. She was in the wrong place at the wrong time. As for your father, his weak heart couldn't take the stress of you going to jail for a crime that you didn't commit."

Dewan wiped his forehead with his sleeve again.

"This is your opportunity to get back at everyone. Join The Promise and you'll be saved from the upcoming apocalypse. You know what you need to do, Dewan."

Something was odd. Dewan was not wiping away tears, but rather perspiration. When Parris looked at Eva, she wasn't perspiring. "Eva, do you feel hot?"

"No, why?" she asked.

"I was just asking." Parris didn't feel hot either. It was something she had not noticed in any previous test subjects. She looked back at Dewan. *God, he's sweating.* She was ready to call the infirmary but thought better not to panic him. She touched

Dewan's shoulder. "Come. Let me help you back to your chair. You'll calm down easier."

He slapped it away hard enough that Parris was tipped over slightly. *Oh Lord, this ain't good.*

She backed off, but like a whip, Dewan's hand gripped her throat. He stood, pulling Parris up with him. A few seconds later she felt her feet dangling. *Oh my God, how'd he get so strong? This has to be some sort of adrenaline rush.* Parris glanced at Eva who sat with her jaw locked open and trembling. *Shit, she's strapped in and can't escape.*

"Dewan!" Parris choked out as she kicked him just below his right kneecap with the tip of her pump. He lost his grip and Parris dropped to the floor. She turned around to run and slipped. She fell, but immediately clawed away on all fours. Two hands locked around her ankles and jerked her backwards. She had no grip on the floor and her palms screeched against the tiles.

Where the hell's security? Hashimoto? What's taking you so long? "Dewan, stop! Please." She could use her martial arts skills. Sure, and risk blowing her cover. Or not defend herself and die. Something was wrong with him. He yanked her from the back of her collar and pulled her up onto her feet. As Dewan continued to tug on the collar, Parris easily slipped out of her lab coat. Luckily, it wasn't buttoned.

She spun around quickly and landed a side-palm strike to the side of Dewan's neck. She could've gone for his face but the neck was a more vulnerable spot—no effect. Dewan threw the lab coat to the floor and grabbed her throat again and squeezed. Parris caught a glimpse of the ceiling as the pressure around her neck crushed her more than she had imagined Dewan was capable of.

She caught a glimpse of the one-way glass behind Dewan, and all she could think of at that moment was about security and why they weren't there yet. *Those idiots behind the glass could see what's going on. Why aren't they doing anything?* There was a madman in front of her—a raging redness in his eyes and growing, bulging veins in his neck. She'd lost Dewan to some monster she may have created.

Parris heard Eva screaming for help to the point that it was inaudible background noise. She was slammed against the wall twice, and then suddenly, she was free. She fell, and then something large struck her, ran alongside her body and turned her. The turning stopped when she was blocked by a much harder and colder surface which didn't yield to her movement. It was only instinct that caused her to sit up. But she was weak and she dropped back to the floor.

She was now at peace and it was the most comfortable feeling. Darkness came down on her as heavy as the weight of a stage curtain, making her unable to move and unwilling to try.

Chapter 11

Hideaki Hashimoto's office at Hexagon Pharmaceuticals

Parris opened her eyes in a series of blinks. She recognized Hashimoto's voice speaking in Japanese. She turned her head and saw the scientists from the monitoring room in front of Hashimoto's desk. A chill under her head jolted her up. That was when she saw the ice pack that had been propped between the back of her head and the cushion. She got halfway up, still feeling some throbbing at the back of her head. It all came back to her—Dewan had attacked her.

"Dr. Parris. Thank goodness," Hashimoto cried out. He rose from behind his desk and walked over to her. The other two followed, but kept their distance a few feet behind him. Hashimoto knelt down on one knee and placed a hand on Parris's shoulder. "Are you feeling better?"

"Better abou-wha? From being knock out, or that it took suh long for you to send someone to help me?" Parris sucked her teeth as her Barbadian accent came out strong. Hashimoto's eyes dilated as he backed off.

Hashimoto shrugged his shoulders. "We were taken by surprise. We alerted security. Unfortunately, Dewan had assaulted you just as they arrived. I apologize for the delay. But you were rushed to Hexagon's infirmary. Our doctor said that you only suffered minor bruises. There appeared to be no internal bleeding or head trauma."

It came back to Parris, in bits and pieces. She remembered lying on the floor as the guards tried to subdue Dewan. It took a few jolts of their electroshock guns to bring him down. Talk about creating a monster from a simple experiment. The next thing she remembered was being rolled away on a stretcher and then waking up in the infirmary.

But they were slow to rescue her. She could've suffered more severe head injuries and could've been lying in a hospital, possibly in intensive care. She still blamed them. She might forgive Hashimoto tomorrow, maybe in two days, after she had calmed down. "Where's Dewan?"

"He's in the infirmary under supervision. The last time I checked on him he was still shaken up. I asked him why he attacked you. He said he didn't know, that he couldn't remember much, but that he felt exhausted and simply wanted to sleep. But why did you show Dewan the article?"

Yup, the sixty-four thousand dollar question. "To test the drug's efficacy. I wanted to see how far I could go without using the visor."

"But the chair's visor is supposed to facilitate that. Once his mind was exposed to all the images, in conjunction with the drug, his mind would become more relaxed and hence be more susceptible to anything you say. The news article wasn't really necessary."

"The new variant of the drug we all worked on was just tested and I think you'd have to agree with my conclusion that it's unsafe to use."

"I can't agree with you fully, because Eva was a success."

"What?"

"The experiment had to continue, even without you."

"You continued with her after what she saw?" Parris asked.

"We had to calm her with a sedative, but then she was fine."

"That was a mistake, and a very dangerous risk. Those aren't lab mice, they're human beings. Why would you risk doing something that could potentially damage her brain after what you saw? The experiment should've been cancelled."

"We're on a tight schedule. But putting all that aside, what do you remember?"

Parris sighed while she shook her head. "I...I can't tell you much...It all happened so fast. I don't even know where to begin." Parris then looked up at Hashimoto. His sympathy appeared genuine, but he had serious ethical issues.

"Don't trouble yourself. There's always another time. We have a video of the incident. The video will be reviewed and hopefully we can learn something from them."

"I'd like to see them, too."

"Another time. You'll take the rest of the day off to recuperate. You've been through a lot. Come back tomorrow when you have a clear head."

Parris stood up and walked to the door.

The brooch. Parris suddenly remembered. She hoped to God that it wasn't damaged, or else she would never hear the end of it from Levickis.

"Get some rest. I'll see you tomorrow with your report of this morning's events."

Parris didn't answer him but heard the door close as she walked down the dimly-lit, carpeted hallway, decorated with small wall lamps.

She got to the elevator and pressed the lower button. It arrived a few moments later, and when the doors opened, her path was blocked by a bulky man in a chocolate-colored suit.

Parris stepped back to allow the miniature camera to catch his face before he walked out. He didn't even acknowledge her presence with a smile, but Parris didn't care. As long as he was caught on camera, he could do anything he wanted. The man walked past her and strode briskly to Hashimoto's office. She had hoped that he would've said something to her. Just a few words from him, and his accent, if he had one, would've given her a clue to his nationality. But she'd have to wait on Levickis.

She walked into the elevator and the doors closed. That's when she unpinned her brooch and looked at it. It looked fine to her, and she pinned it back on. A few unexpected bruises, but the work day was done.

***

Half Kilometer from Hexagon Pharmaceuticals.

Tomas Levickis took another bite from his ham sandwich and rested it on the paper bag on the passenger seat next to him. He chewed while tapping his left foot to the beat of the latest Coldplay single on his iPod. Not having many friends didn't bother him—it helped him concentrate more on his tasks. Ironic as it was, his parents didn't even have a home computer for him while he was in grade school. He had no choice but to use one at school or at his friend's place. Maybe being a second-generation American of Lithuanian descent had something to do with it, having parents who were still stuck with their old habits.

He actually had bought them a desktop computer to get them to start modernizing. They picked at it at first. Then they couldn't keep off of it and were always sending him emails. First, every day, and then every week. Recently it was reduced to once or twice a month, which was more to his liking.

He scratched below his left ear on his beard, as he took a sip of water from his plastic bottle. *God, it's about time I shaved this crap off.* He picked up his mug and finished off the rest of his coffee. It was his third cup of the morning.

This was the first time he had been partnered with Parris in the eleven years he'd been a technical field agent and already it was the biggest task he'd ever taken. The change was good, being that it was also the first time he was partnered with a woman—one that was actually in the middle of the action and not sitting with him in a van or on a yacht doing surveillance.

He watched his computer screen as he saw Nita look at him through her brooch. "It's all right, princess, it's not broken." It was a wonder that it had not broken after the way she was pinned against the wall and then thrown onto the table. Exposed wiring from it would've blown Parris's cover and possibly jeopardized the mission, not to mention her life. *Fuck. Thank God she's all right.*

He pressed replay and saw Nita's face as she examined the brooch to make sure it still worked. He watched her walk backwards until the man in the chocolate suit appeared, at which point he tapped the left key and freeze-framed the image. Integrated in the software was a face-recognition program, and with a few keystrokes, the image of the man became more focused.

It only took three minutes before Dewan's video image was matched up with a picture from the *New York Times* which Levickis had printed out and given to Parris the night before. He would now use the facial recognition search from the CIA's databases. He reclined his seat slightly and undid his belt to give his slight pot belly some room to expand.

He picked up his thermos and poured himself his fourth cup of coffee. "All right, Mr. Brown-suit-man, who are you?"

Chapter 12

Entebbe Air Force Base, 4:23AM, local time

General Downing was the first to burst into the conference room with a file folder, followed by Colonel Bell. Fox and Walsh were already inside as the yelling started.

"How the Sam Hill could they just turn around and put all the blame on us? Whoever's responsible for this attack had to get in the country somehow. Damn it, we could easily turn around and blame them for lax border patrol."

"How the Sam Hill could they just turn around and put all the blame on us? Whoever's responsible for this attack had to get in the country somehow. Damn it, we could easily turn around and blame them for lax border patrol."

"We can blame the Ugandans for lax border patrol and they can blame us for lax security on our own compound," said the Post Commander. "All that's going to accomplish, is to create tension between our two countries. That's something we don't need right now." Bell went to the opposite side of the table from Downing. "We need more allies here in Africa, if we're going to prevent terrorists from gaining ground in these parts."

"Try explaining that to someone who'll listen." General Downing shot a menacing stare at Fox and Walsh—making them feel like two young brothers who were about to be accused of something they knew nothing about. "Any of you men want to trade jobs?" They both looked at each other and then back at

Downing. "I didn't think so." He rested his cane against the side of the table as he took his seat with Colonel Bell. He sighed. "Some things were found at the CDC compound. But they don't tell us much."

"Such as?" asked Fox.

"They recovered the clothes of the deceased," said Downing. "There were the guards, the scientists, and some clothing from the SEALs. Unless the perpetrators were naked there's no extra clothes indicating they were among the dead."

Fox shook his head. "That's a shame."

"Yes, it is," said Downing. "A damn shame that some Russian-speaking individuals managed to sneak into the compound right under our noses, make off with Pandora, and leave everyone else for dead. And so far, there are no leads as to where they are."

"Nor where they're heading," said Colonel Bell.

Fox held back a yawn and rubbed his left eye. "Was there anything else found that was unusual?"

"Just a dagger sitting on the ground inside the dome," said Bell. "As far as I know, none of our boys were carrying it." He handed Downing the folder who then passed it on to Fox.

Walsh turned to Bell. "Any prints?"

He shook his head. "Nada."

"That's no surprise." Fox opened the folder and looked at the picture of the dagger. "But this is."

"What is?" Walsh leaned over to look at the picture.

"It's a D-W73 Cold War dagger." Fox handed the picture to Walsh. "This is a 1950's issue for Russian Air Force officers. There are more modern daggers that could've been used if you wanted to attack someone."

Bell turned to Fox. "Looks like Ares left their calling card."

"It's unusual for them to go to that extreme," Fox replied.

"Was there any blood or other DNA evidence found on the clothing?" asked Walsh.

Downing shook his head. "There wasn't a speck of DNA evidence at the crime scene. There wasn't even any fresh blood on the clothing—just tear marks on one of the victim's clothing, made from the knife attack, we're assuming."

Fox shook his head. *No doubt. Marx said that Pandora will consume everything in order to reproduce.* Fox turned to Bell. "And the video footage before the incident?"

"Wiped clean," Bell replied. "These guys did their homework."

Walsh put both arms on the table and looked at Downing. "Then we should find out more about this Sveta Sokolova chick. I say that we search her home inside out. She's got to have something that could link us to Ares."

Fox rolled his eyes. "That's the first thing Ares would've done. I wouldn't be surprised to find her house burnt down under mysterious circumstances." *Jesus, Walsh, what else do you expect?*

There was a knock at the door.

"Come in," said General Downing.

"What's that?" A faint voice with a strong New Jersey accent came from the other side.

"I said, come on in," Downing repeated louder.

"Right," said the voice.

Fox had a strong feeling who it was, as he looked at the doorway.

The door shook a few times as though the person had difficulty opening it. "The door's locked, sir," the man said.

Fox rolled his eyes and looked away from the door. *Oh yeah, it's definitely him.* "Try pushing the door instead of pulling, Dobbs."

"Right," came the answer, and Bill Dobbs entered.

"What brings you here?" Fox wished he could take that question back.

"You won't believe this. I was in one of the offices set aside for me, trying out this new online computer game, you know the ones with the—"

"I'm sure it was exciting. What's going on?" the General asked. Fox would've cut him off too—Dobbs had a tendency to carry on.

Dobbs paused a moment as though he forgot what he was talking about. "Right. I got some classified info to show you."

Fox chuckled. "Classified? Say it ain't so."

Dobbs ignored him and took out some pictures and documents. He was no stranger to Fox's comments and was often the butt of his jokes.

"Anyway, nearly half an hour ago, about 4:00 AM, a search was run on this man after he was spotted in Tokyo, by one of our undercover agents. He has several aliases, but the CIA databases have him listed as Valerik. He's a former KGB agent and hasn't been seen since the early 1990s."

Fox raised his left eyebrow. "He disappeared around the time the Cold War ended, only to reappear again."

Walsh turned to Fox. "You think he could be involved somehow in the Pandora incident?"

"Uh, guys, that's why I'm here." Dobbs pushed his glasses back up his nose. "As I mentioned, a search was done on Valerik by one of our agents who's currently on assignment in Tokyo. He was spotted at the Hexagon Pharmaceutical Company around 11:00 AM, Japanese time, which would correspond with the multimedia search at 4:00 AM, our local time."

Walsh sighed. "Aw hell, you're confusing me with this goddamn time zone crap, Dobbs."

"I'll give you a crash course on time zones afterwards," said Fox. He turned to Dobbs. "Go on."

"Sure. As I was saying, we don't know why he's there, but I took the liberty to track his latest movements. It turns out that he boarded a plane in Minsk at 12:00 PM earlier today, which is in the same time zone as we are. He only made one connecting flight in Moscow, under a different alias, before he reached Tokyo. He travelled light, one bag of luggage and a briefcase."

Bell chuckled. "Son of a gun. What are the chances of that?"

"That's all he needed," said Fox.

"What's that?" asked Dobbs.

"A briefcase," Fox replied. "If he was involved in what happened back there, then he could've smuggled a sample of Pandora with him, like the one I travelled with."

Dobbs smiled. "It's pretty neat, because we currently have a model type of the briefcase that Valerik was most likely travelling with. It's designed to hide the contents. Does a hell of a job fooling x-ray machines. They've been around for quite a while. First, we had one model and then the Russians developed their version and then the Germans. Of course the British had to—"

"I'm sure they're very nice briefcases, Bill." General Downing sank back in his chair.

"Valerik's probably getting help from Hexagon Pharmaceuticals to reproduce Pandora. They'd be equipped to do so," said Walsh.

Fox breathed a sigh of relief as he held out the picture of Valerik. "Our missing link. So who's the agent who spotted him? I assume we'll be meeting him."

Downing attempted a half smile as he turned to Fox. "You mean *she*. And it's someone you should know pretty well."

"Right," said Dobbs. "Well, there's a man also, but the actual one who spotted him was a woman. The man who's assisting her is a computer specialist like me and—"

"I'm sure he's a nice guy, Bill." Fox turned from Downing and looked at Dobbs. "Who are they?"

Dobbs sighed and dropped his arms beside him. "I was just getting to that. For Pete's sake, why do you guys keep interrupting me all the time? Anyhow, the man's name is Tomas Levickis." Dobbs picked up the manila folder and fingered through the documents until he found the pictures of both agents. "And the woman is Dr. Nita Parris."

Fox raised an eyebrow and looked at Dobbs. "Doctor who?" He didn't wait for him to answer. He got up, walked over to Dobbs and snatched the photograph from him.

"Uh, I said, Dr. Nita Parris. She's a biochemist and used to be a weapons analyst. She's working under NOC at Hexagon." Dobbs's referral to NOC was an acronym for *Nonofficial Cover*— agents that worked worldwide as employees for companies, real or fake, and also as students.

"Their mission was to find out everything about their brainwashing experiment. I haven't met her myself, but I heard she's got nice set of calves. She's also—"

"Born and raised in Barbados and graduated with top honors from Princeton University," said Fox. "She was three-time Ivy League Conference champion in the sprint hurdles both in the indoor and outdoor seasons. She was also pretty quick over the 200-meter dash."

He couldn't take his eyes off the black and white photograph.

All CIA photographs were recent. She had not changed a bit since he last saw her. *Was she a field agent when I met her?* Sure, he could ask Downing and just get the that's-classified response. Somehow he felt that she wasn't, she appeared to be too honest with him. Then again, he's trained to appear the same way to people too.

Downing smirked. "I sent Dr. Parris and Levickis over there to gather intel on her boss, Dr. Hideaki Hashimoto. I want to know what's really going on at Hexagon. I suspect that Japan's Boeisho is looking into them, but I feel more comfortable having our own operatives over there, just in case the Japanese neglect to tell us something." His referral to Boeisho was the acronym for the Self Defense Forces, or Boeisho Boeikyoku. "Come to think of it, I forgot to mention this to them."

Dobbs turned to Fox. "So you've worked with her before?"

Fox was a bit hesitant before answering. He remembered the night that he stood her up, only to learn after that she was carjacked on her way home. Although he learned that she survived the ordeal, it only brought a bit of comfort. But now she was going to be back in his life, and he'd have no choice but to respond to what he did to her. "Well, not exactly."

Walsh chuckled. "Probably dated and dumped her, too."

There was a short silence as he looked at Fox, who looked back at him briefly, and then turned away.

Walsh's head dropped into his hand and he shook his head. "Jesus H. Christ, Fox! I can't believe you."

"It was a few of years ago. She told me she was a researcher."

"And you probably told her you were a travelling salesman. I'm sure she's looking forward to seeing you again."

"She'll forgive me." *Yeah right, dream on.* A few hours ago he was going to officially resign from CIA. Now with Hiller's death, the possibility that an Ares agent has gone rogue, and the involvement of an old flame of his, it's as though life was testing him.

Downing cleared his throat loudly. "You two can straighten that out when you meet. I'll contact my secretary, Ms. Vasell, and have her make the travel arrangements for all three of you.

I'm putting you three in charge of tracking down and capturing Valerik. I'm also interested in knowing what's going on at Hexagon Pharmaceuticals. There's other details that you'll just have to catch up on in the briefing you'll receive, Any questions?" Nobody answered. "Then this meeting's adjourned."

Dobbs was the first to leave as Walsh came up to Fox. "Who's your friend?"

"Who, Dobbs? He's one of the geeks from the Office of Science and Technology. He's an expert in anything with a circuit board and high-caffeine consumption. I heard that his wife's seven months pregnant."

Walsh chuckled. "Looks like he doesn't get out much. I got to say, you know some mighty weird folk."

Fox looked Walsh in the eye. "Yeah, you're right. It's funny how they always wind up working with me."

Walsh's smirk disappeared, and before he could reply, General Downing called out to Fox. "Fox, hang around a minute."

Colonel Bell turned to Downing. "I'll see you later."

"Sure thing, Fred."

Fox stood where he was, and he heard the Colonel close the door behind him.

"I want you to share your thoughts with me. You're the only one who found it strange that the culprits would use that particular dagger and leave it behind."

"It doesn't make sense, sir. If someone wanted to cover their tracks, why would they unleash Pandora, risking their own lives, and leave the dagger. Another thing I didn't bring up in the meeting—it was reported that the culprits spoke Russian. Were they actually heard in the background speaking Russian when the SOS was sent? Why would they risk being heard when our voice recognition computers could isolate their voices and potentially identify them? Anyone in Ares wouldn't have been so careless."

Downing nodded approvingly. "You're right."

"We should consider the possibility that someone's trying to mislead us, and is attempting to send us on a wild goose chase."

Downing rocked in his chair and smiled. "This is what I like about you, Ridley. When you're on the ball, you're really on it.

And that's the reason why I haven't reassigned you yet." Downing stopped rocking in his chair. "Now, I'm not going to ask much of you, but just that you keep your emotions out of what happens from here on. Or else, assuming you do come back alive, I may have you re-evaluated and reassigned. Is that understood?"

"Yes, sir."

As Fox turned away, Downing looked up at him. "Oh, Fox?"

Fox turned back to him. "Yes, sir."

"Is there anything else you want to talk to me about?"

Fox hesitated for a moment. He knew what the General was referring to, but now wasn't the time to discuss it. He couldn't afford to miss the chance of finding Hiller's killers. And he wouldn't be able to sleep knowing that Parris was also connected to a major player. "No, sir. You were very clear on the situation at hand and what needs to be done."

Downing closed his eyes, pursed his lips, and nodded. "All right then. I was only asking because the last time we were in this room, I thought there was something important you wanted to tell me before Walsh interrupted us with the bad news."

Fox looked back into the General's eyes. There was no point in turning away from the old spymaster, because Fox knew that it would only confirm that he was hiding something. "It was nothing important." *There, no denial that anything's on my mind. That should put the issue to rest. Downing wouldn't be digging anymore.*

"That's good to know."

Fox was about to leave when an idea came to him. He turned back to his superior. "Oh sir, I don't normally make requests."

"What is it?"

"I'd have a much better chance at controlling my emotions if Ms. Vasell could arrange that both Walsh and Dobbs flew on a different flight and stayed in a different hotel than me. After all, I recall the time that the roof of the church she attends needed emergency repairs, and that they were short on funds. I also recall how my large anonymous donation helped them out."

There was a brief silence before Downing smiled curtly and nodded. "I'll make sure I mention it to her."

Chapter 13

D espite having the windshield wipers at maximum, it still felt as though Fox drove through a waterfall in the dark. Pushing speeds that were well over one-hundred-and-twenty kilometers per hour on the two-lane rural provincial highway at night didn't help either. Only a reckless person would attempt driving in these conditions, and that's how many people described Ridley Fox. Fuck them. That's their opinion because to him this was a Sunday drive.

The flashing red, blue and white lights Fox saw through the downpour became his guide. He didn't bother to turn off the engine or shut the door after he pulled off onto the shoulder. He just ran towards the flashing lights. His hair now clung to his forehead and the side of his face. By the time he reached the yellow barrier tape, Fox was literally carrying rain in his clothes. He ripped through the tape and two police officers ran towards him, each grabbing a shoulder to restrain him.

"Whoa, back up! This is a crime scene. Where do you think you're going?" yelled one of them. Both cops were over six feet tall, just like Fox. Had anyone other than these two men been stupid enough to attempt what they just had, Fox wouldn't have left them standing for long.

Small waves of water spattered around them, as Fox struggled to fight off the officers. "Goddamn it! I'm Captain Warrant Officer Ridley Fox. That's my fiancée over there so get the hell off of me!"

"It's all right, let him through," said a man on the inside of the yellow tape. He was dressed in a trench coat and wore a brimmed hat.

Fox shoved the two officers aside. He darted past the man in the trench coat who was about to identify himself. But Fox didn't care for that right now—a black body bag was being wheeled away from an overturned vehicle by two paramedics.

The EMTs backed away as Fox skidded to a stop at the gurney. He fumbled for the zipper and yanked it downwards, exposing her. His head fell onto her breasts. "Oh my God! No, no, no!" He lifted his head, looked beyond the heavy rain that pelted him and hollered as loud as he could. If God heard his cry and felt his anguish, then it was apparent in the series of lightning flashes that streaked across the sky at that precise moment.

Someone nudged Fox. It was the man with the trench coat. "Mr. Ripley."

"Mr. Ripley," said the stewardess as she nudged his left shoulder. He never really cared for this pseudonym. He woke up to see her pleasant warm smile and almond-shaped eyes.

Again that nightmare—he couldn't remember the last time it occurred, but it was bothering him again.

"You'll have to fasten your seatbelt. We'll be landing at Narita Airport in less than ten minutes."

Fox put his left hand to his forehead, he was sweating. "Domo arigato gozaimasu." Which meant *thank you very much* in Japanese.

There was the usual long wait at customs once he got off the plane. Fox collected his luggage and was in the terminal corridor when a blow to his right shoulder and arm nearly made him spin around and drop his luggage.

"Sorry," the man immediately said in Japanese, and then moved on. Typical—just bump and move on. But at least this one apologized.

Fox tightened his grip on the handle of his suit bag, swinging it over his shoulder when the word *pickpocket* came to mind. He immediately felt for his wallet and detected its shape through his pocket.

All right, so he didn't steal my wallet. Then why were the man's hands were around his shoulders? Another thought came to mind. He felt inside the breast pocket of his blazer. His fingers touched a piece of paper that was not there before.

He looked a few feet to his right. The mens room sign stood out from all of the other neon-lit names that were found along the corridor. Fox walked through the curved open door entrance and headed to the last stall. He locked it and hung his suit bag on the hook.

Amidst the background noises of automatically flushing toilets and running water, Fox took the folded piece of paper from his breast pocket and read it. It was a simple message written in English: *Do not trust anyone in the Boeisho. They're waiting for you outside. Go with them to avoid suspicion. I'll meet up with you soon.* There was no signature or any other indication as to whom it was from, and Fox hadn't recognized the man. But the Boeisho was here and most likely would be there to wait for Walsh and Dobbs also. The worst case scenario would be for them to be detained and questioned by the Boeisho.

Fox took out his cell phone and texted a message to Marie Vasell, advising her to arrange that Walsh and Dobbs be flown to Okinawa Base. When he was done, he put away his phone, tore up the paper and dropped the shredded pieces into the toilet—the automatic flusher took care of the rest.

Once he reached the atrium, he looked through the windows at all the green taxis lined up at the curb. People crisscrossed in front of him constantly. A young woman, stood out—probably a student. She rushed to meet an older couple who he assumed to be her parents. He also took notice of several men in expensive-looking suits, either pulling their luggage behind them, or carrying a single briefcase. Then there was the individual complaining behind him and the man to his left who was upset at hearing his flight was delayed.

Fox glanced at a digital clock hanging overhead—it was 12:45 AM, meaning that it was 5:45 PM at Entebbe. He was used to the time zone changes, and the twelve hour flight on the Boeing 747 had given him enough time to rest.

The exit loomed just ahead when he was caught off guard by

two black-suited men as they accosted him.

Fox glanced at them. "Are you here to welcome me?"

"Come with us, Mr. Fox," said the man on Fox's right. Then they both stepped aside and gestured Fox to pass between them.

Outside, the powerful smell of exhaust fumes struck his nostrils. The other man circled around Fox's left and redirected him to the right. "This way. You should know where to go from here." At the front of a row of six taxis, were two black fleet sedans.

When they got to the second sedan, the man on Fox's right extended his arm. "Your bag?"

Fox handed it to him. "So are you going to tell me who you are, or can I assume that you're Boeisho?"

"Please, step this way," said the other man.

Not too talkative.

He opened the back door for Fox, while the other placed his suit bag in the trunk. When Fox bent down to get inside, he saw the occupant and paused in the doorway.

"Good evening, Mr. Fox. Welcome to Tokyo," said the man dressed in a navy colored suit. His receding hairline exposed an almost square forehead, and his cheekbones glistened when he smiled. Fox knew there was more to him than his cunning grin. On the outside, he appeared to be a warm and friendly man, but there was the other side—the one which held onto many secrets that one would kill to know.

Fox spotted a brown manila envelope in a holder attached to the side of the front door.

"Come in, you must be exhausted from your trip."

"You can say so." The door was closed behind him and the driver slowly drove off.

The man smiled. "I'm Head of Section, Yuji Tanaka. We knew it was only a matter of time before you'd arrive." Tanaka produced a ceramic vase-like flask that Fox recognized as a tokkuri and two small cups called oshokos.

"Sake?"

"Sure." Fox took an oshoko from him. "I've heard many things about you. Congratulations on your recent promotion."

"It was well earned" He lifted the flask. Being no stranger to

Japanese customs, Fox held out the oshoko with his right hand while supporting it underneath with his left, as Tanaka poured him a cupful. Fox put his cup down on the stand, was handed the tokkuri, and did the same for Tanaka. Once he finished serving Tanaka, he put down the tokkuri, picked up his cup and took a sip. He preferred the ceramic oshokos to the wooden ones which had a tendency to mask the non-chilled sake's true aroma.

Tanaka lifted his oshoko. "I hope I made the right selection. Junmai-Shu is to your liking?"

Fox put down his oshoko. "It's good to know I still have buddies in your organization who like to talk about me." It was nice that Tanaka knew he preferred the low fragrant, but explosive impact that Junmai-Shu made once it was swallowed, as opposed to the weaker flavors.

"Yes, especially a female agent or two who would love to be here right now." If there was one thing Fox noticed about Tanaka's face, it was definitely his glistening cheekbones.

"They still haven't gotten over that yet? Nothing more than an occupational hazard, that's all I have to say about it. So why did you come out here to meet me?"

"The office tends to be a bit boring after a while. I came to meet you myself, primarily because of the delicacy of the situation. The fewer who know of it, the better."

"So delicate that you had me followed?"

"I won't discuss our methods of intelligence gathering."

"I wouldn't expect you to."

"But on to the subject." Tanaka then crossed his leg. "Tell me—in your opinion—what would someone have to do to be the most powerful man on earth?"

Fox thought about the question and wondered what this had to do with what happened in Uganda, assuming that Tanaka was referring to that.

"I'd say it'd be someone who'd have the greatest amount of influence over people and who stands to gain a lot and lose practically nothing at the same time."

"Such as?"

This has to be going somewhere. "It would be someone

who exercises his resources in the most efficient way, so as to blackmail, if not control, a small or even a large group of people. A community even. The most common forms of influence are money and weaponry. Then there are religious cults that use spiritual influences and brainwashing techniques to aid a selected group to share the worldview of their leader, for example."

Fox saw Tanaka's eyes glisten at the mentioning of the religious cult. He was definitely onto something. Tanaka slid into the corner where he now faced Fox at an angle. "This has something to do with a cult, doesn't it?"

"A Doomsday cult, to be precise. For the past eight months, the Boeisho has kept a close watch over a particular cult called The Promise. Its leader is a man named Hideaki Hashimoto. Interestingly, he's also the CEO of Hexagon Pharmaceuticals. He's done an excellent job keeping his private life out of the public. All of his recruits are between the ages of sixteen and twenty-five and live in his mansion in West Tokyo. Practically all of the members have, at one time, either brought shame to themselves or to their families and Hashimoto convinced them of their own self-worth. They've all become militant and are prepared for the end of the world to come to the rest of society, but he will be their savior." Tanaka took a short sip of his sake.

"That's when we stepped up our surveillance. We've had a few incidents in the past with cults—you probably remember attacks in the subway and shopping centers—so we weren't going to let this one get out of hand. Hashimoto isn't without his own personal protection, too. He has his own private group of ninjas. We had three agents infiltrate the cult. Two weeks ago we lost contact with them. But before we did, we were able to find out that they were going to steal a bio-weapon from a secret facility somewhere in Europe."

"How did The Promise know about this facility, and what made them so sure that they could break into it? For them to be able to pull this off they'd have to have someone on the inside."

"They did." Tanaka handed Fox the brown manila envelope from its holder. The envelope was left unsealed and Fox pulled out a familiar picture.

"The man you see there is—"

"Valerik, ex-KGB."

"You know him."

"He's the reason I'm here, but I guess you've already figured that out. How's he involved?" Fox took a sip of his sake.

Tanaka continued. "He's one of Hashimoto's followers, but before that he was, and may still be, associated with a consortium called the Arms of Ares, which he joined soon after the fall of the Soviet Union. He's Hashimoto's chief strategist and he was going to provide the cult with the necessary information and technology that would allow them to carry out their plan." Tanaka sipped some more of the sake. "Tell me what you know about Pandora. We already know that you've been to one of Ares's facilities and destroyed it. You must know what it can do."

"I've been briefed on what it can do, and I'm sure you have, too. You only wish you knew about Hashimoto's plans before Valerik was able to make off with it and arrive here in this country undetected. So when were you planning on sharing that information with us?"

Fox took Tanaka's silence into consideration. "That's okay. I understand it must be embarrassing for you." He looked at the second picture of the man he assumed was Hashimoto.

"So, when you find Valerik, what do you plan to do? Kill him?" asked Tanaka.

"No, I thought you'd let me question him before you all do that."

"That we can do."

"Then I'll keep that in mind. But I'm guessing your visit to the airport was more than coming to meet me. Am I being recruited to join you guys in the hunt for Valerik?"

Tanaka chuckled. "You have many talents, Fox. You've lent us your assistance in the past. You were a tremendous asset and for that we're in your debt."

"Thanks, but that was a long time ago. I prefer working alone now. So, if you don't mind, I'd like to get out."

Tanaka's surprise was evident in his facial expression. "So soon?"

"You seem to have all the resources you need. You don't need me."

There was a moment's pause.

"As you wish, Mr. Fox." Tanaka leaned forward and tapped on the glass partition. Fox watched the driver's eyes look back through the rearview mirror and Tanaka motioned him to the side of the road.

A few seconds later, the car came to a stop.

Fox opened the door and turned to Tanaka. "I'm sure I'll be hearing from you or one of your men soon." The trunk was automatically opened from the inside when he got to it. Fox removed his suit bag and swung it over his shoulder. He didn't hear Tanaka's door open amidst the other sounds of cars, horns, and even a police siren. He closed the trunk, and turned to walk away when he heard Tanaka.

"We lost three good men to these people. Do you think they'll treat you any different?"

Fox walked away without looking back. "I don't know because that's the least of my concerns."

"You ought to be concerned. It's what might keep you alive, as your friend Hiller would still be right now. May he rest in peace."

Fox stopped abruptly. He turned around and faced Tanaka.

"Both of you worked together to help us."

Fox used his free hand to brush back a few strands of hair that fell in front of his left eye. The air in his mouth got drier with each passing second as he slowly took a step back towards Tanaka's vehicle. Tanaka was calmer and his cheekbones did not glisten as they did before.

"Come work with us again, Fox. And we'll find Valerik together."

Fox was about to take another step. *Remember the note. It obviously wasn't for nothing.* "As I said, that was a long time ago. I work alone now." Fox turned and walked the other way and hailed the first taxi about to pass him. It swerved to the side and screeched to a halt. Fox got in and the cab sped off into traffic.

"Akasaka Imperial Hotel, please," said Fox in Japanese. He let his head fall back. The only thing on his mind at the moment was getting a hot shower. Probably watch a movie or two while in his suite. It was a relief to be away from Tanaka right now, but Fox knew that Tanaka's men would be tailing him. He would have to lose them in a large crowd. "You know what? I need excitement. Take me to Kabukicho instead." This area was Japan's largest red-light district, an area Fox frequented whenever he was in town. The driver nodded in response.

Fox looked through the rearview mirror to see if he could spot the second black sedan. Nothing was in sight. There had to be a second unmarked somewhere in the traffic—it wasn't the first time he'd been tailed—nothing a quick change of clothes and a little makeup couldn't fix. Losing them would be easy. The hard part would come once he set up another date with Dr. Nita Parris.

Chapter 14

Hexagon Pharmaceuticals parking lot, 9:00 AM

V alerik muttered to himself as he walked through Hexagon's parking lot, got into his blue hatchback, and slammed the door. *A day later and Hashimoto still can't tell me why Dewan acted up yesterday while everything went normal with Eva.* He grabbed the top of the steering wheel and tapped it with both index fingers. Again, Dr. Parris was on his mind. *What did that woman do? What was she holding back?*

Valerik started up his car and backed out of the handicapped spot, barely missing a female Hexagon employee, and drove off. Valerik's car felt a bit lazy as he tried to accelerate to the entrance, when suddenly it sped up again. The occupant of a passing car caught his attention so that he almost rear-ended a car that was stopped in front of him. Valerik slammed on the breaks, missing the back bumper of the car in front by inches.

Dr. Parris was in the passing car, and she did a double take as she passed him. He couldn't help notice the change in her facial expression. *Was she scared or just curious?* Regardless of what it was, his danger radar was on high alert and it warranted following her. Fox's interference at destroying the Groznyy facility was a minor setback. He couldn't afford any more, not at this point when they were so close. And if she was going to be a liability, then she must be taken care of at once.

He exited the parking lot onto the two-lane road where he

would drive for a few miles before he found a place to stop. He'd then call Hashimoto and let him know his thoughts on Parris. He wanted to be alerted the moment that she was about to leave Hexagon. The car began to jerk aggressively again, and then sputtered until it coughed itself to a stop. The rodeo ride ended as he looked at the fuel gauge.

"Ahueyet!" *What the fuck!* Valerik stared at the empty fuel gauge. *Impossible. I filled the tank this morning.* A loud roaring noise closed in on him. Valerik checked the rearview mirror above the dashboard and saw an SUV, seconds before it came up on his driver's side and then swerved in on him. The seatbelt bit into his waist and chest as his car was thrown.

His car did a three-sixty spin once and came to rest. Valerik heard the roar resume before he saw a pair of white taillights as the SUV reversed towards him. The collision should've ripped Valerik out of his seatbelt and thrown him through the passenger-side door. Instead, the car slid sideways like a hockey puck across the ice.

When the car settled, Valerik fumbled for the seatbelt buckle while he was in a dizzy state. He heard men's voices speaking in Russian, seconds before someone undid the seatbelt for him, yanked him out of the car and threw him onto the concrete.

They found me. But how? Valerik pondered that, as he watched two jean-covered legs from behind. One man was bent over inside his car. There was another one, and his running shoes were visible from underneath the car as he paced back and forth. He heard what sounded like the car seats being torn apart. *What the hell are they doing to my car?*

He clenched his eyes shut and when he opened them he looked at his assailants. He recognized the one closest to him who stood over six feet tall. It was Pyotr. He had a cleft in his chin and a buzz-cut hairdo. Based on his athletic physique, he could easily pass for a soccer player instead of the vicious assassin he was.

"Have you found anything?" In Russian, Pyotr asked the other, whom Valerik still couldn't see.

"Nothing," came a reply. That voice had a familiarity to it as well, but Valerik was too disoriented to put a face to the voice.

Valerik tried to get up, but there was no use, he was weak and hurting. Even if he could limp he wouldn't be able to get too far. Pyotr walked to the back of the trunk, flung it open and dug around inside. He wouldn't find anything in there except for the spare tire. And Valerik knew it when he saw him back away from the trunk and turn to the other man, still out of sight.

Pyotr approached Valerik. "Let's go. Come help me carry him."

The dirt-stained running shoes stopped a foot away from his face. He knew what was going to come next and before he had a chance to turn his head he saw the tip of the shoe flying right towards his head.

***

"Eh, comrade. End of the line. Wake up."

Valerik felt his face thrown against a cold hard surface. His right eye could not open well. It must have been where he had been kicked. There was a coldness of the window on his right cheek. If he had a prayer, Valerik would be able to shoot his way out of this situation. He wasn't surprised to find his gun missing.

Pyotr—who was sitting beside him—slapped Valerik with a backhand to his cheek. "Come on. You didn't think you'd still be armed, did you?" He could only see the back of the driver's head. Through one eye, he stared out the window. There were large stacks of metal crates on either side where they drove. Then he saw a large cargo ship. And that smell, that marine smell, he caught through the open window up front. They were at the Tokyo harbor.

The car came to a stop alongside another red sedan which faced the waterfront, with the downtown city skyline on the opposite side of the bay. And that's when Valerik saw the man he hated at the edge of the dock. He was so arrogant that he had to dress in his trademark gray suit while the rest of his thuggish entourage wore jeans and old plain jackets.

Pyotr pushed Valerik out the door, showing off his Micro-Uzi to him. "Come on, out you go."

He then saw the driver. It was Demyan. He knew firsthand that he had been about to be committed to a mental institution after being dishonorably discharged from the Russian military—until

Ares had recruited him. He was a few inches shorter than Pyotr, had put on a bit of muscle, especially around his shoulders, since the last time he had seen him. He still had a thinning hairline and unkempt stubble.

Pyotr nudged Valerik forward with the tip of the Micro-Uzi. "Do you remember when we used to take orders from you, comrade?"

Valerik didn't answer as he watched them both laugh. *These lowlifes are enjoying this.* As he walked, he tasted the salty, metallic blood in the space where three of his teeth used to be. The shove he got from behind made him lose his footing and he stumbled to the ground—to the shoes of the real sadist. *Typical of these men. They always took pleasure in abusing their victims.*

The white-haired man approached him, pen twirling in his hand. "Valerik, my old friend. Look at you. Once a decorated KGB operative and a notable agent of Ares. Now you're a crazed fanatic."

"And you," said Valerik, swallowing a small amount of blood and coughing a few times. "Profiting from the demise of the Soviet Union. You and your group are no more than terrorists. Shameful, petty terrorists."

The white-haired man chuckled and stopped twirling his pen. "Is that how you see us? You betrayed us because you think we're terrorists?" The white-haired man then turned around, walked back to the waterfront and stopped short, a foot from the edge. The only sounds heard were the lapping of the water, a dragging boat horn, and blurred city noise in the background.

"You had an excellent plan to use your rank to infiltrate one of our labs and destroy it. But I doubt you'd be so obtuse as to destroy the only supply of Pandora without saving some for yourself and for your friends at Hexagon Pharmaceuticals."

How did he know about Hexagon? It must be Ares's mole within the CIA. It was the only explanation. My God! The girl—Dr. Parris—she's got to be CIA.

The white-haired man turned around with such dramatic flair that he appeared to cause the small breeze that sent a chill deep through to Valerik's bones. The white-haired man got down on one knee so close to him that Valerik could hear the clicking his pen made as he twirled it close to his ear. "Where is it?"

Valerik began to get up slowly, but he felt a sneaker dig into the back of his neck and push him back down. There was no sense in trying. These men always kept their victims down. He knew it was over for him, so there was no sense giving in to them.

"I have no answers for you. Your time will soon be over. You'll pay for your crimes against humanity." Valerik swallowed. "All of them." He knew what was coming next, but there wouldn't be any joy among them, and that was all the satisfaction he needed. He saw it in the flustered expression on the white-haired man's face as he looked at his henchmen.

"Do you hear that?" said the white-haired man as he looked at the others. "The words of a true dreamer."

What happened next, occurred so fast that all Valerik heard were feet shuffling on the ground. A lot of dust was thrown in his face and a sharp pain wrapped around and dug deep into his neck with the tightness of a knotted balloon. His face hit the pavement once and then there was a moment's view of the dock as dirt got kicked into his eyes. With his arms at his side, he had no way to loosen the vise-like pinching of his esophagus, as it cut off the flow of air, and the pain sank deep down into his neck. The pain dug deeper, he felt it sink into the bone. Darkness closed in.

***

The white-haired man unwound the wire from around Valerik's neck and dropped the body back down to the ground. He released one end of the pen and the inner wire was dropped back inside along with the cap. He tossed the pen up in the air once, caught it, fit it back into his breast pocket and sighed. "Pathetic."

"Do we toss him in the bay?" asked Pyotr.

"Yes—actually, no. Let's send a message to his group. One that's strong enough to provoke a response. Dump him somewhere where he'll be easily found. I want to watch it on the evening news." He faced the Tokyo Bay and sighed. He heard Valerik being dragged across the pavement while he irrationally took out his pen and began to twirl it. He had lost count of how many lives had been taken with this pen.

There, that felt better.

Valerik didn't squeal. Nothing lost, nothing gained. Other options were still available. Now that Fox was in town, he already knew what the next one would be.

Chapter 15

Azabu District, Minato Ward, Tokyo

For Parris, driving her car from West Tokyo to the Minato Ward at lunch hour would've been chaotic. So she drove from Hexagon and parked close to the Tobitakyu Station, a five minute walk from her apartment building. She caught the train, transferred to the subway to Akabanebashi Station where got into a taxi.

Going out to lunch wasn't her style, what with all the news reports on E. coli and salmonella poisoning every few months back in the US. Had she been at work, she would've prepared a tuna-fish sandwich. This was second to her favorite, flying fish, if only it were readily available in Tokyo.

She had no plans to go into town. She was here only because of the designer vase filled with a dozen long-stem red roses that sat in her cubicle when she stopped by the office that morning to give Hashimoto her report. She got the hint that something was up the moment she stepped off the elevator to her floor. All of her colleagues smiled and giggled when they saw her. The sender's name was Scott Ripley—it was a code to let her know that a fellow operative wanted to meet with her.

She wondered why Levickis didn't inform her of this, and it made her leery about being followed—this, coupled with the unsettling feeling she got when she passed Valerik at the entrance to the parking lot earlier. The advantage of being in a city like

Tokyo was that the subways were a surveillance nightmare. With thousands of people commuting by the hour, it would be very easy for Parris to lose anyone that followed her, so long as she avoided being captured by the closed-circuit cameras that were found throughout the city. Throughout the trip she did not spot anyone suspicious.

While Parris was driven through the Azabu District, she took out her compact, looked in the mirror to make sure that her make-up and headband covered up her facial bruises. There was nothing to worry about.

The narrow street they drove on had a tan-colored stone wall on one side. The driver turned into the open-gate entrance where the name *International Tea House* was stapled on the wall next to the gate, in both Japanese characters, and also in English underneath them. Beyond the gate, Parris saw the two-story stone mansion. The building was obscured from the street by several different trees, as the other homes were. The number of trees surrounding the place ensured privacy from anyone on the outside. She thanked the driver while she handed him a few bills, and got out of the cab. She closed the door, opened up her umbrella against the light rain that had started to fall. She turned towards the double doors to the mansion, about ten feet away.

She was a bit nervous meeting this mysterious Scott Ripley, the man who had sent her the flowers. Levickis told her earlier, that the person did not want to identify himself for personal reasons. But with the lavish surroundings, Parris got the hint that her meeting could possibly also be social.

One of the double doors opened and a short, plump young woman appeared, dressed in a cherry blazer and black pants. "Good afternoon, Dr. Parris. My name's Sora."

"Hello, Sora," Parris replied as she closed her umbrella and walked quickly past her. *What is it with these bright cherry blazers? They're so out of place.*

Parris came to a carpeted hallway with some doors on either side. Not knowing where to go to next, she stopped.

"Mr. Ripley's waiting for you in the dining room. It's the first set of double doors to your left. I'll take your umbrella for you."

"Thanks." Parris handed Sora her umbrella. She would later check it for any tracking devices. If it was bugged she would conveniently forget it in the cab on her way back to Akabanebashi Station.

She heard a set of rhythmic chords on a piano from inside the room she was headed to. As she opened the doors, the chords grew to a crescendo and then diminished. Parris thought that this was the cue for an operatic singer to join in, but she only saw a pianist in front of a baby grand piano. She closed the doors quietly so as not to disturb the player who had his back to her.

Parris looked around the room. It had high ceilings, about thirteen feet high, and the floor was hardwood. In one corner a fifteen inch television was turned on and muted. There was also a small wooden coffee table and two chairs with armrests. The furniture looked European. She felt the television set was out of place. *Where's Ripley?*

The pianist then stopped abruptly, as though he was in error. Parris looked at him as he played the same section over. Again, he stopped.

"Fuck!" Parris heard the pianist say. *He can't be an employee.* The pianist appeared to notice her and glanced over his shoulder.

"Hey, there."

Parris slightly tilted her head to the side. "Mr. Ripley?"

"You're talking to him. Any trouble finding the place?"

"No. It was a bit out of the way for me, but not much trouble getting here."

"Good. What kind of tea would you like?"

Instead of answering, she continued to stare at him as she approached him slowly. *That voice, should I know him?* The melodious texture of his voice numbed her mind.

"Dr. Parris," he said a bit louder. He continued to play, but more quietly.

"Yes," she replied as she swung her purse over her shoulder.

"Your tea? They have all kinds."

Oh what the hell, just say anything. "Jasmine."

"Will that be Oolong Jasmine Tea or Green Tea with Jasmine bulbs?" came a voice. Parris turned around and saw Sora smiling in the doorway.

"I'll have the Oolong."

"And I'll have the Earl Grey Pot de Crème," said the pianist. Sora bowed and then left, closing the doors behind her.

The man stopped playing, swung around in his swivel chair to face her, and stood. Parris felt a cold shiver ripple through her, and she swore that her heart rate tripled. *It's him. What's his face? The man from Germany who claimed to be in Washington on business when she met him at Max's Pub in DuPont Circle in D.C. almost two years ago.* Only now, he didn't have a German accent, nor the blonde, shoulder-length hair. The man in front of her had trimmed, auburn hair. He was still clean-shaven and had the same square jaw.

She walked to him and stopped less than an arm's length from him, close enough to smell his cologne. *Lord, he's still wearing the same cologne.* "Who are you?"

"The name's Ridley Fox, and yes, that's my real name. But you can call me Ridley." Fox smiled and extended his hand. "It's nice to see you again, Nita."

Parris's kept her hands to her side. "What are you doing here?"

Fox lowered his hand. "Hoping to find the same thing you're looking for."

"Really? And what do you know about what *I'm* looking for?"

"Your partner, Tomas Levickis, ran a database search on a man I'm after. You saw him at Hexagon."

Parris paused. Her heart was still racing but she managed to bring it under control as she looked into his clear, hazel eyes. She sighed with a smirk. "Really?"

"The Boeisho is trying to keep tabs on me. You don't have to worry. I already checked the surroundings, there's no sign of them."

She looked back up at Fox and went to smack him but he caught her wrist. *Damn, he has quick reflexes.*

"As I said, it's nice to see you again, Dr. Parris." She kicked him in his left shin. Fox dropped down on one knee. "Jesus, woman! What's gotten into you?"

Parris turned around and stormed away for a few steps, paused, and then walked back to him with gnashing teeth.

"Nice to see you too, *Ridley*," she said with a menacing emphasis on his name. "You can't imagine how long I've been waiting to do that. Tell me, *Ridley*, was it fun? Toying with me the way you did?"

Fox shook his head. "I didn't mean for that to happen, it just did."

"Is that all you have to say? You stood me up? Sure, it can happen. Guess what? After I waited on you for almost two hours. I left, only to be carjacked and beaten up at gunpoint on my way home. Do you know how many weeks of counseling I had to go through?"

"I was called on assignment. I—"

"I've had my emotions messed with in the past by other men, long before I was part of any agency. You had a responsibility then, as you do now, and trying to get involved with me was very irresponsible. Now get up, I didn't kick you that hard."

"I beg to differ."

Parris didn't reply.

"Great. Of all the women I could've met, it had to be the one who holds grudges," muttered Fox.

"I heard that. And yes, I can hold a grudge."

"It was an observation."

"Sure, fine, whatever." Parris looked over the table that was set for both of them. On it was a nice little bonsai plant, a lit candle, and some cutlery on a white cloth napkin. She looked back, over in the corner where the television was, and only then did she notice what was on. It looked like Curly, Larry, and Moe. She looked at Fox in bewilderment. "*The Three Stooges?*"

"I kind of like that show, all the old shows actually. The Avengers comes on later, and oh, you just missed *I-Spy*," Fox said as he took a few steps.

"So this is how you spend your free time when there aren't any women to toy with? Watching reruns?"

"I'm actually quite diverse," Fox said with a Barbadian accent. If that was a way for him to get her attention, he just got it.

"Yeah, and trying to play the piano too, I noticed."

"Hey, I wish I had the time to play the piano and the violin as much as I did when I was younger," continued Fox without the accent.

"So, you're an amateur musician."

"What do you think so far?"

"I can't say. I wasn't really paying attention."

Fox paused and shrugged his shoulders with a slight chuckle as though his feelings were hurt.

I couldn't care less for how he felt.

Fox walked back to the piano, sat down, and played a different tune. It was more thunderous and definitely less romantic and gentle than what he had played before. Parris wasn't a connoisseur of modern piano music, but she was sure she'd never heard that piece. She walked over to the back of the baby grand. "Why'd you do that?"

Fox looked up, but not enough for her to see below his eyes. They had lost some of their warmth. "Do what?"

"Change tunes."

"Oh, you noticed?" Fox's eyes disappeared as he lowered his head. "I thought you weren't paying attention."

"Not entirely." She advanced two steps along the side of the baby grand and stopped. "But I prefer it to what you're playing now."

"You could've fooled me. I thought that was your way of telling me that I suck."

"I wasn't. I...I'm just not familiar with classical music. Who composed it?"

"Some noteworthy composer," Fox answered. "We all have ways of dealing with stress and our emotions. Some people swing a golf club, others go to the firing range, as for me, I'll play an instrument."

Parris took a step closer. She wanted to see into his eyes. She watched as he kept playing, although now, it was more like he was banging on the keyboard. She wouldn't yell above the piano. But a few moments later, he seemed to calm down. What he played now almost sounded like what he played earlier. Was this his way of reaching out to her? *My God, is he playing this to impress me?*

He looked up at her again and she felt a dryness at the back of her throat that made her immediately look away from him.

The double doors opened and both Sora and a young man came in. *Perfect timing.* The young man carried two plates and Sora had a tray containing two small teapots with hot water, two separate tea balls beside each, and a carafe of cold water.

"Hello, Dr. Parris," said the young man as he stopped and bowed in front of her. "I'm Yoshirou."

"Hello." Parris bowed, not knowing what else to do.

"How about some curried chicken roti?" asked Fox. "That's still your favorite, isn't it?

Oh my gosh, he remembered. Parris watched as Yoshirou set the table. "What's going on here?"

Fox had a half smile and he ended his rendition with a few gentle chords. "Lunch."

"It seems out of place."

"I know it seems weird finding West Indian cuisine here, especially at a tea house. But I'm good friends with the owner of this particular franchise and I put in a special request."

Yoshirou assisted Parris with her chair as she sat down facing the television. He helped Fox to his seat while Sora placed the small tea pots and cups, the Oolong Jasmine tea bulb for Parris, and the Earl Grey Pot de Crème for Fox.

Fox and Parris thanked them both and the two waiters retreated to the door.

Fox looked up at Parris with the fork in his hand. "Bon appetite."

"Thank you. But I know you didn't travel all this way to apologize and pamper me with this meal. So, where were we?"

"As I said, I'm following a lead."

"Really, and abusing The Company's budget by sending me expensive flowers and reserving this place. Tomas could've taken any messages for me. So how did you manage to pull this one off?"

"I'm a member. As I said before I'm good friends with the owner," said Fox as they both dropped the bulbs in their individual tea pots.

"Bet you are."

"Yeah, it's a pretty nice concept they have. They've got these home-type establishments here in Tokyo, London, Amsterdam, Cairo, New York, and also Hong-Kong. I'm thinking of opening one in Montreal, my hometown."

"Oh really?"

"Is that a work-related accident by the way?"

Parris's hands shot up to her headband. *Was the Band-Aid showing?* She felt around. *No, it wasn't.*

"How did you know that?"

Fox sliced into the roti shell with his knife. "I didn't. That was, of course, until you reacted the way you did."

Parris sighed in embarrassment. "Yes, I was attacked at work yesterday morning."

"Attacked?"

"Yes."

"By who?"

"One of my subjects. The new mind-control technique Hexagon has developed didn't go too well."

"Any idea what went wrong?"

"Not yet, but it appears we'll stick to the original drug we used before. Ironically, it's been named Clarity."

"How does it work?"

"By blocking the RAS's normal function, along with the amygdala and hypothalamus."

Fox crossed his legs and held his chin in his palm and tapped his lips with his finger as he chewed. "The RAS?"

"Yes. It's the Reticular Activation System responsible for screening unnecessary info into the brain."

There was a moment's silence and then Fox looked back at Parris as she began to eat. "Right."

"What's wrong?"

"No, it's nothing. It's just that biology isn't my forte."

I guess you won't be impersonating a scientist anytime soon. "Anyway, in order for us to effectively brainwash our subjects, we have to disrupt the reasoning, personality, and drive regions of the brain."

"Yes, of course, in the hindbrain," said Fox.

"No," said Parris. "That would disrupt their sight. Personality's found in the forebrain and human drives are in the thalamus. With those areas disrupted, the subjects are then more susceptible to suggestion. That's where our device comes into play."

"Which device?"

Parris told him about the chair and its function. "Before we developed the latest variation of the drug, patients would have to undergo several sessions with the chair before they were completely brainwashed. We were hoping to reduce that amount with the latest version."

Parris then cleared her throat. "Now, tell me more about the man you're tracking."

Fox poured himself a glass of water and poured a glass for Parris. "His name's Valerik and he's raised a few red flags since you spotted him yesterday morning. A little over a day ago, a temporary CDC compound in southern Uganda was attacked. The main suspects may be members of an organization called the Arms of Ares. Have you ever heard of them?"

"Of course. Everyone's watching out for them. The CIA, FBI, Homeland Security, you name it."

"They've recently raised the bar on bio-warfare. They've been researching a very deadly microbe."

"What type of microbe?"

"It's called Pandora." Fox took a sip of water. "Sound familiar?"

"Yes. I was a weapons analyst back in the days the Defense Department was researching it. But wasn't that project cancelled several years ago?"

"It turns out that some people didn't want that. Ares is trying to market Pandora. I managed to stop them from selling it to Sudanese government officials who were going to use Darfurian locals as guinea pigs. But we believe that Valerik has obtained samples of Pandora and has given them to this man."

Fox reached into the blazer that hung on his chair and pulled out a rolled-up legal-sized brown envelope. He handed it to Parris. She opened it and removed the pictures.

"I believe you're well acquainted with him?"

Parris stared briefly at the picture. "Of course. He's my boss."

"Small world, isn't it? Several years ago he was believed to have helped the Soviets develop a brainwashing program. Today he's a cult leader. I've been informed that the Boeisho has been keeping close watch on his cult. Three of their agents infiltrated the group. Lately, they've all gone missing."

She stared at the photo. "If he's involved, then it's possible that all of our test subjects who've been given the drug could be recruited as cult members. They'd be easy, vulnerable targets. All this time I thought this talk of a cult was part of the experiment."

"It's very real. Your experiments were nothing more than a front."

Parris raised a hand to cover her mouth. "Oh, Lord."

"Don't be too hard on yourself, Doctor. You would've found out sooner or later. Valerik's picture's there as well."

Parris took out his photograph. "Yeah, I saw him yesterday as I was leaving Hashimoto's office. He didn't look too friendly. I also passed him on my way to work this morning."

"He has a history. He went off the CIA's radar several years ago—"

"During the Cold War, only to resurface now. Yeah, I've learned that much from Tomas. If he stole samples of Pandora for Hashimoto, then he could easily hide it at Hexagon." Parris poured herself a cup of tea. She took out a navy blue handmade table napkin with yellow frilled borders. She placed it on the corner of the table, when suddenly her jaw dropped and she looked past Fox.

"What's wrong?" asked Fox.

Parris leapt from her chair and dashed over to the television in a few long strides. She turned up the volume—Valerik's picture was on the screen. She heard Fox's chair sliding in the background and heard him approach. She couldn't understand what was being said, but seeing Valerik's picture could only mean bad news. Her thoughts were later confirmed when a multi-car pile-up on a highway was shown.

She glanced over at Fox before looking back at the television. "What just happened?"

"For starters, he's dead."

Parris rolled her eyes. "Now tell me something I couldn't have guessed for myself."

"An eye-witness claimed that his body was dropped from an overpass into oncoming traffic late this morning, which resulted in the pile-up."

"Any idea who did this?"

"My guess is someone who couldn't stand him, considering the way he was disposed of."

"You mean, you don't know."

Fox gestured to the television. "Hey, I'm seeing this for the first time like you. We're bound to find out more later on."

The news report ended. They both returned to the table.

Parris continued to eat and then wiped off the corner of her mouth with the table napkin. "So, Valerik's dead. We have an idea of who his allies were. We're just unsure of his enemies."

"There's something else I should add. A few members of the Boeisho met me at the airport. Their Head of Section was the one who briefed me on what happened in Chechnya. But just before that, someone else ran into me at the airport and slipped me a note that said not to trust them. And that he'd contact me later."

Parris sipped her tea as Fox recounted everything Tanaka had told him. "Do you think the Boeisho could've killed Valerik?"

"They could've, but I doubt they would've disposed of him in such a manner. Whoever did this wanted an audience, or to send a message to his colleagues." Fox finished his roti and drank the rest of his water. "Like Ares."

"You think they're here?"

"I wouldn't be surprised. They're pretty resourceful. And they seem to be getting better at it. I'm surprised they were able to track him down this quickly. Hopefully, my informant can tell me more."

"I'd be careful." Parris held a finger to her lip briefly and then pointed it at Fox. "We don't know anything about this informant. He said you can't trust the Boeisho. They were expecting you and knew when and where to meet you, which means that someone tipped them off. And for this informant to know your whereabouts could mean that someone tipped him off also."

"If he's Boeisho, and let's just say he is for argument's sake, he'd have his channels. I doubt that he's working alone."

"And what if he's one of Hashimoto's men? Tanaka told you that he lost touch with his three agents. Who's to say that your informant isn't one of Hashimoto's brainwashed cult members? I know I wasn't involved in brainwashing all of them, but you have to still consider the possibility."

Fox leaned over the table and looked Parris in the eye. "I realize that. But he has something to share with me. And with Valerik dead, it's all we have to go on right now. If someone's lying, then I'll know soon enough."

Parris copied Fox's actions and leaned in herself. "In that case, I'm coming with you to meet him, the next time he contacts you."

Fox dropped his head on a slant and raised an eyebrow. "Say what?"

"You heard what I said."

"He asked for me. That means I should go alone."

"So what. I'll hide. If he's one of Hashimoto's men, chances are I've seen him around Hexagon."

"And if he's not, you risk blowing your cover."

"I'll be careful."

"You'd be doing just that...by not showing up. You don't need to attract attention to yourself. You're NOC, remember?"

"I'm glad to hear you say that. I guess that's why you sent me a boat-size bouquet of roses to my workplace?"

"Do you always have to have the last word?"

Parris got up and leaned on the table towards Fox with outstretched arms, eyes narrowed. "I do, considering I wasn't aware you were put in charge."

Fox stood up and duplicated Parris's actions. "It's not a matter of who's in charge of what. It's about the Boeisho not knowing about you, and its best that we keep it that way. I've done exceptionally well so far."

"You think so?"

"Are you always this argumentative?"

"When I don't agree with something, I'll damn well let you

know it. But if you want to go it alone, fine. You're better off letting Tomas hook you up with one of his gadgets, preferably a mini video camera that can pin to your jacket. At least that way he can run a search on your informant. It's the same way we caught Valerik's image. Is that too much to ask?"

Fox looked away from Parris for a few seconds, to the television which now showed a chewing gum commercial.

"No," he said and then looked back at Parris. "It isn't."

There, at least we actually reached a compromise. She couldn't believe it. Just as they were starting to warm up again he had to insult her like this. *Who's he to tell me that I shouldn't come?* This wasn't working, it was an unavoidable mistake that they wound up working together in the first place. She had to get away from him. Parris looked at her watch and stood up from the table. She grabbed her purse from the back of the chair as though she were in a hurry. "I have to go."

Fox called out as she headed towards the door. "Don't get me wrong, Dr. Parris. I just don't want to see your obituary on the evening news."

That did it. She turned around, and walked towards him slowly while she stared him straight in the eyes. "You expect me to get hurt, don't you?"

"To be blunt, you already have been."

"I'm quite capable of taking care of myself. I've learned that from the past, so I don't need a bodyguard."

She turned and walked back to the door. "You've found me so I assume that you can find Tomas. But let me warn you, he's not as sociable as I am."

***

Fox watched her disappear. He expected to hear the door slam, but she didn't do that. She was feisty, irrational, not to mention cynical and paranoid, and maybe she was better off on her own. He would later get in touch with Tomas, but not because Parris had suggested it. He always thought one way of dealing with unpleasant people was to do or say the opposite of what they would expect. Parris didn't expect him to agree with her on meeting Levickis, so he agreed.

It was the same way he dealt with Jessica. Always act unpredictably, that always calmed her down. He remembered when he had proposed to her. They had an argument the night before about how he put his life on the line all the time and that it wouldn't be conducive to their relationship. He couldn't forget the shock and delight on her face when he had walked into her workplace on her lunch break the next day, dressed in army fatigues with a large garbage bag. Then in full view of all of her colleagues, he had stripped down to his boxer briefs and bagged his fatigues telling her that he's throwing it all away. Never mind the commotion that it caused, even the security guards that arrived didn't bother to stop him. And that's when he got down on one knee and showed her the engagement ring.

Before he realized it, something rolled from his eye and down his left cheek. He immediately wiped away the tear. *Why the fuck is this happening? I've scarred her, and it has changed her life forever. Now she's involved in a life that I was ready to leave.*

His thoughts were interrupted by a knock at the door. He hid his face from Sora. "We're done. Can you please call me a taxi?"

"Yes, Mr. Ripley. By the way, someone dropped this off for you." She walked up to him and handed him a letter-sized envelope.

Fox took the envelope while covering his eyes. "Thanks."

She bowed and as she turned to walk out the door, she paused and looked back at him. "Is everything all right?"

"I'm fine. Thanks for being concerned. I just need to be alone for a bit."

When she left, Fox tore open the sealed envelope and took out the paper that was inside. The handwritten note read, Koishikawa Korakuen Gardens tonight at 8:00 PM. I'll carry a brown paper bag and will pass the Weeping Cherries.

Fox held the paper over the open flame on the table. He let the fire consume it until it reached his fingers, and then he blew it out. He dropped the blackened pieces onto his lunch plate.

This guy knew Fox better than he'd thought. *How'd he know to look for me here?* He had been certain no one had followed him and he had personally swept the premises for bugs or any other listening devices. The place was secure, but whoever this guy was, he was top notch, and if he was on the run from the Boeisho, it would explain why he'd been able to avoid them.

With that taken care of, his attention focused on the meal. *Where else could one get a foreign meal prepared the right way on such short notice?* He reached into his wallet and took out a wad of bills. He had already run out of Japanese currency. The last cab driver didn't complain when Fox gave him two hundred dollars for dropping him off at the mall and then picking him up ten minutes later from another entrance in his new disguise. *Oh, what the hell.*

He tore out a few American bills and tossed them on the table, right beside Dr. Parris's table napkin. *Well, how about that—she forgot her own table napkin. She's too steamed. Better to wait and give it back to her later when she's cooled off.* With West Indian women, it was always about timing. But Parris, as he now learned, was a lot more unpredictable.

He folded it and placed it into the breast pocket of his blazer. He checked the tip on the table. *Three fifties, was that enough?* Fox tore out a few more bills from his wallet. There, an extra hundred should make them happy. *No need to piss anyone else off today.*

Chapter 16

Koishikawa Korakuen Gardens, 7:58 PM

T he park lamps beside the path glowed like individual lighthouses on a foggy distant coast. Fox could not see much from either side as the thick fog obscured everything that was more than thirty feet away. His informant could not have predicted the fog. That didn't bother Fox considering that it would be harder for someone to follow him. On the other hand, it would also be easy for someone to ambush him. Fox sat down on a bench beside a sign that said *Shidarezakura*, which meant *Weeping Cherry* in Japanese. He looked at his watch, leaned on the arm rest and tapped his fingers.

A couple passed by him, hand in hand. The age difference was obvious. *Jesus, another sugar daddy.* They were a few feet away when Fox glanced at them a second time. He'd recognize them for sure if he saw them again.

Why the hell did I get stuck with someone that holds grudges? He rubbed the spot where Parris had kicked him. It still hurt slightly to the touch. *Maybe I deserved that.* An older couple walked by in the opposite direction from the previous couple. *Maybe I should've added ginger beer or the sorrel to the lunch menu today.* Those were popular Caribbean drinks from Barbados. Fox rested both elbows on his knees. *Here I go again, thinking about what I did wrong. Why the hell am I even thinking about her? Why should I even care if she likes me or not?* Fox glanced at his watch a second time.

Maybe things would've been better had he been partnered with an antisocial, like Levickis. He'd be more focused and have no one to pester him, that would work. Thanks to him, he was now armed with a Beretta 92G Elite II regular sidearm, along with its relative, the Beretta 950 Jetfire mini-pistol that was concealed in his ankle holster. Fox then checked the pen in the breast pocket of his jacket to make sure the micro video camera lens was facing outwards. Other than the weapons, the other concealed item he had was a Hexagon Pharmaceuticals guest ID.

At that point, Fox noticed a man approach. His face was partially hidden under the peak of his baseball cap. He wore a green polyester spring jacket, blue denim jeans and slightly worn running shoes. He came close to being five foot five inches tall— about the same height as the man that had bumped into him at the airport. But it was the brown paper bag he carried that gave him away. Fox stood and joined him in his stroll.

"I trust you weren't followed," said the man.

"I trust that you trust me when I say I wasn't."

"I'll take your word for it. You can call me Ken Katori, a Boeisho operative. I'll make this meeting as brief as possible. I take it that you met with Tanaka?"

"Yes."

"I am one of three that had infiltrated a doomsday cult. We had reason to believe that they were planning a major attack on Japan. But our cover was blown."

"Was it Tanaka?"

"Yes, he's the mole for the cult. He blew our cover."

Fox looked at him. "Explain."

"Have you heard of a man named Hideaki Hashimoto, the CEO of Hexagon Pharmaceuticals?"

"Tanaka spoke of him."

"His group somehow got to Tanaka and recruited him," said Katori, as they walked around a curve.

"Why would Tanaka join with Hashimoto?"

Katori dropped the paper bag in a trash can. "He didn't join Hashimoto's group, he was coerced."

"Hashimoto brainwashed him, didn't he?"

"So you know of his alleged involvement with the Soviets during their war with Afghanistan."

"I've been briefed about it."

"Well it doesn't stop there. It appears that he's started up his program again. Tanaka, along with members of the police department and other organizations, were also his victims. My colleagues didn't know about Tanaka until recently. The Boeisho has been keeping a close eye on cults since cult groups were responsible for the wave of pipe bomb explosions and other terrorist activities that rocked Japanese cities back in the mid 1990s. Hashimoto's group was no exception. I was recruited as one of the guards, or a ninja if you wish, and so were my two colleagues. He's recruited people from all over the world to build his group, mostly those between the ages of thirteen and twenty-five, from all cultural backgrounds, and of all types."

Fox checked their surroundings surreptitiously to make sure they were not being followed. "What do you mean by types?"

"Hashimoto hasn't limited his selection to a specific group of people. Along with small-time criminals and juvenile delinquents, he's mostly recruited academics. Not the ones you'd find interning or looking for jobs, but the ones who failed or cheated on their exams. Especially those that were kicked out or who had dropped out of school. There were many from all over the world."

"So Hashimoto's been profiling these individuals. Why?"

"I'll get to that part later."

Both Fox and the informant descended a curved stairway while they continued talking.

"What about the ninjas? Were they brainwashed also?"

"No. They're Hashimoto's own private army, and they're all loyal to him. They will do everything necessary to protect him and his goals. But before my team and I were compromised, we suspected that Hashimoto may be taking orders from someone."

"Like who?"

"We weren't able to find out. But we discovered Hashimoto's plans to assault Ares's Groznyy laboratory to steal a specific bio-weapon, we immediately informed Tanaka. The problem is that he informed Hashimoto and that's when they decided to get rid of us. If only we'd known that Tanaka was on their side from the beginning, one of my colleagues would still be alive."

They both got to the bottom of the stairs and continued along the path.

"But they didn't attack the Groznyy lab after all," said Fox.

"No, they had a change of plan and attacked the Ares lab in Belarus."

"It figures. I didn't leave much behind for them in Groznyy."

Katori looked at Fox. "So it *was* you."

"Damn right it was. What happened to your partner?"

"He escaped with me, but we often don't stay together, to make it more difficult for Hashimoto to track us. His name's Aijima Sato. We still work together and were able to find out that the CIA would get here sooner or later. He'll find you when the time is right."

"I think it's way past that time. If Sato has valuable information then he must give it to me if you both expect me to help you."

"You'll get it. If you want to take down both Ares and Hashimoto, you'll have to do it on our terms. Don't forget we have to be careful. Hashimoto got to Tanaka—Tanaka of all people! And it's no thanks to that former KGB spy."

"Valerik."

"Exactly. My only regret is that we didn't eliminate him earlier. He's the only one who could've provided Hashimoto with enough information to aid in Tanaka's capture and subsequent brainwashing."

"I didn't think the Boeisho would've killed Valerik," added Fox.

"Of course not. His own people did it."

"The Arms of Ares."

"Exactly. I'm surprised he allowed himself to be tracked down so easily."

"It's starting to make sense now. Hashimoto stole Pandora from Ares and now they're trying to get it back. And they've killed off Valerik—"

"For revenge."

"I don't think it's only for revenge," asserted Fox. "They didn't want him talking to me when I found him, or anyone for that matter. This brings me to my next question. I'm assuming you heard what happened in southern Uganda?"

"Yes, a bit."

"Why would Ares risk infiltrating a military-guarded compound to steal back Pandora when they already knew of Valerik's whereabouts? All clues point to them but I always felt something wasn't right."

"Oh that wasn't Ares. It was Hashimoto."

"I don't understand. He already has Pandora, he didn't need any more. Unless he wanted to frame Ares."

"That's exactly what he wanted to do."

"But he obviously knew that the CIA would've figured out that Ares wasn't involved eventually."

"Yes, *eventually*." Katori said. "He'd be way ahead of you by the time you found out that you were on a wild goose chase. Hashimoto would've had someone on the inside. It's my theory that one or more of his recruits were already at the compound at the time. Once Pandora was delivered, they destroyed it."

Fox sighed with a chuckle. "It was all staged. Only one of the scientists had torn clothing, meaning that he was the only one attacked with the dagger found at the scene. Up until now, no one has been arrested at any of the checkpoints set up on all of the highways and airports. The culprit or culprits were on a suicide mission."

"Exactly."

"Tell me a bit about Tanaka. What's he like?" asked Fox.

"There's not much to say about him. He's been Head of Section for the past ten years. He lost his only daughter in a traffic accident about six years ago. He got the news while at a Tchaikovsky recital with his wife on their wedding anniversary. Other than that, he's normally reserved. Why?"

"I was curious. Wanted to see if there was a connection between his..." Fox paused just when he noticed that Katori had stopped walking with him and was two steps behind him. What he wanted to know was if there was a connection between Tanaka and the other brainwashing victims.

Fox didn't have to know what was on Katori's mind. From his body language, he knew that Katori sensed that there was something wrong—as though they were being watched.

Katori pulled the peak of his baseball cap lower over his face and walked quickly in the opposite direction away from Fox.

Fox ran and caught up to him as Katori said to him. "Sato will get in touch with you and tell you the rest." They passed through the exit and walked out onto the sidewalk. Fox had to shout to be heard above the noise from the cars and trucks that zoomed by. "Look, I can get you protection."

"What are you going to do, call them? The Boeisho will trace your phone signal, or worse yet, even block your call. Think. You sat in Tanaka's car. Did it occur to you that he had a recording device to register your voice patterns so they could be used to track you?"

Damn, he's right.

"Besides, it'll do neither of us any good. Not against them. Now I'm warning you, Fox. This meeting is over."

"No, it isn't." Fox grabbed Katori by the shoulder, and he immediately and violently slapped him off. He stared back at Fox with narrowed eyes and heavy breathing.

"Listen, it's always on our terms when either I or Sato chooses to meet with you. We know who these people are and how far they're willing to go. So if you want to stay alive, I suggest you go back to your car and get away from here, and me, as quickly as possible." He turned and walked away rapidly.

While Katori tried to act tough, Fox knew he was scared. All he could do was obey him and nothing else. He watched Katori run off to the curb where he was just in time to catch the bus.

Fox ran the opposite way in a slow jog and snatched his cell phone off his belt clip. With his thumb he switched it off and replaced it on its clip. Its internal scrambler should keep him undetected for a while. Walsh and Dobbs would be pissed off, Walsh more than Dobbs since Fox hadn't contacted either of them yet. But after what Katori told him, it was for their own good. But Dobbs should be able to tell whether or not they were under surveillance. He was one of the best technicians he had ever worked with. In fact, Fox wouldn't be surprised if he knew of every satellite in orbit. The Boeisho wouldn't find him easily. And as long as Walsh stuck close to him, they shouldn't find him either.

The Tokyo City Dome was nearby, and Fox headed that way. There were always crowds in which he could lose anyone that may have been following him. Fox already knew where all of the closed-circuit cameras were along the way. It was all a matter of keeping his face hidden from them.

After having walked through the Tokyo City Dome and its labyrinth of underground connecting corridors, he emerged to the surface from an exit that was reserved for city maintenance workers. Fox's navy sports car was the third car away from the intersection. He used the automatic locking mechanism on his keys to unlock the door, and then got in his car from the street side, where the driver's side was. When he started her up, a blast of warm air flowed from the vents. He lowered the temperature to a cooler setting, turned up the defogger, and threw the gear into drive.

Whenever he parked, he always left enough space between his car and the back of the car in front of him to allow him to simply drive out. This was useful when he needed to make a quick getaway. Nevertheless, that tactic was useless this time.

A vehicle with disabled headlights screeched to a stop beside Fox. The back bumper lined up exactly with the front end of his car and blocked his path. Just as quickly a red sedan screeched to a halt right behind it, blocking the back passenger door of his car.

Fox expected to see a group of Asian men rush out of the two cars, but to his surprise, two Caucasian men dressed in jeans and light jackets appeared instead. It only took seconds before men with Micro-Uzis surrounded him. For sure if they wanted him dead, Fox knew they would've shot him already. These men wanted him alive.

Fox heard a car door slam behind the red sedan, and when he turned to look, Fox saw a man about his height, with thuggish looks and a pair of thick eyebrows that practically joined to become a single brow. He walked up and stood a few feet away from his door.

"Get out of the car. Keep your hands where they can be seen." The heavy Russian accent gave him away. Valerik's killers no doubt, and now they came for him. Fox had no plans to become the cause of another pile-up on a Tokyo freeway, but he wasn't going to be forced to give up intelligence either. This called for a more reckless and aggressive approach. No matter how slim his chances were of getting out unharmed, it was still a chance he had to take

Chapter 17

The man bent over slightly to look Fox in the eye. "I said get out! I won't repeat myself."

With no other alternative, Fox turned off the engine, left the keys in the ignition, and stepped out with his hands exposed. The first two gunmen backed away at forty-five-degree angles beside Single-brow forming a triangle.

Fox stood still, and smirked. "I've got to hand it to you guys, being able to get this far without any help."

Single-brow's eyes narrowed as he threw an underhand punch to Fox's stomach. The blow was so heavy that Fox buckled over and fell to the ground, winded. Too disoriented to stand on his own, he felt himself being lifted up and thrown against the side of his car.

Single-brow frisked him from top to bottom and then struck him in the forehead with his palm. "You weren't told to speak."

Fox breathed hard as he gave Single-brow a threatening stare in the eyes. *That's the last time you'll hit me.* His two Berettas and his cell phone had been removed. No surprise. At least his diversion was enough to distract Single-brow long enough that he forgot to examine the pen that Levickis had given him.

"Now go to last car. You're coming with us."

"What for? I already have a car," panted Fox, still winded. He knew it would provoke Single-brow, and as expected, he threw another punch towards Fox's stomach, but Fox swung his left arm downwards in a semi-circle and knocked his arm sideways, causing him to turn in the same direction. With his opposite hand,

Fox grabbed the shoulder that fell closest to him while he was off balance. He pulled, spinning him around, while he removed the Elite II, all in one motion, and popped off a shot into each gunman before they reacted.

Single-brow couldn't move, not with the way Fox held onto him. He gasped as he stared at the two corpses, blood oozing onto the street from the single bullet hole between their eyes. Fox breathed out a warm breath on Single-brow's neck, just enough to cause the tiny hairs to stand on end, and jammed the sidearm into the small of his back. "No, you're coming with me."

"Let him go!" yelled an angry voice. "You're surrounded."

When Fox looked, four more men with Micro-Uzis appeared both beside and behind him to replace the two he had laid waste to. The man who spoke to him was among the four. Fox noticed how his face reddened under the street lamp above, exposing his buzz cut.

"I'm warning you. Let him go," Buzz-cut repeated.

Fox turned and saw Buzz-cut's entourage. Had they not been there, he would've gotten away. Fox threw Single-brow's gun to the ground and shoved him away.

Immediately, one of the gunmen rushed Fox and pulled him away from his car, shoving him in the direction of the last car they drove. Fox caught a glimpse of his face under the streetlight. He had stubble and a thinning black hairline that he tried to hide with a comb-over that didn't quite work.

Buzz-cut and another man got into Fox's car while the others went back to the remaining two cars. Only Single-brow and Comb-over headed to the back car. Fox saw the other cars take off quickly. That was no surprise since there were bound to be witnesses who saw Fox waste the two men in self-defense. Within a few minutes, the entire block would be crawling with police, crime scene investigators, and paramedics.

Comb-over opened the car door for Fox. As he was about to get in, he saw a more fancy-dressed man in the backseat. Unlike the other thugs, he wore a suit and tie.

"Get in," said Comb-over.

"Wait," said the white-haired man, looking away from Fox

towards Single-brow. "Are you okay, Comrade?"

Single-brow's mouth slanted downwards on both ends as he looked down, followed by a slow nod. "Yes...yes, sir. I'm all right."

"Are you sure, Comrade? Because from what I saw, Fox disarmed you and used you as a human shield. Now three of my men are dead."

"Three?" He looked back at the two bodies on the ground. "Sir, there's only..."

Fox understood what the white-haired man meant, obviously before Single-brow did. The man pleaded apologetically, but the white-haired man was unforgiving. He gave a nod to Comb-over, who aimed his Micro-Uzi at Single-brow with a large grin. A few staccato shots later, his body was thrown to the ground with blood pouring from his face, chest, and stomach. Comb-over then swung the gun at Fox. He grinned again.

"No, Demyan!" growled the white-haired man. "He rides with us, remember?"

Fox couldn't help but notice Demyan's smile drop, followed by a huge sigh. While his weapon was still pointed at Fox, he waved its tip towards the back of the car and stepped aside, allowing him to pass. A hard object struck Fox at the back of his head and the world went spinning.

***

When he opened his eyes, he saw the white-haired man beside him, twirling a pen. He gingerly touched the back of his head as he tried to look around. Fox didn't feel any blood between his fingers, and didn't have to look outside to tell that the car was speeding. *Jesus, how many more times can my head take another bashing?*

The white-haired man turned to Fox. "It still hurts, doesn't it? It could've been worse for you. I noticed that you've made friends."

"Yeah, I was going to invite him out for a drink, but he had a date."

"Don't patronize me with your dull humor. You're a pest and I'm tired of people like you getting in my way. Lucky for you, I'll give you the chance to redeem yourself. Tell me, what did you learn from your friend?"

"He didn't say much. He had to catch the bus. Since you know so much about me, why don't you tell me about yourselves?"

"You know exactly who we are, even though we've yet to cross paths personally."

Fox took a closer look at the pen the man twirled, as he stopped doing so for a moment. "That's all right. From the word, October, that's written on the pen you're twirling, I can assume that you're all members of the October Cell of Ares. Seeing how you're dressed, you're their leader, and like the other leaders of the other cells, nameless. Do you mind if I call you the October Man?"

"Don't antagonize me. I know he shared intelligence with you. You're going to tell me what it is and everything you've found out since you've been here. I've dispatched a squad to go pick him up."

"So you don't need me. I guess I'll be on my way. Driver?"

Demyan spun around in the front passenger seat and aimed his Micro-Uzi between Fox's eyes.

The October Man threw out an arm with an open palm. "No! Not in here."

Fox looked into his trigger-happy eyes. "He's right. You wouldn't want to stain your boss's suit."

Demyan sneered and pointed the sidearm away from Fox towards the ceiling, but kept his eyes on him. Fox knew that he ached to use his weapon, and his face became even more menacing when the October Man did not grant him his wish—this time.

"Joke as much as you'd like to. You may not feel threatened right now. But where we're going, both you and your friend will tell us everything. And I promise that it won't be comfortable for either of you. You're familiar with our classic torture techniques."

"Of course. Come to think of it, in the past twenty-four hours I've had my head bashed in with the butt of gun—twice, I've been kicked in the shins, and punched in the stomach. A good, old-fashioned interrogation should be fun."

The October Man didn't answer. Fox hoped he could stir up his temper. It appeared to distract him. But the one thing that Fox knew that Ares operatives excelled in was their torture techniques—using medieval or ancient methods as a signature. He recalled uncovering one of their victims in the past. The shirtless man had been strapped to a table with a cage on top of his stomach. Fox still had memories of the foul smell in the room before he had seen the large hole in the victim's stomach—with a rat gnawing away inside. Apparently the cage that housed the rat had been heated, freaking out the rodent so that it had burrowed its way through the man's stomach and intestines in order to escape.

The only thing that Fox imagined that could be worse, was a sadistic torturer that maintained the suffering as long as possible, not allowing his victim to die.

The longer the car ride, the more time Fox had to guess as to which method the October Man had chosen for both him and Katori—and something told him that the October Man had already guessed this and would make the ride as long as possible.

Chapter 18

Katori's breath fogged up the window on the side exit door as he waited for the bus to come to a complete stop. The doors flung open and he was out. He made his way back to the taxi stand that was less than two blocks ahead. For now, he would head back to the safe-house both he and Sato *borrowed* from a vacationing couple.

A bright light shone around him, quickly followed by the loud screeching of tires. When he turned, two men—both taller and larger than he—pounced on Katori. Before he could run away, a large hand tightened around his forearm just seconds before he saw a fist flash towards his face. There was impact, then darkness.

Katori woke up to find himself in the back seat of a car in plastic handcuffs, sandwiched between two large men. He was pretty sure they were the same ones who had attacked him. They shouldn't have been able to capture him so easily. He had gotten careless. Along with the two men who sat beside him, there were two others up front, including the driver. All four of them were Caucasian and were dressed like members of a typical street gang. They were not Tanaka's men and most definitely were not Hashimoto's either.

"Who are you people?" Katori coughed up in Japanese. They didn't answer.

A cell phone rang up front. The front passenger held it up to his ear and answered in what sounded like Russian. He was in the middle of a sentence when two explosions shook the car. There was a bounce, and they all flew forward as the driver tried to maintain control when the vehicle spun counterclockwise ninety degrees and crashed into a parked car. Katori heard one of them yell *zaebis*, which he assumed was some form of profanity, as he was thrown into the seat in front of him while being crushed under the weight of one of the thugs beside him. All was quiet, with the exception of the running engine. The driver turned to the passenger to say something, but his partner was too preoccupied fumbling for the cell phone he dropped.

Glass shards burst inwards from the passenger windows and showered everyone, and that's when he saw swift shadowy movement outside. The entire episode took less than ten seconds before screams and shouts of agony erupted around him. Bits of muscle tissue and blood splashed on his face. He was quick to wipe it off until the window behind him exploded inward. Katori was covered in several shards before hard fingers dug into both sides of his face and neck and pulled him through the back as he tried to pry himself loose.

***

Fox tried to listen in on the conversation on the October Man's phone call, but he couldn't catch everything. So far he gathered that something was wrong when the October Man called out the responder's name three times before he switched his phone off.

The October Man turned to the driver, and Demyan, with a head tilt towards Fox. "Dump him."

The car slowed down without stopping. Fox was forced to open the door and was kicked from behind. He flew from the car and rolled over a few times until he crashed into a solid object. He then landed in a cold puddle of rainwater. Fox rolled out of the puddle and quickly got up, ran his fingers through his hair to get out any excess water and scowled as he watched the members of the October Cell speed off, taking his car with them. Next time he'd send them all to the morgue as retribution. He looked down and saw that he hit the edge of the sidewalk. He brushed downwards and hard, on his clothes, to get the excess water off of him.

Fox thought of the oddness of their actions—releasing him,

considering how much danger he was to them. The October Man must have been spooked. Fox figured that if the October Man feared that his men were being followed by the enemy, then dumping Fox would divert the enemy's attention away from them. As the saying went, if you and your friend are trying to outrun a lion, you don't have to outrun the lion—you just need to outrun your friend.

After what Katori had told him, phones would have to be on hold for now. But there was one more option, and Fox was most uncomfortable thinking about it. He wasn't going to spend the night on Dr. Parris's couch—he just had to talk to her in person.

At first, he walked down the street, and then he broke out into a slight jog. He didn't know the name of the street that he was approaching, but several cars flew by, so a taxi was bound to pass by anytime soon. As he approached the cross street, a black stretch-limousine drove into the intersection and stopped. The tinted glass prevented him from seeing who was inside, but he already guessed that whoever it was wasn't there to help him. At least, that's what his instincts told him.

Fox heard more than one engine gunning behind him, so he quickly jumped to the side and onto the sidewalk thinking he'd be run over. A black motorcycle shot past him and screeched to a halt, with its driver facing him sideways. Before he was able to look at the driver, another motorcyclist charged him on the sidewalk, forcing him to jump back onto the street. The first motorcyclist revved the engine a second time and drove slowly around Fox while the second did the same, putting Fox between them and the limousine.

The Yakuza-style ambush was not unfamiliar to Fox, and although he couldn't see their faces beyond their dark helmets, he knew that they were not there to attack him unless he provoked them. With him unarmed, they had the upper hand.

Okay I get it. I'm walking to the limo. Fox looked over his shoulder at the limousine again, and this time the rear window lowered. Through it, he saw the familiar smile and high cheekbones. He walked sideways towards the limousine while keeping an eye on the motorcyclists. They followed him on their bikes at the same pace in order to maintain their distance from him.

"Come inside and join me," said Tanaka. "It's not safe for you to be out there. But you've already figured that out, haven't you?" He laughed when Fox turned to look at the two men as they simultaneously revved their engines, reminding him what was in store if he didn't do as he was told.

Chapter 19

Doctor Nita Parris's Apartment, Chofu-shi, West Tokyo, 9:12PM

Parris entered the elevator to her apartment building and put down the two grocery bags. The doors closed and she paced within the small space, her hands on her hips. *Why did Dewan attack me? What did I do? And now he's become a complete angel, changed even more than those so-called born-again Christians.* At least, those were Hashimoto's findings when he spoke to her earlier over the phone. It didn't make any sense.

The thoughts kept revolving like a treadmill through her mind. Then, there was Fox, the man that started it all. Her life as a field agent could be traced back to the moment he dumped her. *How could I have been so naïve as to believe that he was interested in the book-smart goody-two shoes that I used to be?* She'd always been viewed by many guys the same way. Throughout high school, university, especially at her track meets.

But Fox seemed different. She didn't know what it was about him that intrigued her, but she sensed it when she met him earlier—especially when he played the piano. *He couldn't have written that piece for me...yeah right, wishful thinking. Why would I even think that in the first place?* It was only then that she realized that the elevator wasn't moving.

She hit the seventh-floor button on the panel. *That's a sign that I'm thinking too much.*

When the elevator stopped, she gathered her belongings and

walked to her apartment. All she thought of doing was preparing something light to eat and then heading straight to bed.

Parris reached over to the wall and flicked the light switch. As she removed a can of corn, some green peas, and then a bag of noodles from her grocery bag, she heard the door buzzer. *At this hour? It must be Levickis.*

She walked to the front door, where a ten-inch monitor was mounted on the wall. It showed a live camera shot of the entrance to her building. Levickis stared back at her, looking exhausted. Parris pressed a second button beside the monitor to buzz him in. She then unlocked the front door and headed back to the kitchen.

By the time Levickis arrived, Parris had downed two glasses of cranberry juice, finishing off the two-liter bottle. He walked into the kitchen as she took out another bottle of cranberry juice from the second bag and put it into the refrigerator. "Juice?"

Levickis unzipped his jacket. "No thanks." From inside his jacket, he took out his PDA and then threw the jacket over the back of a chair.

Parris looked at him and noticed how he fumbled with his PDA. "You look worried. What's wrong?"

"Everything. Something's happened to Fox."

"Really? And he was concerned about me not being able to take care of myself."

"I lost contact with him after his meeting."

"Who'd he meet with? Anyone in the agency files?"

Levickis tapped the screen with the miniature plastic wand. "I ran a face recognition search on his contact. Nothing's come up yet. My guess is that he's Boeisho."

"Did you find anything else?"

"It looks like he's been kidnapped. He was in a scuffle and his camera—my camera—got broken when he was thrown from a moving vehicle."

Parris tried to get a look at his PDA. "My God, is he all right?"

"It appeared that he got up and walked a bit before the camera stopped transmitting. So he's fine. You, on the other hand, had the decency to fall headfirst so as not to damage yours when Dewan went berserk on you."

"I'm going to ignore that last comment."

"Ah, here we are," said Levickis, as he brought up the video caption at the point where Fox was accosted at his car. He then handed the PDA to Parris.

"Let me guess, you ran a face recognition search on these men and it turned up nothing."

"Not quite. Fox managed to get three of them on camera. Two of them were once in the Russian Air Force, up to about a year ago. Both of them were dishonorably discharged. Now they're known members of Ares."

"Yes, I see." Parris walked as she read the PDA. "Both of them were involved in drug trafficking to the Russian Mafia while in service. They were arrested and charged, but managed to escape custody, due to what may have been an inside job."

"What do you know about Fox?"

"He's a jerk, but I'm not going to get into any of that right now."

"Sounds like your type of guy."

"You wish."

A ringing came from her belt clip. Parris removed her cell phone and flipped it open. "Hello."

"May I speak to Helen Pierce?" It was her contact and Helen Pierce was the signal.

"I'm afraid you have the wrong person, maybe you want to speak to Sheldon Spears."

"Ain't he still at work?"

"He is. I'm his sister."

"So you've been briefed on our arrival?" said Walsh who was careful not to use her name and keep the conversation curt. Although they both used secure lines designed by the tech guys at the Office of Science and Technology, or OST, in Langley, Virginia, the precaution was necessary. Their cell phones, as well as their PDAs and any other communication devices, had to be changed every few months, since less friendly nations had their own tech guys who did nothing else all day long but try to break through the secure lines of other nations—especially those in the United States.

Parris handed the PDA back to Levickis. "Yes, we have."

"Is the computer nerd with you?"

Parris glanced briefly at Levickis. "He is."

"Good. Any word from Sheldon? The bastard ditched us." Parris understood Sheldon was code for Fox.

"That's what both of us are trying to find out. We've just learned that he's run into some bad company."

"Oh, Christ. This ain't good." Walsh then spoke to someone else in the background. "Listen, both of you need to get over here ASAP. We're staying at a different hotel than before. I'll have my guy send the computer nerd our location to his PDA."

"I'll let him know." She hung up.

"What was that all about?" asked Levickis.

"That was Walsh. He's sending us a meeting location."

Less than five seconds later a tune came from the PDA and Levickis tapped the wand to the envelope icon on the screen. "They're at the Shinigawa Empress Hotel, room 305."

"I'll go change." Parris left the kitchen and walked to her bedroom. First, she had learned that her experiments were part of a recruitment ploy, as of this moment, Ares had their agents in town, and now Fox was missing. Parris knew that she was in for a long night.

Chapter 20

Shibuya Ward, 10:20 PM

T he black stretch-limousine cruised between forty and fifty kilometers per hour through the streets of the Shibuya Ward, a major fashion district of Japan and also a major nightlife area that teemed with young people and countless garishly-lit neon lights and billboards.

"I thought you'd be happy to see me. After all, we rescued you," said Tanaka. His bodyguards flanked Fox while he sat opposite them.

"Yes, you did. Only now I've been kidnapped in luxury and without any sake to serve me this time. It's an interesting scheme Hashimoto has going on. You keep the Boeisho in check so that he can carry out his plans. If only you knew what you were doing."

"What makes you say that?"

"You must admit that it's hard to believe an important person within the Boeisho could be swayed by the teachings of a cult."

Tanaka laughed. "I hope you weren't too taken in by what your contact told you. His understanding of things is, how should we say, limited. He most likely blew things out of proportion." Tanaka sighed. "May he rest in peace."

Fox was not surprised. He feared the worst once he saw the October Man panic. He said nothing but just stared angrily at Tanaka.

"Poor soul. It was the only way to put an end to his state of confusion. We can't allow people like him to spread lies about us. It was for his own good, and, you could say, for ours as well."

"Ours? I don't see anything good about your so-called beliefs, so I guess you'll have to kill me, too."

Tanaka laughed again. This time he sighed louder. "It's a real shame that you don't understand the way things should be, at least for now. It was the same for everyone at first, including me. But that'll change, and trust me, you won't regret it."

"Is that why you're keeping me alive? So that I learn the teachings of Hashimoto? My God, he's really warped your mind. Sooner or later the Boeisho will discover you're a mole, responsible for the deaths of your own men, which will leave you either court-marshaled or executed without trial. But I'm guessing that you've accepted that as part of Hashimoto's plan."

"It's the final outcome that matters. If I should die before then, I will have gone down as a martyr."

Fox didn't say anything else, but noticed that they were slowing down, and he looked out the window to see where they were. Outside was the glitzy entrance to a nightclub. *Cylinder* was written, in both Japanese and English, in large, green neon lights above the entrance. The line-up was the same as with most nightclubs, long enough to go around the block with probably a sixty-to ninety-minute wait.

"Does this remind you of your high school years?"

Fox stared at the crowd. "It sure does. I never had to wait in lines though, since I always knew someone on the inside. It's always helped, just like it's helped Hashimoto having *you* on the inside."

When the limousine stopped, a bouncer, the size of an NFL linebacker, opened the door, and Tanaka's two henchmen gestured for Fox to exit.

"No, after you," Fox said to the ninjas. The two men forced him out, causing him to nearly stumble and fall. The two motorcyclists, who had accosted Fox earlier, had parked on the sidewalk close by, away from the crowd.

Tanaka was the last to get out of the car and the same bouncer closed the door. He looked at the two motorcyclists and waved them off. They both responded by revving up their engines and speeding away. Tanaka then straightened his tie as he looked at Fox.

"It's not a good idea to disobey Hashimoto's ninjas, especially since they'll kill on a command from an authoritative figure."

"Well, since it's only you, I guess I have nothing to worry about."

Tanaka laughed once again.

Another bouncer unclipped the velvet rope to allow the four of them to pass through. As expected, the people closest to the front of the line yelled in protest and Fox gladly waved back to them. They walked up a set of stairs and were met by another bouncer who opened the door for them.

Fox noticed that all the bouncers had similar physiques. *Steroids...could they be more obvious?* They were almost cartoonish with their oversized upper bodies and stout lower bodies, sort of like the bulldog from *Looney Toons*. Fox forgot the character's name. Hector, possibly.

The foyer, circular and painted, lit in fluorescent red, ringed the actual dancehall. A clever feature was the smell of cherries, and it made him thirsty. With the massive crowd outside, Fox knew the bartenders would have their pockets overflowing with tips by early morning.

The inner circular wall was covered in mirrors and had four entrances to the main dance floor, all equidistant from each other. Each dancehall entrance had two rows of thick, black-leather curtains that acted as a sound barrier to keep the music inside.

Tanaka turned to Fox. "We should hurry. The young people will be streaming in any moment now." Tanaka led the way to the glass-enclosed elevator, which was on the outer circular wall of the foyer.

Along the walls, were small artificial palm trees in large ceramic pots, filled with sand. Fox dropped down and pretended to tie his shoe. As expected, Tanaka's henchmen grabbed him from behind and pulled him up. However, Fox pretended to stumble and caught the edge of one of the pots with both hands. Again, Tanaka's men were too occupied pulling Fox up onto his feet to notice him dipping a hand into the sand and then dropping some of it into his pants pocket. He could've flung it in the eyes of Tanaka's men right now, however he wanted to meet Hashimoto, and letting Tanaka lead him was the easiest way to do so.

Once they got in, they rode the cylindrical elevator up all five stories. They exited the elevator into an area that was similar to the street-level foyer, except the walls were fluorescent green and actually emitted a strong lime scent. A powerful blast of House Music overwhelmed them when Tanaka pulled open the second leather curtain of the doorway.

This floor of the dance club was empty, and it resembled a cylindrical-shaped prison with fluorescent surroundings. The fifth floor was fluorescent green, the fourth floor was yellow, the third was blue, and the second, purple, then the bottom floor was red.

From where he was, he saw that each floor was ring shaped with the exception of the bottom floor and that there were bars that surrounded the inner ring. Then there was the most spectacular feature. Five cage-dancers, three young men and two women, each dressed in fluorescent red, purple, blue, yellow, and green bodysuits. As they danced, their individual cages were randomly lowered and raised in the open space of the cylinder.

Fox walked on with the others as he observed the surroundings. *A front for recruits, no doubt.* According to what he knew, Hashimoto was recruiting people in the age group he saw lined up outside. It didn't matter what happened behind the scenes at this nightclub, but Hashimoto had no right to be around anyone this age. And if things went Fox's way, he'd burn the place to the ground.

Fox saw an area separated by a glass enclosure. Even the inner ring of that section had its bars replaced by glass. Tanaka opened the glass door, and when it closed behind all of them, the loud music was left behind as well.

Tanaka stepped aside and gestured to the others to walk past him. "Ah, much better, much quieter, wouldn't you agree?"

"Actually, I liked it out there. I was about to have a John Travolta moment."

For the first time, Fox noticed that Tanaka didn't laugh.

Obviously he didn't seem to understand the joke.

Unlike the dance floor outside, this room was a cocktail lounge complete with booths and round tables with a glass vase and candle on each. All of the tables were empty, except for the last table where Fox saw the silhouette of a person. The person sat alone, facing away from them.

Fox squinted as he tried to discern the shadowy figure. "So, you've brought me to meet Hashimoto personally."

Tanaka laughed again, and Fox rolled his eyes. "Hashimoto? That's not Hashimoto."

Fox took a second look at the person, but still couldn't identify who it was. *Of course, Katori told me that Hashimoto reported to someone else.*

"I thought I told you to watch your back, Fox," said the silhouetted figure.

Fox stopped where he was. *Hold on, I know that voice.*

The two guards were close to Fox as he was made to stand about eight to ten meters away from the booth, where he finally saw the woman, confirming his guess.

"Surprised?"

He was surprised, and Fox's blank stare probably didn't hide it. "I thought I'd learned everything tonight, until now."

Dr. Tabitha Marx took a sip of what Fox thought to be a Black Russian. "There's a lot that we need to talk about."

"Really, where would you like to start? Do you want to talk about how you managed to recruit Japanese secret agents into your organization? Or would you rather talk about your acts of treason and how many years back they go?"

Marx relaxed into the cushiony seat and took another sip. "The recruitment process wasn't much trouble. We help people see things as they are. Once they see the alternative that we offer, they're practically on hands and knees begging to join. It might surprise you to know how resourceful I really am. Given the right moment, I could even recruit you."

Fox smirked as he nodded. "Is that right?"

"Oh, I know so. Would you rather hear it from Tanaka instead? Or would you prefer to hear it from the police commissioner?"

Fox lost his smirk once he heard this.

Tabitha's smile grew as she saw his expression change. "By the way, the word on the street is that you're a murderer. A vicious assassin, I might add. Five, no, in fact nine men in total this evening. All of them believed to be of Russian origin and one of them Japanese, all ambushed and slaughtered. I'm impressed."

"You would be. And I'll bet that my fingerprints magically appeared all over the victims and the murder weapons that were conveniently left at the scene of the crime."

"Correction. *Scenes* of the crimes."

Fox chuckled and turned to Tanaka. "So are you going to offer me more sake, then lift my prints from the oshokos to frame me for another murder? Or do you have enough?"

Tanaka laughed.

"Oh Fox, it's good to see you can still keep your sense of humor, or sarcasm, or whatever you want to call it," said Tabitha. "No, if I wanted you thrown in jail or executed, I would've already given the order. But I need you alive, not just because I admire your presence, but because there's something I need from you. And within the next few minutes I'm going to have it."

Chapter 21

Shinigawa Empress Hotel, Shinigawa Ward, Tokyo, 10:25PM

The drive was long, and Parris wasn't a fan of vans, especially the eight-year-old one that Levickis drove. Simply put, she did not feel safe in it whatsoever. Its base was too narrow for its height, like some of the vans she saw on the roads in Barbados that looked like they would flip the moment they flew around a curve. Levickis's van was similar, and she sat firmly into her seat with one hand gripping the hand bar above her passenger window and the other on the seat next to the gear. On top of that, she wanted to reach over to the volume dial and turn down the loud music he played, too.

Levickis glanced over at Parris. "You're safe, you know. That's what the seatbelt's for."

"I feel much safer hanging on." Parris's grip tightened just as Levickis took a curve without slowing down. "Will you turn down some of that noise?"

Levickis quickly glanced at her. "This *noise* is what's keeping me awake. You wouldn't want me to fall asleep and crash, would you?"

"Trust me, it's not the music that'll make you crash this van." Parris held her breath as he overtook a motorcyclist. "For now, I'm not in the mood for any song that keeps repeating the verse, *'It's the end of the world as we know it'*."

Levickis sighed and turned down the volume. "I've been

wanting to ask you something. What's your problem with Fox?"

"Problem? What are you talking about?"

"Come on. I asked you before what you knew about him. You didn't have anything nice to say."

"We had a falling out in the past, and that's all I'm going to say." She saw him glance at her out of the corner of her eye, but she wouldn't look at him. *Now he wants to bring up Fox.* Levickis remained silent for the rest of the ride.

When they made it into the Shinigawa ward, the breathtaking view of the Tokyo Harbor with its high-class restaurants and hotels instantly made Parris forget about the ride. Levickis found a parking space a block away from the Shinigawa Empress Hotel. Parris was more than anxious to get out of the van and was ahead of Levickis as they crossed the street.

The hotel's lobby bustled with tourists—even at that hour—most of whom she figured were meeting in groups to spend a night on the town. Just as well that nobody knew what was going down. She shuddered to think of the mass carnage that could tear the city apart.

They both rode the elevator to the third floor and quickly found their way to suite 305, where Levickis knocked on the door.

There was the sound of fast approaching, heavy footsteps towards the door before it was opened. Walsh's haggard but robust figure, stood before them. "Come on in."

"Good evening," said Parris as she walked in.

Levickis merely nodded his head.

As they passed him, Walsh pointed to Dobbs who was seated at the coffee table in front of his laptop. "That's Bill Dobbs. He's helping us with tech."

She looked at Walsh. His hair was a mess, and his tie undone. "What happened to you? Bad flight?"

"More or less." Walsh moved the second chair away from the coffee table. "The flight was over-booked and I ended up riding in coach beside some woman who must've been going through a damn mid-life crisis. She wouldn't stop talking to me and complaining to the stewardess. God knows how many hours of sleep I need to catch up on because of her."

"That's why I never got married," said Levickis.

Walsh frowned at Levickis's comment. "Our relief came when we got word that our connecting flight was changed, and we were redirected to Okinawa. It was longer, but Downing must have had a good reason."

Walsh gestured to the two single beds. Parris first told them everything that she had learned from Fox about her experiments, the cult and Hashimoto's connection. She then told them about Fox's contact at the airport.

Walsh crossed his arms. "I'd personally like to know how Ares tracked Fox to this location so quickly."

Levickis answered, "My guess is that they must have obtained airport security footage, the same way Dobbs was able to trace Valerik back to Minsk, where he boarded a plane to come here to Tokyo. And how they knew when and where to find him, they must've planted some kind of tracking device on him."

Dobbs looked up from his laptop. "A tracking device? I know Fox, and trust me no one can simply plant a tracking device on him."

"Unless, it's done underhandedly. Like from someone he knows," said Levickis.

Dobbs looked back down at his laptop. "Then whoever it is, they'd have to be a real pro."

Parris turned to Dobbs. "Maybe it wasn't planted on him. Maybe he was unknowingly tagged."

Walsh looked at Parris. "What do you mean?"

"Back in the 1970s and 1980s, it was discovered that East German agents, the Stasi, had used radioactive sprays to track dissidents," Parris answered. "Stasi agents sprayed their clothes or belongings with Scandium-46, which emits highly dangerous gamma radiation but harmless beta radiation. The agents would then carry miniature radiation detectors in places such as their armpits, which would vibrate if the unsuspecting victim ever came near."

"If you're saying that Fox was sprayed with such a dangerous isotope, wouldn't he be dead?" asked Walsh.

"I didn't say that he was sprayed. Secondly, not all radioactive isotopes are harmful. For instance, doctors use Iodine-131 radioactive dye to help them in treating thyroid cancer. If Fox got close enough to someone, he could've been tagged with a harmless radioactive isotope. A kiss, or a handshake, maybe something that he drank, could easily allow it to be absorbed into his bloodstream."

"Exactly how would he be monitored?" asked Walsh.

"By satellite," said Levickis and Dobbs in unison. Levickis walked over to Dobbs. "One specially equipped to detect radioactive isotopes. That's assuming that the Japanese have perfected a satellite that could zero in on their target without having interference from other radioactive sources in the environment."

Dobbs looked up at Levickis. "I wouldn't be surprised. The OST's been trying to contract with American companies to develop one for years."

Walsh sighed. "Well, ain't that a goddamn mess! With Fox running off like that, God knows how many people he came in contact with. And what's even more frustrating, is that we didn't think of tagging him in the first place so that we'd know where to find him, or if he's even still alive."

Dobbs continued to type away at his laptop without glancing at the others. "My guess is that he still is. I've worked with him before. Trust me, he's a survivor."

"And I hope he's vexing his captors the same way he's done to all of us," quipped Parris.

"But wait a second." Walsh pointed towards Parris, his mouth slightly hung open for a few seconds. "If Fox was tagged and he's being monitored by satellite, whoever's been watching him would've seen everyone he's come in contact with. That means they'd be watching you too."

Parris glanced once at everyone in the room before she stood up and began to pace around. "Oh Lord. What do we do now?"

Levickis raised his hand to stop her. "Calm down."

"What do you mean calm down?"

"Satellites work by capturing either an infrared image from a person's body heat signature or by taking an actual photograph," answered Levickis. "They would've started observing you the moment you left Fox. But, they couldn't have taken photo images of you because it was cloudy today, and you would've had your umbrella. And even if they decided to follow you by infrared, your image would've been lost in the subway. You're sure you weren't followed?"

Parris raised her right hand to her temple and sighed with relief. She then sat back down. "No, I wasn't. That I'm sure of."

"As for Fox, let's hope that he gets himself out of whatever crap he's gotten himself into," said Walsh.

Parris looked up at Walsh. "If and when he does, he'll contact us. That's when we have to warn him."

"But if the tag is in his system, how would he get it out?" asked Walsh.

Parris rested her elbows on her knees. "Normally, a tagging isotope would decay over time. But as for the one affecting him, it could range from several hours to a few days. So to be on the safe side, he'd have to ingest a masking agent to neutralize the detection properties of the tagging isotope until it decays."

Walsh glanced at everyone. "We don't have masking agents on us. Where will we find one at this hour?"

"I have access to Hexagon's labs so I can create one tonight," answered Parris.

Walsh cleared his throat. "Well, I was with Fox in Uganda, so you better make one for me too."

Parris glanced at everyone. "As easy as it was to go after Fox, Ares could've gone after us too. They haven't yet, so to be on the safe side I'll get enough masking agents for all of us."

"Just to add to that, the room's secure," said Dobbs. "I've got anti-surveillance equipment setup close to all the windows. So if anyone were using any type of equipment to eavesdrop, I'd know about it. I can tell you about the time that I was in Brazil, and the hotel I was in was located right next to—"

"You can tell us about it later, Dobbs," said Walsh covering Dobbs's mouth with his hand. "Anyways, moving on. Regardless of this unexpected situation, we've received new instructions from Downing, and some of them especially involve you, Dr. Parris. You'll have to access everything you can find in Hexagon about Pandora."

Parris ran a hand through her hair. "I'd have to break into Hexagon's high security level, better known as the Safe."

"Downing gave us the green light," said Walsh. "As you stated in your last report, you believe the Safe is the repository of all of the intel. From what you told us earlier, my guess is that not only might you find intel on Pandora, but also of the cult's contacts, the whereabouts of other possible laboratories, warehouses— everything we'd need to know in order for the CIA to raid all of these facilities and shut them down permanently."

"Yes, I do." She then looked at Levickis and Dobbs. "But I'll need special clearance to enter the Safe."

"You'll have it." Dobbs got up and brought over a series of printouts from his laptop and placed them on the opposite bed, side by side, to form a layout. Parris and Levickis stood up to take a closer look at the layout as Dobbs pointed things out with a pen as he glanced at Parris. "Have you actually seen the area around the Safe?

"No, I just said that I don't have clearance for that area."

"This is where you'll get off the elevator." Walsh pointed out the area with a pen. "You'll enter a room with a guard sitting at a small monitoring station. From that room you'll access the Safe directly, but you'll need an access card and you'll also have to punch in a four-digit code into a keypad."

Parris turned to Dobbs. "What about cameras? Someone's sure to recognize me and know that I'm not supposed to be there."

"Levickis and I will be in control of that. We'll actually be underground, but outside Hexagon, where we'll gain access to the mainframe computer and to all of the cable and video feeds throughout Hexagon."

Levickis turned to Dobbs. "We'll loop a segment."

"Correct. So anyone else watching will only see a recording of the security guard instead of you," Dobbs replied.

With his index finger, Levickis drew a circle around the area of the guard's workstation. "But we'll allow her to be seen by the security guard from his monitoring station in his room, of course. We'll just block out the other viewing areas."

"And we'll still be able to maintain contact with you via your earpiece, until you enter the Safe," said Dobbs. He referred to the microprocessor-controlled receiver that was small enough to nestle in the ear canal. One would need a flashlight to find it. Inside Parris's jacket lapel would be a voice transmitter of the same size. The transmissions would be burst UHF, making them next to impossible to track. Even if one were to track it, the transmissions would still be scrambled.

"What do you mean, until she enters the Safe?" asked Walsh.

"Because it really is a safe," Parris said. "It has high-end anti-surveillance equipment which will interfere with all communication to the outside of it, knocking out both audio and video. I'll be on my own from that point on, until I leave."

Dobbs then handed her a disc. "This SCSI CD contains a virus which will eliminate all the firewalls and other security features that prevent hackers on the outside from breaking in. It'll actually trick Hexagon's system into thinking that the security protocols are still active. Think of it as unlocking a window from the inside."

Walsh then pointed to the disc as he turned to Parris. "Once uploaded, Dobbs and Levickis will hack into the system and download all the info we need."

"Once this is done, the CD will automatically reset all of the security protocols," said Dobbs.

Parris played with the disc in her hand. "Anything else I need to know?"

Levickis cut in. "Yeah, don't damage the earpiece."

Chapter 22

Fox was forced to sit down in front of a round table. The ninjas had no intention of allowing him to get any closer to Marx and literally shadowed his every move. Tanaka stood opposite him, leaning against the side of the booth next to her. She got up and walked towards Fox, stopping about five feet from his table's edge.

Dr. Marx rested her drink on another table close by, just as a momentary blast of loud music caught his attention. When Fox looked at the entrance to the cocktail lounge, he saw a waiter enter with a glass on a tray.

"Care for a drink?" asked Dr. Marx.

"I'll pass."

"I insist." Marx motioned to the waiter to put the drink down in front of him. She then crossed her arms.

There was a moment's blast of loud music as the waiter left the lounge. Fox put the glass to his lips and tilted it towards him, but didn't drink any of it. For all he knew, she had slipped something into his drink. He needed to be in fighting form.

"So where do you fit into all of this? No, don't tell me. You plan to sell Pandora to the highest bidder and beat Ares at their own game."

By the way she raised an eyebrow, Fox got the impression that he had insulted her.

"Sell? Pandora belongs to me. The only reason Ares ever got it is because I let them take it."

"You mean to tell me you just gave it away?"

"Yes, as a matter of fact. I had no choice but to let them have it." Marx paced slowly from side to side. "It would've been difficult to weaponize it on American soil while keeping my cover at the CDC. Thanks to Valerik, I was able to let Ares do the job instead. When the ice man was accidentally discovered two years ago in the Arctic, I was once again given the chance to continue my work. I extracted a Pandora sample from the ice man and gave it to Valerik, who then gave it to Ares. Valerik told Ares of his retrieval of the perfect weapon."

Fox sighed. "And Ares fell for it."

Marx smiled. "Of course they did. Valerik and I kept in touch so that I could monitor its progress from a safe distance. Ares never really knew the origin of Pandora. All along they thought that they were dealing with a weapon that was created in the CDC labs several years ago. The Americans had a chance at controlling Pandora because of my genius. I remember when the Defense Department needed me back then. When my project was terminated, so was my necessity. Do you know how it feels to be someone's puppet?"

"No, I can't say that I do."

"Really? You, an instrument of your government's political ideals? Please, you're a puppet and don't even know it." Fox sensed the iciness in her voice, as she uncrossed her arms. "You're just like my parents, the way they lived their secret lives. My father worked for the CIA, whereas my mother for the KGB. Guess what?"

Fox remained silent.

"My father gets killed in a Soviet air raid over an Afghan rebel training camp, thanks to my own mother. I never knew this at the time, obviously. It's ironic that I later accepted an offer from the Defense Department to work on a bio-weapon that was to be used against enemies of the state, giving me the chance to avenge my father's death. Now I was the one keeping secrets from my mother. All of a sudden, the US signs the Biological Weapons Anti-Terrorism Act. I show up at work one morning to discover that all of my research was destroyed, then get handed a letter stating that my services were no longer needed."

Fox lowered his head. "Who are you to compare me to your parents? You don't know anything about my life."

"On the contrary. I know that at one point in your life you wanted to stop serving your home country to settle down. The things that love can do to a man."

Fox's stare would've frightened the average person. But not Marx, she was way too psychotic. In fact, Marx's smile grew the longer Fox stared at her. "Do you still dream about her, or am I correct to assume that they're actually nightmares? I know you must have them from time to time."

She'd caught Fox off guard.

Don't let her gain control over me, whatever I do.

Marx took a sip of her drink. "Come on, it's no secret that you were once a Warrant Officer in the Canadian Joint Task Force Two, and you quit to settle down and take a teaching position. You were even about to get married. All of that was cut short when a so-called traffic accident took your bride-to-be away from you."

She's trying to rattle me. This could be a precursor before she administers the Clarity drug. Just as Parris described.

"You must have spent several sleepless nights blaming yourself for not seeing it coming. Knowing that it was something you could've prevented. Am I right?"

Fox looked away from her so that her eyes would have less effect on him.

"Your pain drove you over the edge. You couldn't bear to have her killers get away with it. You travel around the world with a gun hoping to bring down an organization that has links in many governments worldwide."

Fox still didn't say a word. *The nerve to bring up Jessica's death—fuck, there I go, letting her get to me.* Fox looked past Marx at Tanaka. "I suppose it helps having friends in the intelligence community."

"And why not? I make it my business to know as much about the enemy as possible. I've learned from my mistakes."

"Is that right?" asked Fox.

Marx downed her drink. "Absolutely. For instance, I wish that

I had known that my mother was the enemy before she confessed everything to me. It was painful to hear that her actions got my father killed. But it was even more painful to learn that she knew of my involvement with the Defense Department and that she was under orders to kill me."

Fox still didn't look directly at her, but the sound of her voice spoke volumes. In it there was a mixture of both rage and sadness. In fact, there was more rage. But he couldn't allow himself to have sympathy for her. She was playing with his mind, that's all.

"Coincidently, she had developed severe heart complications, and was never able to carry out her orders. Whether the CIA murdered her in revenge, the KGB did so because she never carried out her orders, or it could have even been natural causes, I don't know, and frankly I don't care. Not anymore. You intelligence operatives, you're all the same—just mindless puppets."

Fox chuckled as he shook his head. "And you're supposed to be the puppet master?"

"You can call me what you want. Have you ever heard of Neil Kirkpatrick, the industrialist? Actually, come to think of it you would've been finishing high school at that time he was well-known."

"Actually I knew of a Neil Kirkpatrick. I've done my background checks on you too, Dr. Marx. It's strange how he died while horseback riding in rural Pennsylvania. Doctors said he had a heart attack, right after being given a clean bill of health. He must've been thirty years older than you at the time."

"Yes, he was. He also was a huge donor to the politicians that voted in favor of ending my research on the bio-weapon we now know today as Pandora. "

Fox closed his eyes briefly. "So you had him killed, didn't you? On the side, you took advantage of the fortune that he had left you with."

"We all have our skeletons, Fox. It's funny how our lives are intertwined."

"Really? How so?"

"Don't you see it? The Cold War ends, hence terminating my chances of getting even with the Soviets. The Soviet Union collapses, and the KGB dissolves. Some of their agents go on to form the Arms of Ares, who later kill your fiancée. You're recruited by the CIA, who help you to avenge her death. But along the way your friend, Pat Hiller, gets killed in Uganda. Now you've come after me."

"You're right. It's a shame neither the Defense Department nor the CDC figured out that you were a psychopath in the making. Otherwise you'd be sitting either in a jail cell or an asylum right now."

Marx's eyes dilated to the point that she appeared to be insulted. "Me? A psychopath? Don't you realize that we're both the victims of other people's agendas? When you lost Jessica, you chose to be a government agent. I, on the other hand, chose to be a free agent. I wasn't going be a part of any regime—whether political or religious—that causes the same problems that we both want to end, through different means."

"So what is *your* way of ending the world's problems?"

"It's simple. Use Pandora to end all wars."

"Now you've lost me."

"Think about it. We've experienced two World Wars, the Korean War, the Vietnam War, the Cold War, the Gulf War. Where has it gotten us, Fox? And now the wars in Iraq, Afghanistan, or the so-called war on terrorism we heard so much about at one time, God knows how long it will last."

Fox looked down at the table in front of him, in deep thought. He then looked back up at Marx. "You're going to target certain countries using Pandora? You want to be in control of the arms race."

"No, Fox." Marx laughed. "You know you really are naïve, despite what I've been told about you."

Fox thought about it for a second, but the only thing that came to mind was far too unbelievable to accept. "I don't think so. You want to be the puppet master, therefore, having Pandora gives you a sense of control."

"Wrong again!" Her explosiveness even startled Tanaka and the guards. "The world needs Pandora and a whole lot more than you're willing to admit."

"Oh yeah, tell me how?"

"Do you remember how the Second World War ended?" Dr. Marx giggled before Fox could answer. "Of course you do. Two nuclear bombs, code named *Little Boy* and *Fat Man*, were dropped on the cities of Hiroshima and Nagasaki, killing over two hundred thousand people. Of course, the devastation was horrendous and is still one of the most talked about topics in history. What's ironic is that the civilian casualties that resulted from the bombings were far less than the number of casualties that would've resulted had the madness of the war in the Pacific continued. Who knows how much longer the war would've gone on."

The answer then became clear to Fox. He didn't want to believe it for himself, but he had to accept it, given all of the facts. The events of 9/11 were the worst and most unforgettable ever perpetrated on US soil, in a single day that he could remember. Since then, leading world governments and their militaries have been on high alert, while the general public wonders where and when the next major attack will take place.

Now it wasn't a matter of where the next attack would take place, it was all about when. And there was no government or nation who could accept that an even worse catastrophe was in their midst. And up until then, Fox wouldn't have either.

"You want to wipe out the world's population." This was all Fox could think of when he looked at those chilled blue eyes of hers.

"Now you're catching on. It'll be a swift end to the forces that are destroying this world, resulting in a new beginning. I'm a learner. I believe that we as humans are meant to make progress. I've had the opportunity to live in a dysfunctional family with opposing views. What's the end result? A zero-sum, that's what. With the way things are going, the complete and utter annihilation of all life on this planet is bound to happen. It's just a matter of when. I simply plan to accelerate what'll be the inevitable. In the end, the chosen few will remain and we'll all start life again and this time it will be an improvement."

"You can't be serious. You're talking about global genocide."

Marx laughed. "No. A global cleansing. Something about you

told me that you'd be trouble when we first met. Already from our first encounter we haven't seen eye to eye. At the CDC compound in Uganda, you saw the corpses. I saw an organism that can self-replicate at an incredible rate."

"And you're bound to run into a lot more like me. What'll you do, kill us all?"

Marx stared at Fox with a glare that put a freeze on everyone around her. Even Tanaka lost his smile. But then she curved her lips inward, exhaled, and rested one hand on the table beside her glass. "Too blind to see things for what they are, aren't we? But you don't have to worry because it's perfectly normal. There's a reason I've kept you alive this long." She signaled with a hand gesture. "You know things. You're of no use to me dead, at least not until I have an idea of what you know."

Again there was a short blast of loud music that signaled the waiter's return. This time he carried a small metal box on his tray. He placed the cigar-box-sized container on the table beside Marx's glass. He then walked away, the short burst of loud music soon followed.

"Can you guess what's inside?"

"Sodium Pentothal, or Truth Serum, its more common name. But of course, you, a scientist, should know the dangers of mixing drugs with alcohol, so maybe it wasn't such a good idea giving me this beverage."

"Don't worry, you'll be under constant supervision." She opened the box and took out a syringe.

Fox smirked. "You'll need more than that."

"Oh, please. Look beside you." Marx glanced briefly at the two ninjas while she held up the syringe. "I could have the truth beaten out of you or maybe have you taken back to the lab where I'd have you converted. If you haven't guessed it yet, I love having fun with science. Especially when living specimens are involved."

Fox felt that she appeared to be overconfident. She might expect him to resist while being held down for the syringe but probably nothing else. The burning candle in the centerpiece, he could use that. Dr. Marx was rather insistent on him drinking. Let her see what she wants to see. He could still get away. Alcohol on an open flame might not be much but it should distract them long enough for him to tackle Tanaka and grab his gun. But the two ninjas would be quick to respond.

"So let me get this straight. Your brainwashing drug, should you choose to use it, would disrupt my reasoning abilities in the RES?" Fox specifically did not refer to the drug by its real name, Clarity, since it was only Parris who had mentioned that to him. Marx looked at him with a half-smile as she raised the syringe to eye level. "The RAS, Fox. It's not called the RES." She tapped the syringe causing the remaining air bubbles to surface. "And that is the area which screens out conflicting information going to the brain. This will first disrupt the ability to reason, along with personality formation."

"In the hindbrain." Fox raised the glass and stopped short of his mouth.

"No, the forebrain and the hypothalamus."

"Oh, I'm not so sure of that." Fox held the glass in hand and turned to the ninja to his left. "Do you mind checking that out for us? I'm curious to know who's right."

"Just give me his arm," snapped Marx.

In that instant, Fox threw his drink onto the open flame in front of him. There was a loud popping sound and a flash of flame and sparks. Fox kicked up his legs and sent the table flying at Tanaka. He launched from his seat and reached into his pocket to grab the sand while he spun around. He then threw it into the eyes of one of the henchmen. At that the henchman doubled over with both hands at his eyes, Fox engaged the other as he blocked off a set of rapid strikes to his chest and face.

Dr. Marx backed away from the melee as Fox temporarily overpowered him, giving him time to tackle Tanaka to the floor and snatch his Sig P226 firearm from its holster, spin around, go down on one knee, and pull the trigger twice. As he expected, the same henchman, already in mid-air flight towards him, caught both bullets in the chest, and crash landed beside him. Fox was about to plug the other henchman when he was kicked in the hand, causing a shot to be fired into the ceiling. Fox was then kicked in the stomach which sent him crashing backwards into a table behind him, knocking it over.

This ninja was no ordinary street thug—he was a trained assassin. But then, so was Fox. His opponent attacked him, but Fox blocked the attacks and soon overpowered him, flooring him. The henchman tried to get up, but Fox had already thrown his leg out and connected the front of his shoe to his temple, knocking him out.

The Sig was still within his reach, and he snatched it up and aimed it at both Marx and Tanaka. "It's time for a change of authority around here." He could shoot them both right now and end this, but it would still leave him at a dead end since he didn't know where Pandora was hidden, not to mention how many locations it could be stored at.

But now that he was in control, he would be the one to ask them questions, not only to uncover where to find Pandora, but also how to undo the effects of the Clarity drug.

"You." Fox pointed the gun at Tanaka. "Get up."

Tanaka's grin faded and he did as told. Fox then pointed the gun at Dr. Marx.

"And you. Go stand beside him." Marx, however, was much slower and obviously didn't feel as threatened as Tanaka. Her stare went cold as she tightened her grip on the syringe as though to crush it in her hand.

"You won't need that anymore, so give it to Tanaka." Her eyes narrowed and the same coldness he felt when he first met her seemed to penetrate his bones, to which he responded by pointing the Sig at her head.

"Now!" Fox said, this time louder.

Marx sighed and handed the syringe to Tanaka. "You continue to impress me. I suppose you're going to force me to take the truth serum to get the information you want. Pity it won't work."

"Oh yeah, why's that?" Fox moved closer to them, stopping short about five feet away.

"I designed truth serum upgrades for the military, as well as their blockers," she answered. "In fact, I'm on one of them right now."

The shot Fox fired grazed Marx's upper right arm, spinning her down on one knee as she grasped the wound with her opposite arm. Fox noticed beads of sweat form on Tanaka's forehead.

With her back to Fox, Marx shot a look over her left shoulder in cold rage. "You idiot!" Her scream stung Fox's eardrums.

Fox then smiled. "Tell me, Dr. Marx. Would you call *this* putting science to use? I got to say I like it. I'm curious to know how many bullets in your arms and legs you'd have to get before you start talking." His sarcasm then lost its bite and his tone darkened as he glared at Marx. "Where's Pandora?"

"You can kill me, but you'll just end up destroying yourself and contributing to the global cleansing." She got up, still holding the wound, and turned to face him. "The plans are already set in motion."

"You're bluffing."

"Am I? Do you honestly think I'd have researched such a deadly microbe without knowing how to destroy it just in case something went wrong?"

"No, but then again if you shared the cult's philosophy, you wouldn't have bothered, would you?" Fox pointed the gun at Tanaka who still held the syringe. "Give her a shot. Or I'll give you one."

Glass shattered at the entrance of the cocktail lounge and an avalanche of loud music flowed inside. Fox counted more than six gunmen pour in quickly, before he ran into one of the booths for cover. When he looked out, slightly above the headrest, he saw Marx, with Tanaka's help, running away.

Flying bullets filled the air around him. Fox ducked back down. He was clearly out-manned and out-gunned, and eventually they would force him to surrender. But that wasn't an option for him.

He took another look to the middle of the dancehall with the suspended cages. That's when a crazy idea came to him. It was risky, but doable. Fox looked below the glass partition and saw the booth that was in front of him. Beyond that there was a chain that suspended one of the caged dancers. It was well within jumping distance and that's where he would make his exit. It looked sturdy enough to support his weight.

He pointed the Sig and pulled the trigger twice. No sound was heard above the loud music but the window pane shattered. He got up and pulled the trigger five more times in rapid succession, in different directions towards the entrance of the lounge. Naturally, the gunmen all dove for cover, and while they did so, he shoved the gun back in his holster and sprinted towards the booth, bullets flying past him.

When he was less than three feet away from the table, he leapt onto it. His foot landed on the windowsill and he threw himself upwards towards the chain with nothing below him but a five-storey drop. Catching the chain was easy, but keeping his grip wasn't. His momentum nearly caused him to fumble on the chain and plummet to his death, but he managed to catch it with his left leg and wrapped it around his shin. He then grabbed the chain securely and let himself slide down until he landed on top of the cage.

A handful of people on the third and fourth floors saw Fox and rushed to the inner circle of the hall. Within seconds, Fox had almost everyone in the club watching him. He looked up and saw a few men rush to the windowsill from where he had launched himself. The gunshots would come soon. He knelt down and slid off the roof of the cage and caught the side bars. Fox watched the girl in the cage shriek and jump back.

He doubted Marx's henchmen would risk hitting the girl, but depending on how desperate they were, they just might. A few seconds passed, but Fox couldn't hear the faint staccato noises from the firearms amidst the loud music. They would have something else planned. As the cage descended, the spectators below cleared an opening for him, and he let himself drop to the floor to the welcoming cheers.

He couldn't stay here. The longer he did, the more he was endangering the lives of others. And it began much sooner than he anticipated. He noticed commotion erupt to his left. People were being knocked over as a huge figure burst out from the crowd and lunged at him. Fox dipped low to the left and swept his right leg across the floor, caught the bouncer by the shins and tripped him. He flew forward in a nosedive and knocked over a few individuals like bowling pins. More bouncers would come, and he could take them all on easily. They were nothing more to him than oversized, moving punching bags. But they could stall him long enough for Marx's other henchmen to get to him. He bolted in one direction and the crowd cleared a path for him.

Fox emerged from the crowd problem free, but knew he had to keep moving because the bouncers, and Marx's henchmen, would be close behind him. In front of him was a peculiar individual that made him come to a halt. He was far from resembling the six-foot-tall, muscle-bound bouncers, but was an average-looking person. He was no more than five foot nine and wore a dark trench coat. But the way he stared at Fox definitely told him something was up. He didn't seem as impressed by him as everyone else was, and Fox's gut instinct told him to prepare for a fight. Years of experience told him that when someone is conspicuously out of place and is eyeing you, it's not because he wants to chat.

Fox rushed him, but the man whipped out a Micro-Uzi from inside his trench coat and pointed it at Fox whose hands shot up so fast that he fell back off balance and onto the floor.

Damn it, not another Micro-Uzi! First Ares and now this guy. Fox scrambled to get up but he knew he was a dead man. There was no way he could dodge gunshots from this distance while he was on the ground.

The man kept his eyes on Fox—there was no anger in them, just a simple blank stare that Fox found difficult to read. Fox could recognize a killer's intention to shoot him by just looking into his eyes, but unless this guy mastered his emotions, he didn't fit the profile of someone who was going to do so.

The man pointed the submachine gun towards the ceiling and fired.

Bedlam!

Screams mixed in with the staccato of shots and a stampede of people immediately followed. Fox got up and was almost knocked back onto the floor as people bumped and slammed into him from all directions. Seconds later, the gunman stopped firing. A hand grabbed Fox by the shoulder, and at the same time he heard a man yell at him.

"Fox!"

Fox spun around and knocked the hand off, and he saw that it was the gunman.

"Come with me quickly!"

Sato?

The carnage spilled outside the club and was all around them as they made their escape. Adding to the cacophony, Fox heard several police sirens closing in on their position. Fox tried to catch up to his rescuer, who had a head start on him. The gunman darted across the street, his Micro-Uzi pointed upwards, and ran around the next corner. He passed about ten cars to his left, when he saw the gunman unlock and open the right-hand side door of a sporty, yellow hatchback and get inside. Fox got to the car, slid between the back of it and the car parked behind, ran to his door and hopped in.

"Ridley Fox, I'm Aijima Sato, Ken Katori's partner. I'm pleased to finally meet you." Sato started up the car and sped out from his parking space, passing a few individuals who hadn't stopped running from the club.

Fox panted as he looked behind and saw the screaming cacophony pouring out of the nightclub. "Yeah, glad to see you, too. Now of all times."

After Sato sped off, Fox heard a faint beeping sound. "What's that noise?" At that moment Sato pulled over and slammed on the breaks.

"Get out, now. You've been bugged." Fox did as he was told, and Sato opened the glove compartment and took out an object the size of a small television remote, complete with antenna. Sato approached Fox on his side of the car and swept him from head to waist, where the beeping increased simultaneously with the light-emitting diode or LED. The frequency increased as Sato brought the device closer to Fox's left arm and stopped above his watch where the device's frequencies maxed out.

"It's in your watch!" yelled Sato. Fox immediately ripped it off and threw it on the side of the road where it fell into a storm drain. Sato swept him again with the detector but there was nothing else.

"You're clean. Let's go." Both Sato and Fox jumped back into the car.

Fox sat there pondering how anyone could've bugged his watch without his knowledge. As Sato raced past other cars through the streets of Shibuya, he thought back hard. If he'd been compromised, then it meant that Walsh, Dobbs, Levickis, and Parris were all in danger. "I need to make a phone call."

"You can't."

"I'm not here alone. The mission's most likely been compromised. Give me your phone."

"I don't have one. And may I suggest that you keep away from them. They're everywhere."

"I'll take my chances."

"Listen. You're not in control anymore, *they* are. And you've seen what they can do. So you'll just have to do as I say if you want us to get through this. Your teammates will be fine."

"Where are we going?"

"Somewhere safe. And when we get there, you'll get to see what we're really up against."

Chapter 23

Dr. Hideaki Hashimoto's Residence, West Tokyo, 12:21AM

Marx wasn't startled even though she could have sworn that a lightning bolt struck, just outside one of the five floor-to-ceiling windows she passed on her way to Hashimoto's office. Her close call with Fox a few hours ago would no doubt cause concern with Hashimoto, who in her opinion panicked too much. The bandage below her right shoulder would be a constant reminder of how Fox had left his mark on her that evening. But Fox didn't worry her—Ares did. They had found Valerik and dumped his body onto a freeway. *How much more blatant of a message could they send that they were closing in on us?* Valerik's capture could only be due to a breach, there was no other explanation. It didn't appear to be too long ago that she had ordered Hashimoto to trick Valerik into visiting him so that his henchmen could ambush him. The gratification she felt when she personally clarified him in the chair was too sweet. Although he was useful, she wouldn't miss him. After all, he was a former KGB operative that worked for the same people that had brought so much misery to her.

As Marx opened the double doors to Hashimoto's office, a crack of thunder boomed as though she had summoned it. The lights in the room began to flicker. Hashimoto, Tanaka, and Commissioner Yushida were already there.

Hashimoto got up from behind his desk and faced Marx. "I

was told what happened—"

"I'm fine," Marx cut him off by raising her hand. Hashimoto got up from his chair and she sat in it. Hashimoto sat in another chair beside the others.

"I'm going to get to the specifics. Valerik's dead, and I think there's a leak. I want your input on where you believe it came from."

Commissioner Yushida pointed his right index finger in the air. "That's assuming that there was a leak."

Marx shot a stern glance at him. "Yes, I do assume. It was either that or Valerik got very sloppy. And I'm not so convinced of the latter. Has your investigation turned up anything on what happened to him?"

"All signs lead to a professional hit," Yushida replied. "The investigation's at a standstill."

Hashimoto crossed his arms. "What about Fox and his CIA cohorts?"

Marx shot him a menacing glance. "I'll ask the questions, if you don't mind." *There's no way you're controlling this meeting.* "Fox is, and should remain, the least of our concerns. As long as we can track him, he can be controlled."

"I have to agree with Dr. Marx," said Tanaka. "We've been tracking him all day."

Marx relaxed back into the cushioned chair. "And has he come into contact with anyone in particular?"

"He did earlier in the Azabu District." Tanaka raised his hand slightly and then dropped it on his leg with a sigh. "But our satellites couldn't capture an image of the individual due to the weather."

"What about infrared tracking?" asked Marx.

Tanaka looked away from Marx as though he were embarrassed. "We lost his contact on the subway."

"That's just perfect," said Hashimoto sarcastically. "Maybe you should've had real men tail him instead of relying on fancy equipment."

Tanaka looked back at him. "We did so initially, and Fox lost them within minutes."

"Then what about his partner, Walsh?" asked Hashimoto.

"We didn't get a strong signal from him to begin with. We had something at first but it faded soon afterwards," said Tanaka.

Hashimoto gave Marx a questioning look. "How's that possible? Didn't you tag both of them?"

"I did." Marx crossed her arms as she gave him a stare that he'd seen once too often. He got the message and shrank back into his chair. "Neither of them suspected anything when I shook their hands at the outbreak site. Unfortunately Walsh had a weaker stomach than I expected. He threw up once he saw the remains of one of the Pandora-infected victims. He must have washed his hands thoroughly before an effective dose of the isotope powder was absorbed through his skin."

"Fox has been useful to us so far," said Tanaka. "In fact, he unknowingly helped us track down and eliminate the agent you were looking for. As a bonus, so were a few members of Ares."

Hashimoto leaned forward. "A few but not all. Valerik's killers will now come for us."

"And that concerns me." Marx crossed her legs and looked up at the ceiling. "But I'd still like to know who Fox met in Azabu."

"It could be Walsh." Hashimoto turned to Tanaka. "You were able to follow him from the airport, weren't you?"

"He didn't arrive at the same time as Fox, nor was he spotted at Narita Airport. I'm assuming that he must have slipped into the country through the American Base in Okinawa."

Marx looked back at Tanaka. "Then we need to concentrate more on keeping a closer eye on whom Fox contacts. Valerik mentioned that Ares has a mole within the CIA, but he didn't know who it was. We can assume that this mole will be keeping tabs on Fox. As long as this continues then Ares will not find us." She glanced at Hashimoto, who had an expression on his face that said *I sincerely hope so.*

Marx leaned forward and rested both of her elbows on the desk as she turned to Hashimoto. "Onto another matter. How's the recruitment process going? I heard that there was a problem during the experiment this morning."

"Not at all. None that wasn't fixed."

Marx raised a curious eyebrow. "Oh really? I tend to believe that when you have two test subjects undergoing the same experiment and one of them goes postal, then there's a problem. A very serious one."

Marx then saw the worry in Hashimoto's eyes. She hadn't seen this look since she first introduced herself to him with evidence of his involvement in human trials several years ago.

"I assure you that there's no problem. Everything's in order, as it should be."

"Then forgive me for not sharing your optimism. In fact, I learned that the young woman who conducted the experiment, Dr. Nita Parris, was injured during the experiment. I also learned that she didn't follow procedure."

"Our findings over what happened this morning are still inconclusive. That's why I've decided to terminate any further experiments with the new variant of Clarity."

Marx brought her hand to her chin as she kept her arms crossed. "That's a bit premature, don't you think?"

"Why do you say that?" asked Hashimoto.

Marx stared at him through slightly narrowed eyes. *You already know the answer.* "What do we know about Dr. Parris?"

"The Boeisho has checked her out," said Tanaka, diverting Marx's attention towards him. "In our opinion, she's clean."

"You see, Dr. Marx, everything that goes on at Hexagon, stays within Hexagon," said Hashimoto.

Marx looked back at Hashimoto. "I'd still continue researching the new variant of Clarity. I still get a feeling that something was overlooked. You just need to look a bit deeper."

Hashimoto nodded. "I will." He then scratched the back of his neck. "In relation to Pandora, you told me earlier that you had something to add to it. To make it more efficient for our cause. Were there any positive results?"

"I've formed my own team of scientists, and I'll meet them later on, after breakfast," she replied. "So far everything looks promising. But to be absolutely sure, I'm going to need to use the young gentleman I had asked you to spare."

The Commissioner looked at Marx and squinted. "You're

going to use a live human being as a lab rat?"

"Why not?" She looked back at the Commissioner. "After all, this is science. Didn't your biology teacher ever tell you that science could be fun?"

Chapter 24

Hexagon Pharmaceuticals

arris rushed into the atrium of the East Wing after having travelled under the overcast and humid conditions outside. But where she headed didn't have any windows, so it could stay miserable outside for all she cared. The large digital clock in the atrium read 8:23 AM. She wasn't expected until ten o'clock that morning so she knew she wouldn't be missed. Last night's visit to Hexagon was a quick in and out. Once Parris made it to Hexagon, she signed in at the security desk in the atrium, got what she needed, signed out with the contents in her purse, and headed home. The masking agent didn't take long to make and she gave Levickis three more syringes in a pouch for him and the others. She kept one for Fox in the glove compartment of her car. Whoever came in contact with him first would give it to him.

Having only slept four hours was murder on her body. Even with two cups of coffee, she still felt groggy. "Hardly anyone in the East Wing this early, guys." There was no answer. "Guys?" she said again.

"We hear you, Dr. Parris." Dobbs's voice boomed through her earpiece, causing her to grab at her ear as she made a face.

"Turn the damn thing down, Dobbs. Lord. You trying to make me deaf?"

"Sorry about that." His voice was a lot quieter. "Is that better?"

Her ear still rang. "Yes. Isn't there a way for you to check your equipment?"

"I said I was sorry."

Parris rolled her eyes. "Sure, fine, whatever."

"Hey, lighten up a bit," said Levickis. "This is no walk in the park for us either. We've just come through the tunnels and have reached the mainframe. It's cold, damp, it stinks, and I know I stepped in something back there."

Levickis's voice became quieter, as though he were talking to Dobbs. "Have you located the POP yet?" This was the point of presence, an access point to the internet.

"I think it's right here," said Dobbs. "I can see the end of the fiber optic backbone cable, router, and switches. I see a free port here. I'll connect the laptop and see if I can ping the mainframe... yup, the mainframe's responding—Packets, sent equals four. Zero percent loss—we're plugged in."

Parris pressed the B4 button. "Anyway, I've just walked into the elevator."

"Great, we're ready to link up," said Dobbs.

Parris looked up at the floor light above the door and watched them all flash. B2, then B3, and finally B4. The elevator slowed to a stop a moment later.

"It's a go, Doc. We're in," said Dobbs.

Just in time. The elevator doors opened. The guard looked up from reading his magazine as Parris walked into the room and nodded. She smiled at him and looked to the left of where he sat and saw the entrance to the Safe. She reached into a pocket inside her tote and took out the security card Dobbs gave her and stopped in front of the control panel.

"The code key is one, zero, four, and five," said Levickis as she swiped the card. When the display above the keypad asked for the authorization code, Parris punched in those numbers. When she heard the beeping sound, she opened the door and passed through.

"It's all yours. We'll hear from you when you get out," said Dobbs.

Parris put the clearance card back into her bag and walked through the door, which automatically shut behind her. She heard static in her earpiece, and eventually the volume was turned down from Dobbs's and Levickis's end.

She stood inside a large white-walled hexagon-shaped room that was about twenty feet all around with an eight-by-five-foot window straight ahead of her. Through the window, she saw rows and columns of discs all tightly stacked together as a cluster.

In front of the window, was a flat screen monitor with the HEXAGON logo as its screen saver, a compact disc drive, and a wireless keyboard and mouse, all on a white fiberglass desk with a white metal-backed chair in front. Everything was where it was supposed to be, just as Dobbs has told her the night before.

Parris sat down at the computer, reached into her tote and removed the SCSI CD, inserting it into the drive. She heard it whirl, and in a few seconds a message appeared on the monitor— the virus was uploaded. *First step done, security is offline.* She tapped the space bar and the screensaver was replaced with the phrase *Please enter file name and code number,* followed by a blinking cursor. Parris typed in the word CLARITY and 60028.

On the other side of the window, a mechanical arm with a razor-thin clamp appeared from below the window level. It moved up and across several rows and columns of discs, and extracted a one-inch diameter disc. The disc was then carried to a drive on the far right-hand side and inserted. Parris removed a second SCSI CD from her tote—one that was specially designed by the boys at the Office of Science and Technology, and only an inch in diameter—and placed it into a second SCSI CD drive. She typed in a sequence of commands to copy all of the contents onto her disc. The message *Copying files* appeared on the screen with a progress bar below it.

Parris didn't want to get too comfortable, but she was curious to know what was on the disc. Sure, Dobbs and Levickis were getting the data uploaded to them at this moment, but it was worth knowing. With the mouse, she opened a window that displayed two file names. Clarity and Pandora. She clicked on the Clarity file first, and another window appeared that displayed several names of individuals under the heading *Subjects*.

Parris leaned closer to the monitor, completely aghast at how many people had undergone treatment using the Clarity drug. Half of them she didn't even know. The list of names was subdivided into various groups. She looked at the last sub-category where she recognized the names of individuals she had worked on, under the later variants of the drug. *My God. This program must have been going on for months.*

She was interrupted when a message that read *Copy complete* flashed across the screen. The two tech guys had their copy, now was the time to get out.

***

Dobbs's and Levickis's flashlight-mounted headbands provided a bit of light. All of their wires attached to Hexagon's internal cable system in a spaghetti-like manner. Water dripped behind them in scattered locations, creating a musty smell in the air. On his laptop, Dobbs saw the confirmation message flash that all data was received. "She did it."

Levickis checked underneath his right shoe again—he knew he'd stepped on something earlier. "Good, the sooner she gets out of there, the sooner we can too." It was then that he heard a clicking sound close by, one that he recognized all too well. He turned around to see two dark figures and a bright flash which was almost simultaneously accompanied by a loud bang and the strong burning odor of gunpowder. A mixture of blood, skull, and brain fragments exploded from the back of Dobbs's head and sprayed all over the monitors and the keyboards.

Dobbs's body was thrown onto Levickis, knocking the wind out of him. If fear and shock could really paralyze someone, Levickis now knew this firsthand, as his arms and chest seized up on him, causing him to breathe short quick breaths. When Dobbs's body rolled off of him, the barrel of a Makarov PM was pointed right between his eyes.

Then the bullet tore through his brain.

***

Demyan held onto the Makarov and dropped his arm to the side. Pyotr stepped from behind him and pushed Levickis's body away with his foot, to make room for himself in front of the two laptops. One of the monitors buzzed with static while the other had the image of the security guard at the entrance to the Safe.

"The girl must still be in the Safe."

Demyan didn't respond. When Pyotr looked up at him, he had a large grin and he breathed excitedly. Pyotr ignored him and pressed the eject button at the side of the laptop and the disc popped out halfway. He removed it, found its casing beside the keyboard, inserted it, and dropped it in his jacket pocket. He then started to type.

***

Time to jet. Parris closed the program. Automatically, the mechanical arm behind the window removed the disc from its drive and replaced it into its storage slot. She ejected her disc, replaced it in its case and dropped it into her tote bag. Just as she got up from her seat, a booming sound reverberated all around her and the room lit up dark red.

What the hell? The word lockdown popped into her head, and she sprinted towards the door, slid to a stop in front of it, and pushed down on the handle repeatedly. The door wouldn't open. She slammed her palm on the door. *Shit.*

She was trapped. *What the hell happened to Levickis and Dobbs? They must have triggered a hidden security feature—or did I do it?* But it wasn't possible. They should have known of any upgrades to the security features. *How could they have missed this one?*

All communications to the outside were cut off, but they'd have to know what was going on now. *You guys better find a way to override the security protocols.* But she couldn't chance them doing so on time. Any moment now, an armed security squad would be bursting through that door.

Parris pulled off her right shoe and turned the heel towards her. She pinched in a camouflaged lever and a thin compartment similar to a miniature compact disc drive popped out—one that was specially designed to hide the one-inch-diameter CD. She knelt down and put down the shoe while she tore into her tote and grabbed the CD case. The tote fell on its side as she opened the CD case, removed the CD, fit it into the slot into the heel of her shoe, and closed it.

She got back up, picked up her tote, and slid on her shoe just as the door burst open. Six guards, dressed in black outfits, helmets, and visors, poured in, surrounding her with electroshock guns. The first one who charged into the hexagonal room stepped away from the rest and approached her with his electroshock gun pointed at her chest. He screamed out something to her in Japanese. She didn't understand him, but she raised both of her hands above her head. He reached to her right shoulder and ripped away the tote. Another guard came up from behind her, grabbed her other shoulder and pushed her sideways into the wall. She struck the wall and then felt someone throw their weight against the back of her neck to pin her there.

Hands frisked from top to bottom and then from bottom to top. She was then spun around and had the same thing done to her again. First her shoulders, breasts, then hips. *At least he didn't check the shoes.* She was then pulled away from the wall and shoved towards the entrance to the Safe. She suddenly felt an enormous surge through the base of her spine that caused her entire body to cramp.

The electroshock gun. It was the last thing on her mind as she dropped to the floor and everything else around her faded black.

Chapter 25

Fox forced his foot down on the gas pedal as the heavy rainfall formed lakes that stretched the entire road's width. Never mind that his view was blinded. He had travelled down this road before. He knew of every pothole and sharp curve long before he came close to them.

The bright flashing red, blue, and white lights he saw ahead through the water-covered windshield became his guide. This time he didn't stop until he was nearly up onto the Provincial Police cruiser that blocked his path. He slammed on the brakes and his car careened sideways to a stop, just tapping the police cruiser on the passenger side. Fox bolted from his vehicle without turning off the engine, ran around both cars, and was intercepted by two police officers. They both grabbed him and pulled him back.

"It's all right, let him through," yelled another man up ahead who was closer to the crime scene.

Fox shoved the two officers aside and bypassed the man who allowed him to pass. He rushed to the stretcher and skidded to a stop in front of it, sending a wave of puddle water over it and the paramedics. He ripped open the zipper of the body bag as a lightning flash streaked across the sky and illuminated the ebony skin of the woman before him. It was Dr. Nita Parris, and she lay serenely with her eyes open and lips slightly parted, as the rain pelted her, running off the sides of the stretcher.

"Ridley?" a voice said from behind. Fox ignored it as he slowly put his hand up to Parris's right cheek.

"Ridley." This time Fox felt a hand on his shoulder, which caused him to jump from his sleep so quickly that he nearly head-butted Sato. Fox looked around him. He was still in the car, only now it was daybreak. *That damn nightmare again.*

"You okay?" asked Sato. "You don't look like you slept too well."

Fox put his hand to his mouth to cover a yawn. "It's been rough the past few days. Katori said you'd contact me. I just wasn't expecting you to crash the party."

"And I wasn't expecting you to be a guest. You're a fugitive from the law for murdering Katori. A single gunshot to the back of his head. Your fingerprints were found all over the murder weapon."

"Yeah, so I've been told."

"Welcome to my life. I've been dodging Tanaka for days."

Fox got out the car and his shoe sunk slightly into the mud. He saw that the whole terrain was like this, no thanks to the rain. To his right, he saw the driveway that was carved out of the woods, with tall pine trees on either side. In front of him was a single-storied house, whose exterior consisted mostly of stone and pine wood. Rain water dripped from the edges of the sloped roof into the underbrush that surrounded the sides. The clearing in front of the house was large enough to accommodate about six vehicles. The smell of damp wood filled the air.

"Where are we?" Fox followed Sato towards the side door.

Sato scraped the mud off his shoes on the iron doormat. "We're about two hundred kilometers outside of Tokyo." Fox walked up to the side porch, scraped his shoes and followed Sato inside.

The entrance led them to the kitchen. At first, Fox looked towards the sink. There were no dishes either inside it or in the dish tray beside it. The kitchen table was wiped down clean, with the table mats in the center under a napkin holder. Along the back wall were the stove and oven, along with a small rack of carving knives, a toaster and coffee maker. "So how long are the owners gone for?"

Sato walked over to the counter and grabbed the kettle and pulled it under the tap to fill it. Then he placed it on the stove and turned it on. "For the rest of the month." Sato walked over to a cupboard and opened the door. "There's just regular tea here, hope that's all right."

"I can use some coffee instead." Fox sat down at the table and dropped his head into his hands.

"Actually, yes. I'll make some."

As Sato prepared the coffee, Fox's head got heavy. Last night's events kept coming back to him. He was compromised and was wanted for Katori's death. The Boeisho would now step up their search for both Walsh and Dobbs. Hopefully Parris and Levickis managed to keep their cover. For now, his only ally was the man who brought over a steaming coffee mug and set it down on the table. *God, there was something from the night before, in the nightclub.* He still couldn't place it, but it bothered him.

"Here's your cup of Joel," said Sato.

"That's Joe." Fox smiled as he took the mug.

Sato smiled too, as he walked out of the kitchen into the adjoining room. "I'll be right back. I have to show you something."

Fox took a sip of the piping hot drink. "How long were you and Katori planning on hiding out from the Boeisho?"

"Until we gathered enough evidence to expose Tanaka," said Sato loudly from the other room. "Now you have to do the same."

"I don't plan on hiding from anyone. We both don't have time for that."

Sato reentered the kitchen with a laptop computer. He placed it on the kitchen table and turned it on. "As Katori might've told you, you've stepped in the middle of a battle. You know the truth about Marx, Tanaka, Hashimoto, and The Promise. You ought to know about some members of Ares. I believe this has been your Holy Grail for quite some time."

No way, you've got to be kidding me. Fox put down his mug and nearly stood in excitement.

"It's not a complete list of the entire organization, just the October Cell." Sato spun the laptop around to face Fox. "Do you recognize any of them?"

Fox gazed at the head shots of six men as he took another sip. "Sure I do. That's the October Man and these are his henchmen.

They're the ones who jumped me last night."

"And they're vengeful. Marx stole Ares's most powerful weapon, one that could sell for billions on the black market. *Your* October Man is personally handling the task of getting it back. They've already killed Valerik and they came very close to doing the same to you. But they'll gladly come after both of us, since they know that we possess information that could seriously compromise their efforts and severely damage their organization."

"Is that all? Where's the rest of this evidence?"

"Right in front of you." Sato pointed to the laptop. "On the same disk is a list of more people involved in their network. In addition, there's a list of all of their contacts, hideouts, warehouses, and everything you need to know about any improvements their scientists made to Pandora since the moment they got a hold of it."

"Let me guess. Valerik, being the double-agent he was, stole this information and gave it to Hashimoto. Now you stole it with hopes of passing it on to the Boeisho." Fox quickly scrolled down the list of profiles.

"But then my team had to improvise when we found out that Tanaka wasn't on our side anymore."

Fox glanced at Sato. "You said that Ares made improvements to Pandora. What are we talking about?"

"It's more potent. But Ares was also trying to figure out a way of destroying it."

"Have they been successful?"

"No, not yet," said Sato. "Once it's released, there's no direct way of neutralizing it. However, it can only survive if it's allowed to feed on its nutritional supplement or any living being. Take those away and you reduce its fecundity."

"That I already know. But once Pandora's released, where does the cult plan to escape?"

"There's a bunker on the Kamchatka Peninsula. Its exact coordinates are on file."

Fox raised an eyebrow at Sato as he continued to scroll through the profiles. "The bunker's been in existence since the Cold War where members of the former Soviet Government could escape in the event of a nuclear war. It's one of many that were built. The idea of its location was to be difficult for an enemy to locate. My guess is that The Promise would've been on their way had it not been for what Katori and I know."

There was still something that weighed heavily in the back of Fox's mind. *What the hell was it? Something about last night wasn't right.* Fox was distracted enough that he decided to close the laptop and get up. "We can't stay here. It's time to come out of hiding."

"And go where? You can't contact your people. Everyone's looking for you."

"As I told you before, I have other partners over here. I'll pass the info to them. What you just showed me, can help clear my name." Fox walked over to the door with the laptop and with Sato behind him, when he figured out what bothered him. *Oh my gosh, yes, of course, that's it.*

"Concerning Katori, you have my condolences. You both did the right thing choosing to go your separate ways. Who knows if we'd have met if you hadn't."

Sato closed and locked the door and turned to Fox. "It was the best thing to do."

"Of course." *Just as I thought. And this confirms it.*

They came up to the car where Sato unlocked the passenger door for Fox. While his back was still turned, Fox drew his Sig. His arm was stretched out with the base of Sato's neck in his sights. "Keep your hands up where I can see them and turn around slowly."

Sato hesitated. "What are you doing?"

"Do it!" Sato's hands went up and he slowly turned around to face Fox.

"The next time you show up at a nightclub, you might not want to use a weapon you took from one of your victims."

Sato chuckled. "What do you mean—"

"The Micro-Uzi you're carrying. You showed it off last night. Maybe it's a coincidence, but I noticed that the October Cell members carried the same weapons. And I'm willing to bet that you were among the group that ambushed Katori and his kidnappers. Tell me, was it you who pulled the trigger? Did you kill Katori?"

Sato didn't answer.

Fox's eyes narrowed as he took a step closer to Sato. "Did Marx give you the honor of replacing Sato because you're the one who killed him, too?" Sato remained silent, but a smile slowly grew.

"You don't have to answer. This was the perfect back-up plan Marx had. Just in case I got away, you show up. Had her plan worked, she would have gotten rid of Ares and misdirected us all at once."

"I must commend you on your hunches."

"I'm flattered. Take out your gun, and slowly, because I *will* shoot you if I have to."

Sato took his Micro-Uzi out by the barrel, and held it in front of him with the handle pointed downwards.

"Put it gently on the ground and step away from it." Fox kept his Sig on the imposter, as he did as he was told. Sure, it would've been simpler for him to toss the Micro-Uzi to his feet, but the impact on the ground would cause the weapon to fire uncontrollably.

As Sato backed away, Fox walked forward and picked up the weapon. He then holstered his Sig, keeping the Micro-Uzi aimed at him. "Get against the car and spread your arms and legs." Sato obeyed and Fox frisked him. There was nothing much but the car keys and a money clip with a few bills. He backed off, told Sato to turn around, and then tossed him the keys. "Get behind the wheel. We're going for a ride."

Chapter 26

Parris jumped out of her slumber, only to find she was held in place by metal clamps. She tried to look around, but her head was held in place also, leaving her to stare at a plain, white wall. She knew where she was. The featureless white walls and the strong lemon-scented cleaner the janitors used were common throughout the sub-basements of Hexagon. And she was in the chair.

The door swung open and a blonde woman entered, followed by Hashimoto. She was much taller than Hashimoto, who only came up to her shoulder. The fact that she was the first to enter the room, gave Parris the impression that she was a major player in what was going on. Her complete disregard for even holding open the door for Hashimoto even hinted that she was an authoritative figure. The woman held a metal box similar to the one used earlier when Parris had experimented on both Dewan and Eva.

Hashimoto walked up to Parris. "I see you've rested well."

"You had me zapped, what do you expect?"

"For that I must apologize. The guards tend to go overboard at times, I'm sure you understand. You might find this hard to believe, but we're actually here to help you."

"Help me?" Parris rolled her eyes. "Now that's news."

The blonde woman placed the metal box on the table and turned to Parris. "You could use the help."

"Why's that?" Parris looked at her. "And who are you supposed to be?"

"I'm Dr. Tabitha Marx, Dr. Parris. Assuming that's your real name, of course."

"It is, *Dr*. Marx. Assuming that you've actually earned your doctorate, of course."

Marx crossed her arms and leaned against the edge of the table. "Drop the pleasantries. You're probably thinking that somehow some form of outside help will arrive."

"Outside help?" asked Parris. "Why would I be expecting help from the outside? I'm an employee of Hexagon Pharmaceuticals. There's been a big misunderstanding."

"Really? Because it so happens that our guards found two dead bodies. Two men were shot to death. Are you sure you wouldn't happen to know why they tried to access Hexagon's security? Not to mention why *you* were caught in a restricted area?" Marx leaned so close to Parris's ear that she felt her breath tickle the surface of her skin.

"We know of the files you've accessed. So drop the act."

Marx's last words went through one ear and out the next. Dobbs and Levickis were dead and the thought of it caused tightness in the back of her throat. "What?"

Marx backed away from her. "Your accomplices, I presume."

"You had them killed?"

"Actually, *we* didn't," said Hashimoto. "We both have a common enemy. And they were after the same thing you were."

Marx crossed her arms again. "That's why you're here, because you're going to help us stop them."

"By turning me into one of your brainwashed slaves?" Parris snapped. "Go ahead. Just make sure you stand close enough so that I can do to you what Dewan did to me."

Hashimoto raised an eyebrow and smiled. "My, my, what a temper."

"Indeed." Dr. Marx walked to the table. "We still don't know why Dewan reacted the way he did. We were hoping you'd be able to shed some light on that, since you were the last person in contact with him."

Parris glanced at Marx. "If you believe that, then what's your guarantee that once you begin the procedure on me that I won't do it to myself to escape?"

"Please. You're completely strapped in. Even if, by some miracle, you were to break free, you wouldn't be able to do it quick enough before the guards came in and subdued you." Marx slid the metal box closer to her and opened it. She took out a syringe with its hypodermic needle and cap.

Parris wasn't planning on being injected by anyone today. She kept forcing the clamps in the hope that they might loosen, but it was pointless.

Marx paused and chuckled, as she stared at Parris. "Go ahead. You'll only tire yourself out and be easier to control."

Parris continued to force her bindings, but Dr. Marx got closer with the syringe. Hashimoto watched from a few feet back.

Marx pinched an area at the side of her upper arm, quickly jabbed in the needle and pushed down the plunger. "That's it, keep at it. It doesn't bother me one bit."

Parris breathed hard and stared at Marx with narrow eyes. "Why don't you remove the bindings? You've done what you came to do."

"No, I think we'll leave you just the way you are." Marx pulled out the needle and lowered the visor over Parris's eyes and ears.

"Dr. Hashimoto," said Marx. "Please go check on my team in the other lab. Get them anything they ask." There was silence for a few moments.

"As you wish," came Hashimoto's reply.

Parris couldn't help notice the ambiance in the room between both Marx and Hashimoto. All along she had thought that Hashimoto was in charge, and now this woman comes along, as the obvious leader. It almost appeared that she was controlling him. *Could Hashimoto be on Clarity? If he was, it would be poetic justice, considering that he created the drug.*

She heard footsteps, then the swinging of a door as it opened and closed. Next came the dragging of the metal-backed chair beside her, just before Marx sat down. "It's just you and me now, Nita. We're going to go to a very comfortable place we can both enjoy."

Parris saw the first few images flash in front of her eyes.

Chapter 27

Parris lifted her hand to her forehead, the visor and her bindings were gone. She felt her head spin a bit. Marx stood in front of her flanked by two dark-suited men. Parris looked Marx in the face, there was definitely something different about her. Her hair appeared lighter than it was earlier—in fact her entire face seemed to glow. It was as though Parris were watching Marx through a plasma screen. The two dark-suited men didn't appear to have the same glow, she couldn't figure why. When Marx extended her hand, Parris was more than anxious to take it.

"I hope you rested well."

My god, she even sounded different. She couldn't imagine anything malicious coming from her anymore. It was a wonder how she could've been so mistrustful of her before. She touched her forehead as she closed her eyes and lowered her head. "How long was I out?"

"Not too long," replied Marx. "But you had a lot to say while you were in the chair. You've had a very eventful life. Come with me."

Parris followed Marx out of the room and into a hallway with the two dark-suited men behind them.

"Now that you're one of us, you will be able to appreciate our group's fundamentals." Marx led her around a corner. "For the years that The Promise has existed, we've spent time recruiting and saving young individuals from themselves, and from each other. This is the first step in changing the entire world. The biggest problem in the world today, is that when you have different religions and political ideologies, people will never be able to coexist. Think of Dewan and all of the others. They're all victims of what society has produced—the unfortunate leftovers."

They came to the end of the hall where Marx opened a door. Parris followed her inside and saw Hashimoto, and three other men dressed in white lab jackets. What they worked on she didn't know. The room was a typical laboratory with all the usual equipment found inside one. This lab had an adjoining chamber, separated by a fifteen-by-ten-foot shatterproof glass wall. Inside the chamber, Parris saw a mechanical arm attached to the ceiling.

Hashimoto turned around to greet them. "Welcome back, Dr. Parris. You'll be among the first to witness the new and improved variant of Pandora."

Parris looked at Marx. "New?"

"Yes," Marx replied. "This is where we come to the second step in changing the world. Thanks to the resources of Hexagon Pharmaceuticals, and my research, we have ourselves the perfect weapon that will bring about the change we want."

"With Pandora?" asked Parris. "If we used this we'd also destroy the animal kingdom. There'd be no food."

"That's with the old variant of Pandora. That one was believed to have wiped out populations a few millennia ago, and was what was brought back from the Canadian Arctic," Marx replied.

"Where did the new variant come from?" asked Parris.

Marx smiled. "You'll know soon enough, after the demonstration." She gestured towards the window and looked at Parris. "Take a look behind the glass and tell us what you see."

Parris walked up to the window, as Hashimoto stepped aside. Inside, she saw two men whose faces were so bloodied and mutilated that they were unidentifiable. But then she noticed their different physiques—Levickis and Dobbs had similar physiques. She put both hands to her mouth at the revelation. *Oh my God, it's them.* But there was also a third person beside them, an Asian man. Only he was not in the same condition as the others. Then, there was the small cage beside him, with four mice—the only active ones in the chamber.

She dropped her hands and looked at Marx. "Those are my

colleagues, I mean, *were* my colleagues." Something then caught her eye, it was the Asian man. *His stomach moved...he was breathing.* "That man's still alive."

"Yes." Marx walked up and stood beside Parris. "For now, anyway. But it won't matter. Pandora works just as well on the living as on the dead."

Parris looked up at her. "Who is he?"

Hashimoto approached Parris on the opposite side. "He's a Boeisho agent who infiltrated our group—one of three. The other two have been disposed of. I wanted to have him executed in a traditional style, decapitation by sword, but Dr. Marx thought it best to use him for live human testing."

Marx pointed, with a smirk, to the man. "Your other former colleague, Ridley Fox, thinks that he's with this man as we speak. Now you'll get to see how Pandora's been improved to our standards."

Marx looked at Parris and gestured to a red button on the console. "Would you care to do the honors?"

Parris went up to the console, and she saw some movement in the chamber. The Boeisho agent sat up and looked around him. When he saw Parris, she took her hand off of the red button. Moments later he noticed the corpses and jumped back. Several hours ago she would have done everything to save this man's life. Now she didn't feel the same way. That scared her.

"What's the matter?" asked Marx.

"I...I don't know," she answered.

"There's no court of law that'll punish this man. The world doesn't want us to exist, that's why this man was sent to spy on us."

Parris's hand moved closer to the button.

"This man represents everything we're against," said Marx. "He *must* be punished. Push the button."

She's right. He's guilty. And without another moment's hesitation, she pressed the button.

Parris felt the button vibrate under her hands and she immediately stood back from the console. Red-fluorescent smoke began to blow inside the chamber, from a ceiling panel.

An uncomforting hissing sound soon followed. As the smoke became thicker it also got brighter. The hissing got louder. The man looked up and saw the cloud descending on him. He backed away until he bounced into the window, scratching his arm and chest. When Parris saw him turn around, she gasped at the sight of blood pouring out of his eyes, and then she jumped back. The man screamed and pounded violently on the window, but it didn't give way. He then threw his weight on it, twice, before falling to the ground in convulsions.

When Parris looked behind, she saw that Dr. Marx's assistants had turned away. Hashimoto had his arms crossed while he stared at the floor. Marx, however, watched the entire show without any signs of trepidation. In fact, Parris thought that she saw a hint of a smile curve up on one corner of her mouth. The man's screams were garbled, and when Parris turned back to him, she was in time to see his eyeballs burst from their sockets, spitting out a bloody ooze that rolled down the window like egg yolk.

Parris stormed away, past Marx and Hashimoto, and turned around. "Why me?" she screamed. She caught everyone off guard. Marx's two guards were about to intervene, but Marx raised an open palm to face level, stopping them.

"Why was I allowed to live? I'm far worse than any of the others in The Promise." A few tears rolled down Parris's cheeks.

Marx shook her head. "You must not say those things." She then took Parris by her forearms. "Now look at me. Those men in there who died, they were beyond saving, but you weren't. I believe in you, do you understand me?"

Parris didn't want to understand. *Just give me a scalpel for me to slit my wrists. That should make things even.*

"Nita!" Marx said this louder and got Parris's full attention. There was something about those eyes of hers that she couldn't ignore.

"Yes, Dr. Marx." She nodded. Marx then smiled as she put one arm around Parris and walked her back to the window as she wiped away her tears with her sleeve.

By this time, the entire laboratory had a reddish glow. The cloud on the other side of the window was so dense that nothing could be seen inside.

Hashimoto went to the console and pressed another button. There was another vibration and loud noise that sounded like a series of fans. Less than five minutes later, the cherry cloud thinned out and was sucked into three separate vents above the chamber.

When Parris looked inside the chamber, the bodies of Levickis, Dobbs, and the Boeisho agent were also gone. Only their clothes remained, in a sticky, dark pile of slime. But in the cage, the mice continued to play around. She looked at Marx. "You've genetically engineered Pandora to specifically target human DNA."

Marx smiled with a chuckle. "Human protein chains derived from DNA to be precise. This is the one thing Ares couldn't accomplish."

Marx took her hand off Parris. "When it fell into their hands, they did a lot of research on it. With help from a former member— you should know him as Mr. Valerik—I was able to monitor their progress from a safe distance, while I kept my cover as one of the head scientists working for the CDC.

While Ares played with their samples, I covertly worked on a theoretic approach to engineer it so that it would target humans specifically. It was also important to increase its virulence so that it attacked faster. Once that was done, I needed the original Pandora back, in order to finish my work on it."

"That's when we raided their facility in Belarus," said Hashimoto.

"And now they're going to try to take it back from us." Marx walked slowly away and then stopped.

Parris smoothened out an eyebrow and turned to Hashimoto. "If they murdered my former colleagues, then they'd have a lot of info on Pandora. That's what my former colleagues and I were trying to steal."

"Exactly. Now we have another crisis on our hands," said Hashimoto.

"Calm down." Marx rolled her eyes and turned to Hashimoto, keeping her composure. She then turned back to Parris. "Who else knew of your whereabouts?"

"Walsh knew. In fact, he was in charge of the operation, only he wasn't on site. Levickis and Dobbs were pros. If anyone had hacked our phone calls or bugged them, they'd know. Walsh must have sold us out."

Hashimoto walked away and then turned back, pacing back and forth. "That means they know the location of our bunker."

Parris turned to Hashimoto. "Yes, but if Walsh set us up, then he and his group either think I'm dead or being held hostage. We can exploit that."

"How?" Marx asked.

Parris looked at Marx. "I can meet Walsh, give him a story that I escaped. Then I put a gun to his head and threaten to blow his brains out unless he takes me to the rest of his group."

Hashimoto stopped pacing and faced Parris. "That's risky. You could be killed."

"I've risked my life for the sake of National Security. This wouldn't change anything." Parris then looked at Marx. "Let me go in alone and confront Walsh. He won't be expecting me anyways."

Marx looked at Hashimoto. "I don't have a problem with that. But should you be overwhelmed, I have something special for you to use that will take care of all of them once and for all."

Marx looked her straight in the eyes. "Hopefully you won't have to use what I'm about to give you. But should you have to, you'll always be remembered as a martyr."

Parris remained silent for the next few seconds. She knew what had to be done, regardless of the outcome. It was, after all, for the greater good. "I'll do anything that'll benefit the cause."

Marx smiled as she backed away from Parris and stood slightly in front of Hashimoto with her arms crossed. "Excellent. Then let's begin
"

Chapter 28

Walsh's Hotel Room

W alsh paced up and down in front of the television, not caring that Pyotr tried to watch the Japanese game show that was on. He was on the phone with Pyotr's boss, getting an earful, while Pyotr shifted back and forth on the bed trying to see around him.

"Hey, stop blocking television," said Pyotr.

Walsh ripped off his tie, threw it at Pyotr, and missed. *Don't you start with me too, asshole.* "No, I haven't heard anything from him yet. He's been like this ever since we left Uganda. I bugged his watch, what more do you want?"

"It's no longer transmitting," said the October Man. "Why is it that you don't know where your own partner is? May I remind you of the other things we're paying you for?"

"Hey, if he wants to go rogue, there's nothing I can do about it," Walsh shot back. "But if you want me to get more agents over here to haul him in, hence drawing more attention to us, I'll do it. Is that what you want?"

"Don't get smart with me. We're one step closer to getting back what's ours. Our reinforcements are scheduled to arrive shortly and I won't have this operation compromised—"

There were two beeps that interrupted him.

"Hold on a sec. I've got someone on the other line." Walsh pressed the button, cutting off the October Man. "What?"

"Tsukiji Fish Market in half an hour."

"What? Who is this?"

"Your Canadian connection cannot speak to you directly. Stop asking questions and meet him in a half hour." The line went dead.

Canadian connection? It was Fox, no doubt. And he got someone to speak on his behalf in order to trick Japan's own Echelon system. Clever. He pressed the swap button and all he heard was a dial done. *Fuckin' A.*

He threw the phone on the bed. It bounced once and missed Pyotr, who was about to say something but Walsh cut him off by pointing a huge fat finger at him. "Don't start with me, you and your goddamn reality shows. I've done enough for you people. And take your damn shoes off while you're on the bed. Jesus Christ, you must be the only assassin on the face of the earth too damn cheap to get a decent pair of shoes."

At least it was only Pyotr that tagged along with him back here. He couldn't remember what he had said to convince Demyan not to come back with him, but was glad he did. *Demyan's too much of a wack job.* Walsh felt safer playing tennis with a grenade than having him around. A few more days, that was all Walsh could think of. With twenty million dollars waiting for him in an offshore bank account, he could finally take the early retirement he had dreamt of and disappear to some remote island. He didn't know where he would go yet, but it would be sunny and hot all year round. He'd watch football via satellite and drink booze all day long.

"Ain't there anything else on TV?"

Pyotr sighed. "Poshyel k chyertu."

"Whatever, jackass," Walsh muttered as he waved him off without knowing that Pyotr had called a loser. *Why couldn't he watch good old American Football, like real men do?* Just then there was a knock on the door. "Were you expecting someone?" Walsh whispered to Pyotr, who shrugged his shoulders as though he were telling him that he didn't know. The knocking turned to banging. Walsh then rushed to the door. "All right, keep your shirt on. Who is it?"

"It's me, Nita."

Walsh paused. *What the hell is she doing here?* He turned to Pyotr, who gave him the, *I don't know, don't look at me*, look. Walsh quietly motioned for him to go hide in the coat closet.

"Quit stalling and hurry up," Walsh whispered through gritted teeth. The Russian rushed past him into the coat closet, and Walsh slid the door shut. He then opened the door for Parris, who, with tears in her eyes, rushed past him so fast that he felt a slight breeze. "Jesus, Parris. Thank God you're all right." Walsh closed the door quickly behind her.

***

"Levickis and Dobbs, they've—"

"I know, we lost contact. I figured something happened to them. And I thought that you were a goner too when I couldn't reach you."

"They're both dead, I just know it. I managed to get by one of the guards before more of them rushed downstairs to the Safe."

Walsh moved past her so that her back faced the doorway the way he wanted. "Okay, you can calm down now. It's all right." Walsh steadied her by placing both hands on her forearms. She instantly pushed him away. Walsh stumbled backwards but caught his balance on the edge of the dresser. As he looked up, he stared down the barrel of a HK USP Tactical, complete with a noise suppressor. "Are you crazy? What the fuck are you doing?"

"Don't act like you don't know." Parris approached Walsh. "You set us up. And now Levickis and Dobbs are dead. You didn't expect me to make it out, did you?"

Walsh didn't answer.

He doesn't look too scared having a gun pointed at him. Did he just briefly look past me? That's when she heard a slight creak in the floor behind her. Parris shot her left leg out in a back kick and struck Pyotr in the groin with the heel of her pumps. He cried out and curled over as she spun around and landed the handle of the HK to the back of his head, flooring him. She heard movement behind her. That's when she feinted left, dodging Walsh, and then kicked him in the right kneecap. Had she contacted him a few more inches more to the outside of his knee, she could have easily shattered it. But she only wanted to floor him like his Russian counterpart, which she did.

"Damn it, Parris. You and those shoes."

"Shut up." She dashed around him so she had both Walsh and the Russian in her sight. "Get up, both of you, and get on the bed. And keep your hands where I can see them."

Pyotr was slower than Walsh at obeying her instructions.

"Now!" Parris yelled.

The Russian limped his way to the bed, and Walsh sat down next to him.

"Sit on your hands and face me with your feet apart." It was then that she noticed Pyotr's blackened running shoes, they were damp and the stains looked recent. "So it was you, wasn't it? You set off the alarm at Hexagon."

Pyotr remained silent.

"Don't bother answering. Your shoes told me everything."

Pyotr grimaced as he looked at Parris. "I'll say nothing to you, you worthless, black—"

The HK coughed out a single shot to his throat, and Pyotr flipped over backwards and onto the floor. She then pointed the gun to Walsh. "You want to make a redneck comment too?"

Walsh had his eyes shut when the shot rang out, but now opened them slowly and turned around. He looked at the hole in the wall where the bullet struck—there was blood spatter around it. Pyotr had been thrown back and he hung off the bed from the waist up.

"Jesus Christ, that was dumb! That was a real dumb thing to do." Walsh looked back at Parris.

"Shut up!" yelled Parris with a hard Bajan accent. "You can shoot off you mout' too and you'll get exactly the same t'ing. But I ain't done wit' you yet."

Walsh looked at her with a blank stare as though he would've said something had he understood what she just said.

"Up you get. Don't try anything on me because I'm armed with enough Pandora to wipe out the city, so you best not try anything stupid."

Walsh seemed to understand her that time, since she'd dropped the accent. "What? Are you insane? And where are we going anyway?"

"We're going to pay the rest of your group a visit. Where are they?"

Walsh got up with both hands held high. "We were supposed to meet at the Tsukiji Fish Market."

"When?"

"In half an hour."

"Get dressed, 'cause that's where you're taking me."

Chapter 29

Tsukiji Fish Market, Chuo Ward, Tokyo

Raindrops dotted the windshield as Fox and his prisoner waited in the car, alone in a deserted parking lot in one of the world's largest fish markets. Fox sat diagonally in the backseat where he could keep an eye on him at all times. He was relieved that Sato's imposter had a cell phone—one with a digital voice recorder. The rest was easy. He forced him to record himself with the phrases Fox gave him. Then he called Walsh from a payphone in a discreet location and played back the recorded message into the phone. He did this while he made the imposter face a wall with both arms and feet apart. It was clean and efficient, with the absence of his voice and his and Walsh's names—the Boeisho's own Echelon system would never pick anything up.

Fox couldn't recall the last time he had seen a parking lot that was so clean. Not a shred of paper was seen blowing about. He saw a car approach from the opposite direction, moments after, the imposter turned off the car engine. The other car stopped about fifty meters away. *Why did Walsh stop so far away?* Fox looked past the driver into Walsh's car hoping he could gather a clue. He wasn't able to.

He tapped the back of the car seat with the barrel of the gun. "Get out—and slowly. Remember your hands." Obediently, the imposter stepped out, left the door open and kept both hands held up high as he walked forward. Fox got out too, leaving the Micro Uzi inside, and he closed both his and the driver's doors.

Fox allowed a bit more than an arm's length between him and the imposter before he followed. *Something wasn't right.* He looked around. It was just an empty parking lot. The market itself was deserted. If a sniper had him in his sights, they'd have to be outside the market in one of the surrounding buildings. The chance that his phone call was intercepted was unlikely. Maybe the imposter somehow sent out a distress signal. But Fox had searched him from head to toe, he was clean. He didn't sense an ambush, but his old army instincts kicked in. That's when he noticed there was someone behind Walsh.

"Stop."

The imposter obeyed as his hands began to drop slightly.

"Walsh, why don't you come on out?" There was movement behind Walsh. The back door swung open and out came Dr. Parris with a sidearm pointed at Walsh. Her eyes narrowed and a slight scowl developed as she shook her head slowly. He saw her lips move and Walsh got out. With the opposite hand she shoved him forward, staying a few feet behind him.

Fox felt a slight chill as a gust of wind blew through the parking lot. "Would either of you mind telling me what's going on?"

"She's a traitor, and she's armed with Pandora," Walsh yelled.

Parris kept an eye on both Walsh and Fox. "Go ahead. Shoot me. You'll kill me, yourself, and a few million others."

She better not mean what I think she does. "I see. Do you mind telling me how you got hold of Pandora?"

"Your partner set us up," Parris yelled. "His friends in Ares killed Dobbs and Levickis. They were counting on Hashimoto killing me too. Ironically, he saved me."

It suddenly hit Fox. *I knew it. But wait a minute...of course... the tracking bug in my watch. Only Walsh could've gotten close enough to bug it. He could've done so before I boarded the plane at Entebbe, while I was in the shower.* "So what has Hashimoto promised you? A life of total bliss after the final holocaust?"

"I don't plan to go on with them. I'm just as guilty as you are for corrupting what could've been a perfect world," Parris asserted.

Fox noticed the imposter's hands drop a bit more. "Keep your hands up. I'm still watching you." His hands went up quickly. "Let me get this straight. We've both, in our separate times, helped bring down terrorists and other criminals, and now you're saying that we were doing more harm than good?"

"You're a fool. Marx said you wouldn't understand."

"Maybe not. But what I *do* understand is that you've been brainwashed by a psychopath. And I also know that the real Dr. Nita Parris wouldn't be easily persuaded unless she was under someone else's control."

Parris smirked. "You're always full of answers, aren't you?"

Fox clenched his teeth. "You studied Clarity, you know what it does. The only thing is, you don't want to admit that you're a victim, do you?"

Parris nudged Walsh below his neck with the tip of her gun as his hands started to drop. They went back up again quickly.

"It's too bad I didn't get a chance to get to know you too well," said Fox. "Although we started off on the wrong foot, I figured you for the type of woman that wouldn't bend to someone else's will." Fox saw the instant change in Parris's eyes and knew he'd better move quickly. The imposter certainly saw the same thing and both he and Fox dove to opposite sides a split second before he heard a loud *bang* which was instantly followed by an invisible object that flew by his left ear.

Parris was about to take a second shot when Walsh swung out his right arm, caught her arm underneath, sending the second bullet into the sky.

Fox was kicked to his lower back and fell to the ground, causing the Sig to fly from his hand. As he tried to get up, he received another kick to his stomach that flipped him over onto his back. This was not the position to be in, leaving himself at a disadvantage.

The imposter stood above him, with his right leg raised as though to drop a kick on him, when a splatter of blood along with small pieces of bone, muscle, and intestine exploded from his stomach. He dropped to his knees and keeled over onto the concrete as a red ring of blood formed around his torso.

That was the last shot from the HK before Walsh managed to grab hold of Parris's arm, pulling the gun out of her grip and throwing her onto the hood of the car. Very quickly she spun around and kicked the suppressor from Walsh's hand before he had a chance to fire a shot. While he was knocked off balance from the impact, Parris spun around the opposite direction and connected a second crescent kick to his jaw, making him stumble the other way. She charged him with a series of combo punches, too quick for him to block. As he stumbled back she pushed as hard as she could against the ground with her feet and propelled herself into the air. With a slightly arched back, she transferred her energy into driving her right knee upwards and struck Walsh in the chest with a flying knee attack. As though he was struck with a sledge hammer, Walsh buckled and fell to the ground.

Fox stared into the eyes of the imposter as his blood poured closer to Fox's fingertips. His chance of getting any information from him was lost. Fox got up on one knee and felt a hot metal object press against his left temple.

"To answer you, Fox, I'm not bending to anyone's will. And guess what? I won't bend to yours either."

Fox slowly looked up and stared into Parris's cold eyes, as though a lifetime's accumulation of anger seemed to fill them. "So that's it? You're just going to shoot me?"

"Were you expecting something else?" Parris asked. "Typical of you. You're so damn arrogant."

For a short moment, she glanced at his chest. Fox glanced down to see what it was. *Holy shit. Her table napkin.* It hung partially out of his breast pocket. He then looked into her eyes. "I wanted to give it back to you, hopefully when we were on better terms. You want it? Take it. I know how much it meant to Nita Parris. I hope you don't mind giving it back to her."

She blinked rapidly and her lips trembled, the scowl vanished, and she breathed hard. She appeared to be struggling, her focus dwindling, as though part of her wanted to shoot him and another part didn't.

Slowly, Fox got up, keeping both hands held up to shoulder

height. He could've easily disarmed her, but what then? She might resist, possibly having the same adrenaline rush her test subject did and overpower him. *Better keep the table napkin visible...it's definitely affecting her.*

He smiled at her. "I'm sure this table napkin must bring back some fond memories. The times you ate with your mother, or maybe it was a gift to you. Maybe the last thing you got from her before she passed away."

At that moment, her hands trembled with the HK. The last thing he needed was for her to accidentally pull the trigger. He slowly inched to the side and lowered his right hand over his breast pocket, took the table napkin and held it out. "Take it. It's yours."

With her free hand, she reached over and took it as she lowered the HK. She brought it close to her face and took a deep breath, as though its scent gave her strength.

Fox reached out calmly and took the HK from her without resistance. He tossed it to the ground, pulled her into him, and tightly embraced her.

Parris sniffled as the tears poured. "I killed them. I killed them all."

"Don't say that. You haven't killed anyone."

"I watched their bodies being eaten by the microbe. I'm the one who released Pandora on Levickis, Dobbs, and the Boeisho agent. Fox, he was still alive and I watched him die right in front of me!"

"You said Walsh set you up," Fox reminded Parris. "That it was Ares who killed them."

"But there was an experiment." Parris wiped away a tear. "Hashimoto's not even the main person we're after. He's working for Dr. Tabitha Marx, and she's bio-engineered Pandora so it only targets humans. They gave me a demonstration. They dragged in Levickis's and Dobbs's bodies, along with a Boeisho agent they captured, and there were mice, and I pushed the button to release Pandora on all three of them. I killed them, Fox and I didn't even feel sorry for them. I murdered an innocent man in cold blood, I—"

Fox grabbed Parris's face gently and forced her to look into his eyes. "Listen. You were under their influence. They were controlling you so you would think the way they wanted you to think. That wasn't *you* who killed them. That was someone else they created. But now you're Dr. Nita Parris again, and as traumatizing as it may be, you're going to have to let that go. There was nothing you could've done to save any of them. And although I didn't want to admit it when I first met you, I need you. Especially now, because what Marx is planning is huge. With Ares around, it doesn't help. You're the only person I can rely on right now, so we're going to have to take down both Ares and The Promise on our own. Do you understand me?"

A few seconds went by, and then Parris nodded. There was something about the way that she stared at him, with her lips slightly parted. Raindrops fell, one by one, off each cheekbone and ran like dew on a newly formed leaf. It was just like in the dream. The difference was that she was alive this time, and Fox would never let anything happen to her. But that stare, he hadn't seen her stare at him like that since...when they first met. As the inside of his mouth moistened, his head slowly gravitated towards hers.

The danger radar went off in his head. From the corner of his eye, he saw movement, enough to make him shove Parris to the side so hard she fell to the ground. He dove for the HK, rolled over on the ground once with it, and shot Walsh three times. Walsh, who was partially standing, lost his grip on Fox's Sig when the first shot landed below his right shoulder. His spin was counterbalanced by the second shot below the left clavicle, and the third shot went straight to the sternum and threw him back-first onto the hood of the car. His lifeless body rolled onto the ground.

Fox kept his gun aimed at him, somehow expecting him to get up again. *How or when did Walsh turn?* Fox didn't have the answer. It made him think back to when he was with Sveta. She had told him that she trusted him because he couldn't be led astray by Ares. Now it was Walsh. *Were there anymore?* He wouldn't know for now. It was doubtful that Walsh would've known all of

Ares's spies.

He didn't even notice that Parris had already gotten up and was kneeling behind him, calling his name.

"Fox," she said, and from the tone of her voice it was as though she had already called his name a few times. He felt her hands on his shoulders.

Fox breathed heavily. "I'm here, Jessica."

There was a moment's pause, as though she didn't know how to answer. "I...I know you are."

The drizzle stopped, and another chilly wind gust blew over him, but it was counterbalanced by the warmness of Parris's arms wrapped around him. As the wind blew stronger, her grip around him got tighter. Fox then felt a hand slide along the length of his arm to his hand and gently pulled away the HK.

"Are you all right?" she spoke softly into his ear.

Fox didn't reply at first, but instead, he held onto her embrace as he calmed down. She maintained her hold on him. His heavy panting eased. "I'm better."

She didn't let go of him yet, but he didn't want to let her go either.

"Fox?"

He turned and looked over his shoulder at her. "Yeah?"

"Thanks."

He stared at her for a moment. *Was this the same woman?* Yesterday they were fighting and now he was in her embrace.

"Yeah, you're welcome." He sighed and dropped his head. Whether or not she had feelings for him, he couldn't let that distract him. He shouldn't have allowed himself to nearly kiss her. It was completely out of line, even for him. But Parris brought something out of him that no other woman did. It's what made him serenade her yesterday, made him want to protect her now. He didn't know what it was, but it made him feel comfortable around her.

They both got up, and Fox turned to her. "We've reached a dead end. We don't have either Walsh or Hashimoto's henchman to question for information on Pandora's whereabouts."

"I know." Parris walked two steps away and then turned back

to him. "By the way, how'd you figure it out?"

"Figure what out?"

"You brought me back to the way I had been before Clarity. How'd you know the table napkin would bring me back?"

Fox took a step towards her. "To be honest, I was buying some time so I could figure out a way to avoid being shot. The last thing I needed was another conflict."

"I see." Parris turned around and put both hands on her hips and walked away slowly. She took six paces and then she stopped, turned around and looked at Fox. "What did you just say?"

Fox didn't want to answer too quickly, and blushed. "I was stalling to avoid being shot, I didn't—"

"No, no, no, after that. You said something about not wanting another conflict."

"Yeah, I think I said something like that."

Parris smacked the heel of her right palm on her forehead. "Oh my God! That's it." She smiled with a laugh. "That's how you bring them back. That's why Dewan went berserk."

"Not with the table napkin?"

"No, you got it wrong." Parris dropped her hand by her side and continued laughing. "Just before Dewan attacked me we were talking about his sister, the one person in his family he was closest to. He said that she and I wore the same perfume. The smell of the perfume obviously held some deep sentiment for him, as the table napkin did for me."

"But how come he attacked you? And why didn't you go berserk and shoot me?"

"Two different situations. I was well under the effects of the drug when I saw the table napkin. Dewan was in the process of being brainwashed at the same time he smelled my perfume. There must've been some kind of mental conflict that caused him to rebel. The drug is even more powerful than we had originally conceived. Had I gone through more sessions, you might not have been as successful in breaking its effects on me so easily."

"Too much conflict. The only way he knew how to deal with it was to attack you. A means of self-defense for the brain."

"Exactly."

"Do you think Marx knows this?"

"I don't know, but I doubt it. Both she and Hashimoto have other things on their minds."

"Like sending you out to kill me? They must be getting desperate, because the man you accidentally shot was posing as one of the escaped Boeisho agents Tanaka was hunting. He gave me false info about Pandora's location, in order to lead me off course, so The Promise could make a clean getaway."

"You weren't first on my list. My main objective was to get Walsh. Ares stole the info I collected on Pandora and everything related to The Promise's plans. I was supposed to kidnap Walsh and have him bring me to Ares where I would release the—oh Lord, it's still on me!"

Parris reached into her inner breast pocket and took out a metallic container, the shape of a small cigarette box. She sighed with relief seeing that it was undamaged. "It's fused shut. It can't get out unless I smash it."

"So I can breathe now?"

"Yeah. Walsh was supposed to bring me to meet members of Ares, and I was going to take them out with this." Parris held the container for Fox to see. "But he tricked me and brought me to see you instead."

"Yes, a meeting I had arranged with him after I took that imposter hostage."

Fox saw Parris look at Walsh. "With Walsh and the ninja gone, how do we find Ares or Pandora?"

"Actually, Fox, it's not a total loss. I have a copy of the files Walsh stole."

"You do? Where?"

Parris looked down at her shoes and clicked her heels, reminding him of Dorothy in the *Wizard of Oz*. "I've got a disk. I've also learned more about Pandora—so much more that I think I might know a way to destroy it. It's a long shot, but the possibility's there."

Fox smirked. "There's a laptop in my car. We can look at what's on the disc." Fox walked over to Walsh's body, grabbed his cell phone from inside his jacket, picked up the Sig which lay on the ground and then walked over to his car. He noticed that Parris ran back to hers.

"I almost forgot something," she said. She climbed into the front seat and appeared to be searching for something in the glove compartment. When she got out, she had a syringe in her hand.

"What's that for?"

"It's for you. I think you might have been tagged."

"I know—my watch was bugged. Walsh must've done it."

"Yes, which would explain why Ares was able to track you all the way here, but it's possible that you may have been tagged with a radioactive tracking isotope. It would've been done inconspicuously, so you better inject yourself with this just to be on the safe side."

Fox took off his jacket and rolled up his shirtsleeve. Parris injected him in the arm, and he rolled his shirtsleeve back down and put his jacket back on.

"How fast will this work?"

"Very quickly." Fox headed to his car while Parris went to the passenger side.

Fox got in and closed the door. "So how do we do it? How do we destroy Pandora?"

Parris pulled her door shut and grabbed the laptop from the backseat. "I have a theory. The new variant is engineered in a way as to not touch any other foreign proteins other than those found in humans. This leads me to believe that any non-human proteins might be poisonous to it. If I can produce a serum derived from non-human proteins, we might have ourselves a silver bullet."

"Might?"

"Yes, *might*. I can only be sure once I've had the chance to test it. I have a sample of Pandora and its data, and now I have a laptop."

Fox started up the engine. "I'm guessing we're on our way to Hexagon."

"How fast can you get us there?"

"Pretty damn quick."

Chapter 30

Fox slammed on the breaks and blasted the horn as someone cut him off.

"Are you okay there?" Parris asked, grabbing the laptop before it was thrown off her lap.

Fox cut in on the inside lane to overtake the offensive driver. "I'm fine. So was I right about the Kamchatka bunker being a hoax?"

"Right you are. The real bunker is located on an island in the Sea of Japan. According to these notes, construction on the bunker in the early 1980s wasn't even completed, but was left abandoned. Hexagon moved in to complete its construction."

Fox hopped a lane. "Where exactly is the island?"

"I'm not checking that right now, I'm taking notes in order to make the serum."

"How long will it take?"

"If all goes well, under an hour."

"What about security?"

"We'll use your makeshift keycard instead of mine. That should buy us some time. As for the rest, don't look at the guards or the cameras. But you already knew that, right?" Parris answered with a smirk.

Fox glanced at her and then back at the traffic. "Of course I did."

When they approached the security checkpoint at Hexagon, Parris flashed her employee pass while Fox flashed Levickis's makeshift pass. The guard waved them through. Parris directed

Fox to the parking lot of the East building.

Fox followed Parris down the elevators to the fourth basement floor, into the same testing laboratory where she had been earlier. She took two steps into the room and then stopped.

"What's wrong?" Fox asked.

"This is where it happened, where—"

"Parris, stop." Fox patted her lower back. "Stay focused."

"Right." She grabbed a lab jacket from one of the hooks near the entrance and put it on. "I'll start working on the serum. Everything I need to make it is in this room. I just need you to hand me the tools and items as I work. Oh, and another thing. You should grab a lab coat, too."

Fox obeyed her and took one. "Yes, ma'am."

There were dozens of mice that were used for experiments kept in the laboratory. Both Parris and Fox had enough to extract blood samples to fill ten test tubes.

"That's all we need for non-human proteins," said Parris as she returned the last mouse to its cage. "What we have in here is similar to what's found in some modern high-tech laboratories. Various chemical compounds and elements must be preserved in different environments with temperature and lighting control. Those chemicals are found in various rooms throughout this sub-basement. The concept is much like your typical candy vending machine. You put in your money, look at the code that's listed under each candy, then you punch in the code on the keypad, and the chocolate bar drops off the shelf."

Fox followed her to the computer workstation where she typed in her personal access code.

"Except in here, you order from this computer terminal. The difference is that you also have to specify the exact volume and concentrations. Based on the notes I read from the files, I've been able to compile a list of ingredients and their precise amounts needed to make the serum. I have them all written down on this piece of paper I took from the glove compartment." She took the folded paper from her pocket and showed it to Fox. "I'll order the first to show you how it's done." Parris demonstrated. Within a minute, a message flashed on the screen. *Compound ready.*

Please collect.

She walked over to a corner, beside the isolation chamber, to a one-by-one-foot metal door located in the wall. She opened it and took out the corked Erlenmeyer flask from the conveyer belt.

"And to think that I spent three hours in chemistry lab class making compounds from scratch when I could've done it here in half the time," said Fox.

"Well, now's your chance to spoil yourself. Gather all of the compounds on my list and be mindful of the specific volumes and masses I've indicated. They must be precise. I'll set up the rest of the equipment."

"Yes, Professor Parris," Fox said sarcastically, with a smile.

Parris glanced back at him for a second before she shook her head.

They both started working.

"So tell me, Doctor...not to bring back any bad memories, but what was it like being on Clarity?"

Parris took a big breath as though she was in deep reflection.

"It's scary thinking back on it. You don't feel any different from how you are now. It's just the way you think that's different. It's like anyone who's gone through a brainwashing procedure, except this procedure's more efficient than traditional methods. Clarity is remarkable, but in a negative sense."

Those words instantly reminded Fox of when he first met Dr. Marx, especially when she described Pandora's self-replication rate as wonderful. But Dr. Parris wasn't the deranged woman Dr. Marx was.

"How's it more efficient?" asked Fox.

"While under Clarity, and with the assistance of the chair, Marx's words all meant something, the way she was able to make me go back and talk about traumatizing events in order to mold me into what she wanted, the way she used my previous experience with you to..." Parris immediately bit down as if to stop herself from saying another word, but it was too late, Fox already knew the rest of what she was about to say. Her head dropped, as she seemed to recognize that. She put the flask down on the counter in front of her, and she sighed. "I'm sorry."

She had struck a nerve and Fox felt the sensation all the way up his spine.

"No, Dr. Parris. I'm the one who's sorry." Fox sighed now too, as he shook his head. "How about that. Marx made you talk about our brief relationship. She made you remember the pain and anger you felt when I stood you up and disappeared from your life. You agreed with her that your pain and troubles could be traced to those who've wronged you, including me. Now you've become the person you are because of me."

"I'd rather not discuss it anymore. That's the past. Let's move on."

"Agreed."

A minute passed, but for some reason Fox still sensed that Parris was somewhat restless. Then again, he couldn't let that distract him. But it was not long before he heard a glass smash on the floor. When he turned to look, he saw Parris staring at the broken beaker at her feet.

"Don't worry, I'll clean it up," she said with a wave of her hand. She walked over to the corner, opened a closet door and took out a broom and dustpan.

As Fox listened to Parris sweeping up the glass, he got restless himself, knowing she wanted to say something else to him. *Keep working, this needs to be finished quickly. Oh who am I kidding?* He stopped what he was doing and looked at her, and before he could say anything, Parris began to unload herself.

"You called me Jessica."

"What?"

"You referred to me as Jessica, back at the fish market."

"I did?"

"Yes. It was right after you shot Walsh. You were slightly delirious."

Fox thought back to when they were at the parking lot. The way she had looked at him as he held her, so reminiscent of the way Jessica had looked at him on the stretcher in his dream. Could he have been thinking of Jessica that whole time?

"Oh, that's nothing. It runs in the family. Kind of like how an aunt or uncle means to call you by your name but ends up calling

you by your brother or sister's name. It was that sort of thing."
Fox laughed hesitantly. He didn't want to talk about Jessica right
now, and the only way to avoid the subject was to pretend it didn't
exist. But he saw that Parris wasn't buying any of it. *Who am I
trying to kid here?*

"Fox?"

He turned to her. "Yes?"

"Stop." She rested the broom against the side of the counter.
"Don't you see what's happened to you? You've intentionally
inundated yourself in the mission as a way of covering up your
past. You just don't know it yet."

Fox crossed his arms, his head slightly tilted, as he looked at
Parris. "Really? Why do you say that?"

"Dr. Marx told me everything. She convinced me you became
some sort of loose cannon after what happened to your fiancée.
She knows quite a bit about you."

Thanks to Tanaka. "She doesn't know anything about Jessica.
And neither do you."

"You're right, I didn't know her. But I wish I did. Because the
fact that you were about to give up your career in an elite Special
Forces unit to settle down with her, she must have been one hell
of a woman."

Damn her. Why'd she have to go for my soft spot? He turned
to the counter and leaned on it with outstretched arms, facing the
isolation chamber. "You know what? Being a part of the JTF2
wasn't even part of my life's goal. I was your typical spoiled kid,
born with a silver spoon in their mouth. There was so much that
I could've been in life—or should I say—what my father wanted
me to be. I threw it all away and joined the army."

Parris slowly walked towards Fox. "You joined the army to
rebel against your father?"

"Yeah, that's pretty much it." Fox smirked and glanced at
Parris. "Then I met Jessica. And everything changed."

Parris stopped a foot away from Fox. "What was she like?"

"She was something else. We had our arguments, she was so
damn feisty. She always tried to prove that she was the one that
wore the pants in the relationship. Kind of what you'd see your

parents arguing about from time to time."

"I wouldn't know."

Fox looked at her over his shoulder surprised. "What?"

"I never had the chance to see my parents argue because I never knew them."

"Parris, I didn't—"

"It's okay, I've had this conversation before. My mother died when I was young and I never met my father. My aunt raised me."

Fox hesitated for a moment, wondering how appropriate it would be to continue talking about this. "Do you ever wonder where your father is?"

Parris shook her head. "No, and I don't want to either."

"To say the least. I haven't spoken to either of my parents, or Jessica's, since...the incident."

"Why?" She then took his right hand. "Do you blame yourself for her death?"

He pulled himself from her grip and turned away from her. "I should've seen it coming. After all the training I'd undergone. I'd learned so much about assessing a situation. Yet I couldn't spot something suspicious about the company Jessica worked for."

"We all make mistakes." Parris walked up to him and turned him around gently. "I'm sorry I was so nasty to you yesterday. You were right. I *was* listening to you play the piano. I understand that you were trying to make up for the past—I just didn't want to accept it then. For the record, I'm not mad at you anymore."

Fox again felt a warmth in her voice and he responded by holding both her hands. "After what happened to you...I mean... the night I stood you up and you being assaulted and all. Don't you regret becoming a field agent as a result of what I did to you?"

Parris smiled at him. "You're not the reason why I'm here. I'm here because I want to be here."

Fox didn't say anything else. She was the first woman since Jessica to come close to making him come out of his shell. But he would never allow himself to get too close to her. Walsh's attempt at taking both of them out at the fish market was a stark reminder as to why he could not allow himself to fall in love again, not while people like Ares and Dr. Marx were out there. He looked over the equipment in front of him. It was time to finish this.

Fox assisted Parris for the first half hour until there were no more compounds to collect, at which point Parris continued on her own. While Parris worked, Fox sat at the computer and reviewed the information she stole from the safe that she didn't have time to read during the ride.

Parris then held up a one-thousand-milliliter beaker with a blood-red solution within it. "I'm done. Now we need to test it."

The casual observer would mistake it for tomato sauce, but it wasn't as thick. She carried it to the counter in front of the isolation chamber where she put it down. Fox watched her as she picked up a scalpel. Alarms went off in his head when he saw the blade pointed inward towards her opposite hand. Without another thought, he snatched both of her wrists.

She looked at him with her mouth agape, as though perplexed. "What are you doing?"

"I was about to ask you the same thing."

"Pandora feeds on human red blood cells to self-replicate, so I'm volunteering myself. For heaven's sake, I'm no longer under the effects of Clarity. Would you rather I cut you instead?"

Fox looked into her brown eyes. *Yeah, I'm overreacting.* He smiled and released her wrists. Parris jabbed herself in the heel of her left palm and held it over a Petri dish. Six drops of blood fell into it. She opened the first-aid kit she had on the counter behind her and helped herself to the rubbing alcohol, cotton, and a Band-Aid.

Below the window, on the far left side of the isolation chamber, was a small slot with a button beside it. Parris pressed it and the door flipped outwards. An inner airlock door also opened, making a hissing sound. Ten seconds later, a tray slid out on which she placed the beaker with the serum, and the Petri dish with her blood onto the tray. She also reached into her breast pocket and took out the metal container which held Pandora. Parris momentarily hesitated as she held it. She looked at the beaker with the serum and then placed Pandora between the serum and the Petri dish. She pressed the same button and the tray slid back, the door closed, and the tray reappeared on the other side of the window a few seconds later.

Parris walked to the console and picked up a glove with several metallic pieces attached to it from off a plastic rod that was attached to the console. The glove controlled the mechanical arm inside the isolation chamber. It weighed much more than an ordinary glove. It was wireless and it gave Dr. Parris complete freedom of movement when she wore it. She pressed a button on the glove that was located under the base of the palm to activate the robotic arm, which then mimicked her hand and finger movements.

She looked inside the chamber as she brushed a few strands of her hair that dropped to her left eye. "Here it goes."

Fox stood beside her as they watched what went on inside the chamber.

The robot arm mimicked Parris's movements and picked up the Petri dish and poured the blood on top of the metal container. She then brought the mechanical arm above it, made it point the index finger downwards, and then lowered it to crack it open. Blood leaked into the container and within seconds a reaction was evident. The combination of crunching and rattling sounds grew louder and a thick, smoky red cloud streamed from the container.

With the robotic arm, Parris picked up the smoking container and dropped it into the beaker, where it floated on the surface of the serum. Parris curled her fingers but kept her index extended and held the robot arm above the beaker with its index finger pointing downwards above the container. She then directed the robot arm to push the container to the bottom of the beaker. She raised the robot arm, pressed the button on the glove to deactivate the robot arm and placed the glove back onto its rod. The beaker shook as it bubbled and belched out the red smoke in huge puffs. It wasn't too long after that the entire chamber filled up with the red cloud. Nothing else was visible it was so thick.

Both Parris and Fox looked around as their surroundings were illuminated by a bright red, much like the cloud that swirled in front of them on the other side of the window. Parris pressed the off button on the glove and returned it to the console as the inner chamber filled to capacity with the red cloud.

A minute went by and the red cloud was still there. Parris

slammed her right fist onto the counter in frustration and spun around with both hands on her hips. "This should've worked! Now what are we supposed to do?" She put both hands to her temples as she paced the room.

Fox remained silent as he continued to stare into the isolation chamber. "I'd say you should make some more of that serum. Take a look."

Parris turned around and swallowed hard when she saw another chemical reaction occur inside the chamber. The cloud began to fade, along with the sound of crunching and rattling. Several seconds later, all that remained were trace amounts of leftover serum inside the beaker, the cube inside it, and an empty Petri dish. Her arms dropped to her sides as she looked up at the ceiling and breathed out a big sigh of relief.

Fox then turned to her. "How soon can you prepare more of the serum?"

"I've already done so." She smiled as she gestured to the side counter where she had a rack with two small vials and picked them up to show him. "From the notes I read, vials similar to these in both shape and size will be used. They've built a device, ironically named Pandora's Box, which will be used to disperse the microbe. These vials are to be inserted into the device. We'll each carry one." She walked over to the counter and brought back the vials, their stoppers, and two small metal cases. She then handed one to Fox. "You'll also need one of these to hold it in, just to make sure you don't break it."

Parris handed him a small metal case. Fox took it, opened it and saw that the vial was meant to fit inside it diagonally on a padded surface. He put the vial in, closed it and dropped the case inside his inner jacket pocket. Parris did the same.

Parris then looked at him, suddenly remembering something. "By the way, I hope your JTF2 duties included knowing how to fly a helicopter?"

"You bet."

"Good. Because we'll have to steal one from the lot."